Harper's Bride

by

Alexis Harrington

A TOPAZ BOOK

TOPAZ
Published by the Penguin Group
Penguin Putnam Inc., 375 Hudson Street,
New York, New York 10014, U.S.A.
Penguin Books Ltd, 27 Wrights Lane,
London W8 5TZ, England
Penguin Books Australia Ltd, Ringwood,
Victoria, Australia
Penguin Books Canada Ltd, 10 Alcorn Avenue,
Toronto, Ontario, Canada M4V 3B2
Penguin Books (N.Z.) Ltd, 182–190 Wairau Road,
Auckland 10, New Zealand

Penguin Books Ltd, Registered Offices:
Harmondsworth, Middlesex, England

First published by Topaz, an imprint of Dutton Signet,
a member of Penguin Putnam Inc.

First Printing, October, 1997
10 [illegible] 5 4 3 2 1

Printed in the United States of America

Janet Brayson, Marg Vajdos, Catherine Anderson . . . what would I do without all of you? I treasure your encouragement and friendship.

To WBP and RWP, thank you for giving shape and form to Dylan and Melissa.

ACKNOWLEDGMENTS

My thanks to Matt Zaffino, meteorologist, for explaining the path of the Midnight Sun.

Chapter One

Dawson, Yukon Territory
June 1898

"No more credit, Logan. Not a dime. You already owe me one thousand two hundred dollars and fourteen cents. I'll forget the change, but I want the rest of it. Now."

Melissa Logan stood just inside the door at Harper's Trading Company, a rough, two-story log building on Front Street. The combined smells of wood smoke, tanned hides, bacon, and raw log walls clung to the place. Holding two-month-old Jenny in her arms, she watched the tense exchange between her husband, Coy, and Dylan Harper. At the end of the counter, a friend of Harper's named Rafe Dubois regarded the proceedings with obvious bland amusement.

Twelve hundred dollars . . . Melissa could hardly conceive of such a sum. Although prices in the Yukon were unbelievably high, she hadn't realized that Coy had acquired such a debt. And they had been in Dawson for only six weeks.

It was plain that Coy had made the man angry. But, then, Coy had a genuine talent for making people angry, and he got mad at everyone else. He straightened his skinny length and adjusted his one suspender, clearly offended. The seat of his dungarees drooped beneath his flat backside like an empty feed sack. He gestured behind him in Melissa's general direction. "I got me a wife and baby to feed. I can't do that till I make my big strike. You wouldn't see them go hungry, would you?"

On the other side of the plank counter, Dylan Harper towered over Coy, his long, blunt finger anchoring a page in a ledger book in front of him. He was a wild-looking man, Melissa thought, tall and lean, with long, sun-streaked sandy hair that brushed his wide, muscled shoulders. His buckskin pants were decorated with a short fringe down the side of each leg, and she saw some kind of Indian amulet around his neck, which remained mostly hidden under his shirt. At his waist he wore a long-bladed knife she suspected he wouldn't hesitate to use. From a high window a shaft of sunlight fell over him, highlighting his sharp, masculine features in muted amber, and making his eyes shimmer like hard green stones.

Instantly, she realized what Coy most obviously did not: he was a fool to cross this man.

"You didn't come in here today to buy them something to eat, and you didn't charge over a thousand dollars' worth of food. You bought tobacco, nails, a *case* of champagne"—Harper paused to look him up and down, as if wondering what a man like Coy Logan would do with even one bottle—"kerosene, and a lot of other things. But mostly you bought whiskey, three gallons of it." He glanced briefly at Melissa, then turned his unforgiving gaze back on Coy. "There's nothing written here against your name that would feed a family, Logan. Anyway, it's pretty hard to make that big gold strike when you're cutting wood for the North West Mounted Police." He tapped the ledger page with his fingertip. "I'm calling your debt. You'll pay or I'll bring in the Mounties, and they'll have you chopping on their woodpile again."

Melissa felt her face get hot, and knew it was more than just the stifling summer heat. Coy had already been in trouble with the iron-handed law in Dawson for public drunkenness. The police had sentenced him to two weeks of their standard punishment—hard labor on the government woodpile. Until now, she hadn't realized that anyone else knew about it.

Coy shifted his weight, and his tone took on a whining edge. "I know you give credit to some of the others at the diggings—Moody, Black-Eyed Charlie, Mose Swindell. And they run up lots bigger bills than me. You ain't made them pay."

"I like those boys, Logan. I don't like you." Dylan Harper's low voice rang with finality.

Melissa knew Coy would not be able to wangle his way out of this. She looked at the sleeping child she held in her arms; if Harper had Coy arrested, what would happen to her and the baby? Jobs up here were hard to come by, and anyway, who would hire a woman with an infant? Melissa didn't know if she had the courage or the strength to face it if things got much worse. Going hungry herself was one thing, but what if her milk dried up and Jenny began to starve as well?

"I'm telling you, I ain't got nowhere near that much money," Coy said, pushing down his dusty bowler hat on his head. "I ain't got nothing but—" He stopped then and turned to consider Melissa. His long, narrow face and cruel mouth perfectly reflected his shiftless, unreliable character. Often, she wondered tiredly why she had married him. She certainly didn't like the speculative glint she saw in his red-rimmed eyes now. Suddenly, Coy reached out and grabbed her arm, yanking her forward. Jenny shifted in her sleep and then settled down. "All's I got are her and the little one."

Harper stared at him with a blank expression.

Coy gave Melissa a push that thrust her forward for inspection. She lowered her face in embarrassment. "She's a quiet type, not like some gabby females, and it don't take much to keep her in line. The baby's quiet, too. Lissy sees to that. She can cook and keep house—" He glanced at her and rubbed at a smudge on her cheekbone, making her flinch. "And she ain't bad to look at when she's cleaned up and her face is washed."

"What's your point, Logan?"

"Well, I'm a thinking man, Harper," Coy said with a sly grin, and tapped a dirty finger against his temple. "I'm always thinking. Maybe you and me can work a trade. This gal and the baby for the bill in your book, there. All fair and square, and the Mounties don't need to know a thing about it."

Melissa's head came up and she gaped at Coy. Dylan Harper pulled back as if he had just been offered a box of scorpions. Rafe Dubois chuckled and shook his head as he leaned an elbow on the plank counter.

"What the hell do— Are you crazy?" Harper demanded.

"Coy!" Melissa cried, so startled that for a moment she forgot to keep quiet. "You can't mean . . ." she broke off, unable to finish. She must have misunderstood him—he couldn't mean that he would actually sell his wife and his own flesh and blood to this man Dylan Harper. No one would do that, it was . . . it was immoral, it was . . .

"Not a word out of you, girl," Coy warned her in a low voice, and pointed a finger at her. "I ain't got time for none of your foolishness." He turned to Harper and continued. "Now she's all right, I s'pose, but she's holding me back. If it wasn't for her, I could be panning heaps of dust. This is my big chance and I aim to grab it."

Melissa ducked her head again, mortified. She could hardly believe the horrifying, humiliating situation she was in. Marrying Coy to escape her drunken, abusive father had been her chief mistake. Not long after the wedding she had discovered that her husband and father were very much alike. But she had compounded that error when she followed Coy to this wilderness. She'd had to cross the snow-bound Chilkoot Pass when she was six months gone with Jenny, only to deliver her in a tent on the frozen banks of Lake Bennett. It was a wonder the baby had survived.

Unable to keep the scorn out of his voice, Dylan Harper gave a low laugh and said, "I came to the Yukon to make money, Logan. I'm not interested in your offer." He considered the weaselly little bastard in front of him and thought he'd never felt such contempt for a man. He only wanted to be paid, not assume the burden of this silent, haggard-looking woman. Damn, Logan offered her as though she were nothing more than a head of livestock. And a baby too?

In this business Dylan had run across his share of lowlife no-accounts, but if prizes were given for the lowest no-account, Coy Logan would definitely win. Dylan hadn't been lying when he said he didn't like Logan. From the moment they met, he'd despised him and had found no reason to change his mind since. That was Dylan's sole reason for calling in the debt. In the scope of the Yukon economy, where kerosene cost forty dollars a gallon and a dozen eggs could bring eighteen, Logan's twelve-hundred-dollar balance wasn't that large. In fact, others owed Dylan more. But he trusted them to pay him back. He didn't trust Logan at all.

Let him dump a wife and baby on him? Hell, no.

Dylan had come North two years earlier with one

purpose in mind, and he wasn't about to let anything get in his way. A worn-out female and her child were not part of his plans. He couldn't tell how old she was exactly, probably younger than she appeared. She was thin and pale, with hair even lighter than his own falling out of a loose knot at the back of her head. Her clothes were old; the pattern in her calico dress was so faded it was nearly indistinguishable. And except for the moment she'd dared to say something—if he could call her small, soft protest speaking—she seemed as indifferent as a rock.

But when he looked again at the woman Logan had called Lissy, he paused. She mostly kept her gaze lowered, and she didn't talk. When she stole a glance at Logan, though, something in her dove gray eyes—a glittering hatred combined with forlorn fear—made him think twice. That was no dirt mark on her cheekbone, as Logan would have him believe. It was a bruise, probably a souvenir from her husband's fist. Dylan had a hunch that was Logan's method of keeping her "in line." The thought made him tighten his jaw.

"Dylan," Rafe Dubois said then, and motioned him to the end of the counter. Rafe's breathing was rattling today, as it did sometimes. "You know he'll either keep beating her, or he'll sell them both to someone else who might treat them even worse," he drawled softly.

The same thought had already crossed Dylan's mind. Still clenching his back teeth, he cast a glance over his shoulder at the woman again. He didn't want to feel sorry for her, damn it. A woman and a kid? He drew his gaze back to his friend.

Rafe leaned closer. "I was about to go next door to the saloon to see if I could interest a miner in some high-stakes poker. You all can come along, and I'll preside over a little hearing to dismiss Logan's debt and transfer, shall we say, the bonds of matrimony from him to you. That is if the lady is amenable to the idea."

Dylan gaped at his friend. "What would I do with a wife? Jesus, Rafe, none of it would even be legal."

"Well, that's a fact, now isn't it? But it would get her and the baby away from the pusillanimous son of a bitch."

"If the Mounties got wind of it, we'd all be sentenced to that damned woodpile of theirs or worse. Besides, you don't even practice law anymore."

"A trifling point in this case, don't you think?"

"If you believe it's such a good idea, why don't you take her?"

Rafe shrugged. "It's not my debt to settle. But where I come from, chivalry would demand that she be rescued." He reached into his breast pocket and extracted a slim, dark cigar.

Dylan tried one final argument. "This is the Yukon, not New Orleans."

"That doesn't matter, does it," Rafe said. It was not a question.

Dylan breathed an exasperated sigh and glanced at the woman again. He knew Rafe was right. Although his friend had a whipsaw tongue and a cynical view of life, his Louisiana upbringing gave him a curlicued code of honor. But Dylan's honor ran just as deep. If something was to happen to Logan's wife, and that seemed like a certainty, his conscience would give him no peace. And with Logan being the lowdown scum that he was, the chances were pretty good that something serious *would* happen.

While he wished mightily that fate had chosen another man to take on this woman and her child, he was the one standing here.

He turned to face Logan again. "All right, Logan. I accept your offer, under two conditions. One, the lady has to agree to this—"

Logan hooked a thumb in his suspender. His attitude had turned suddenly cocky. "Oh, she agrees just fine."

Dylan fixed his gaze on her blond, downturned head. "I want to hear it from her."

Coy Logan prompted her. "Go on, girl, answer him."

Finally, she looked up, and once again Dylan was unsettled by her piercing gray gaze, as if she was measuring his stature as a man. Then she cast a last glance at Coy Logan. "I agree," she said softly, and touched her cheek to the sleeping baby's head.

Dylan nodded. "The other condition," he added, pointing at Logan, "is that you will never bother her again."

"Well, now, you don't got any say-so over—"

"Yes or no," he interrupted. "I forget the debt, or you go chop wood. It's your choice."

Logan scowled. "All right, all right, she won't see me again. Who needs her anyway?"

"Fine, then," Rafe said, slapping the countertop. "If you'll all accompany me next door."

They trooped through the mud to the Yukon Girl Saloon. Throngs of men wandered the street as they passed, some with purpose, but many others with an oddly lethargic look in their eyes. Melissa's sense of terror was so great, she felt as if she were marching from one level of doom to another. Never had she felt so friendless or so alone, or so without choices.

Inside the saloon Rafe Dubois took command of a table in the back. The rest of them crowded around it as though it were a judge's bench.

"Mr. McGinty, a bottle of whiskey here, if you please," Rafe called to Seamus McGinty, the saloon's owner, "and a pen and paper."

McGinty, a burly, loud-voiced man with a rich brogue, brought the bottle and the other things Rafe had requested. But when he saw Melissa and Jenny, he said, "Jaysus, Rafe, if the Mounties find out I let a woman and her babe in here, they'll be closin' me up for sartin!"

Rafe reassured McGinty, then poured a tumbler of whiskey for himself and a shot for Dylan while he worked out the details of their agreement. Melissa took note of her surroundings. She was no stranger to saloons; her mother had sent her in search of Pa often enough when she was young. This one was big, filled with rough men just in from the gold fields, those on their way out, and those who wished for nothing more than to return home. A tinny player piano jangled in the corner, and on one side of the room a crowd was gathered around what looked to be a roulette table. From the walls several stuffed moose heads surveyed the goings-on with staring glass eyes.

How she wished that she and Jenny were back in Portland and had never come on this foolish journey. Dawson was not a lawless place—the Mounties saw to that—but it was dirty and crowded and filled with desperate men.

Two thousand five hundred miles she had traveled to be abandoned by her husband and left to the keeping of Dylan Harper. Life with Coy had been miserable and difficult, and she would not miss him. She had little confidence that Dylan would be a better man. Coy's irresponsibility had put her in this position without choices. Melissa had learned to hide all of her feelings, but fury bubbled up in her for a moment. It wasn't her debt, and yet she was the one being punished.

She cast a sidelong glance at Dylan. He was very tall, much bigger than Coy, broad at the shoulder and hard-muscled. His square jaw and full mouth were not unpleasant to look at, she supposed, but there was a savage edge to him that she could not define. He had a temper like ice and fire, they said. Slow to ignite, but merciless in its vengeance. And while it was illegal to carry a gun in Dawson, she'd heard that he kept a big meat cleaver behind the counter in his store. More than one man had been threatened with it, they said. At least he seemed to be a sober man, which Coy was not.

"Now, then, Coy Logan," Rafe began, pulling Melissa's attention back to the moment. He read some lines that he'd scribbled on a piece of foolscap. "For the debt of one thousand two hundred dollars that you owe Dylan Harper of Harper's Trading Company, you do offer in exchange Melissa Reed Logan and the child, Jenny Abigail Logan. Is that correct?"

Coy eyed the whiskey bottle, which he had not been invited to share, and scratched his chin. "I don't see why we have to go through—"

"Is that correct, sir?" Rafe barked. He was rather fearsome, too, Melissa noted. Thank heavens Jenny slept on in her arms.

Coy jumped. "Yeah, that's right, yeah."

The proceedings came to a halt when Rafe Dubois was overcome by a coughing fit that left him gasping into a handkerchief. "Pardon me," he said finally, clearing his throat. "Very well, then. Let's continue."

When he reached the part that dissolved her marriage to Coy, Rafe murmured so that only Melissa could hear, "I doubt that the North West Mounted Police or anyone else with the Canadian government would appreciate our little procedure here, madam. However, I suspect that you won't mind the opportunity to escape from this philistine?" He was a young man, but so thin and cadaverous that when he smiled, he reminded Melissa of a pale, grinning jack-o'-lantern. But his eyes were kind, and he had the voice and manners of the finest of gentlemen.

She only glanced at Coy—she knew better than to look him in the face. A blur of memories crowded upon her, of pain and worry and indignity. Dylan gave her an even stare. She shook her head. "No, I won't mind."

Rafe looked pleased. "As I supposed. Whatever else he may be, Mr. Harper is a gentleman." He spoke a few more words, and Melissa Logan became Melissa Harper. "You are free to leave, Logan, and I'd advise you to do so now."

Coy gave them a mocking, smart-alecky salute and headed toward the swinging doors with a bouncing step, as if he did not have a care in the world.

"Court is adjourned," Rafe said, and lifted his glass of whiskey in a toast. "Best wishes to both of you, Mr. Harper *and* Mrs. Harper. Now you'd better escort her to the door, Dylan, before poor old Seamus has an apoplectic fit."

"All right, let's get out of here," Dylan grumbled and led Melissa through the crowd toward the open doors. His broad shoulders blocked out most of the daylight, though, as she passed among the men who eyed her with both curiosity and something more.

Outside on the duckboards that were meant to serve as sidewalks, Dylan steered her toward a sheltered recess between his store and the saloon, and away from the rough, milling crowds that wandered aimlessly up and down Front Street. Backed into the corner, she was forced to look into his set, chiseled face. Dylan Harper was a frightening man. Danger and an iron will were plain in his eyes. She dropped her gaze to his hands where they hung at his sides. They were large—broad and long-fingered, and they looked as if they would make sizable fists. Oh, dear God, she hoped that agreeing to leave Coy would not prove to be an even bigger mistake than marrying him had been.

Dread made her grip Jenny tighter than the baby liked, and she issued a little squeal of protest in her sleep before settling down again. Melissa felt her wet diaper seeping through the blanket against her arm. Jenny was bound to wake up soon, and even the best babies cried when they were wet and hungry. Men hated crying babies. Dylan glanced at Jenny, and Melissa pulled farther back into the corner. He looked impatient and cross as he eyed them both, and a knot of fear swelled in her throat.

"Look, this is how it's going to be," he said. "Since I let Rafe talk me into this damn-fool arrangement, I plan to take advantage of it." The weight of dread settled more heavily on Melissa. "I keep the store open long hours, and my days are hard. I need someone to tidy up the place, do my washing and cooking. My place upstairs isn't very big, so brooming it out now and then shouldn't be too taxing. I'll pay you, and I'll look out for you and the baby, here. But this is only a business deal, and a lousy one at that since I'm still out my twelve hundred dollars. You can call yourself Mrs. Harper if you want, so people won't think you're just living with me, and I won't deny that we're married to anyone who asks. But that's as far as things will go between us. You're not going to be my wife, and I won't expect to claim any rights as your husband. And I don't know much about babies, so don't expect me to change diapers or any of that. I'm up here to make money, and when I have enough for my plans, I'm going back to Oregon. I'll give you some cash for a new start here or wherever you want to go. That's all right with you, I hope." The words all came out in a terse speech, as though he had rehearsed it in his mind and didn't want to forget something.

She nodded and kept her voice low. "Yes, it's fine." His proposal sounded fair, and though relieved that he would not expect her to sleep in his bed, Melissa was very wary just the same. He could be lying about everything. His handsome face could be just a mask that hid a dark heart, and certainly, his well-known reputation in Dawson made him a man to be feared. At any rate, both her father and Coy had taught her that she could not take at face value anything men told her. But she knew better than to show it. She knew not to show *anything,* not hurt, not anger. If Dylan meant what he said, she intended to earn enough money, to do whatever it took, so that she would never have to depend on a man again. For now, though, she knew she had to make the best of this.

"What do you want me to call you?" he asked. "Lissy?"

She had never liked being called Lissy, although everyone except her mother had done so. She gazed up into his face again. "No, please . . . will you call me Melissa?"

"All right, then, Melissa. Let's go," Dylan said, and turned to lead her back to the store.

Just then, Jenny began to stir, her wet diaper getting the better of her good nature. "Mr. Harper," Melissa murmured, clearing her tight throat, "I don't have my belongings with me. No clothes for me or the baby. Not even an extra diaper. Coy has them all."

He sighed, and his frown only served to remind her that getting her and Jenny instead of his money was not what he wanted at all. "Maybe it's none of my business, but how the hell did you end up with a bum like Logan?"

She lifted her chin slightly and summoned all the dignity she could muster, but her cheeks grew warm. "We all make the wrong choice sometimes, Mr. Harper." She could see by his expression that a whiff of the baby's urine-soaked pants had reached his nose.

"Well, come on, then. My stock caters mostly to miners, but maybe I can find something for you."

She had another view of his broad shoulders as she followed him back into his store, where he managed to find three flour sacks, and a blanket for Jenny. "These aren't the best, but they'll work for now." He pulled out his huge knife and slit the sacks into diapers with such wicked dexterity, Melissa flinched. Then he cut the wool blanket into pieces that would fit a baby. He started to hand them to her, but tucked them over his arm instead.

"I'll take you down to the market on Wall Street tomorrow. Since the spring thaw, steamships have made it upriver with everything from ice-cream freezers to safety pins. I expect we'll find something for you and the baby to wear. For now, I'll show you the upstairs."

They had to go back outside to reach the side stairway that led to his room, and the mud was nearly knee-deep. Melissa struggled to keep her balance while the sucking mud pulled at her thin shoes. She jumped when Dylan Harper grasped her elbow to steady her. His hand felt big and rock hard, the firm grip of his fingers burning through her sleeve.

A team of Angora goats slogged by close to the duckboards and nearly brushed her elbow while it pulled a sled laden with supplies. On these swampy streets horses were useless and wagons sank to their wheel hubs. During the journey to Dawson she had seen all manner of animals pressed into the service of hauling goods, including sheep, burros, dogs of every breed, even dehorned reindeer.

Melissa hoped Dylan would release her when they climbed the narrow stairs, but instead he fell back only one step so he could continue to hold her arm. When they reached the landing at the top of the stairs, he let go of her to push open the door, allowing her to pass through first.

Inside, after Melissa's eyes adjusted to the gloom, she saw a stove, a corner for washing, a table and chairs, and one big bed. There was no extra space for another.

"Where will I sleep?" she asked, fearing she already knew the answer.

He shrugged. "There's nothing we can do except share the bed. I told you I won't touch you." Apparently, her disbelief showed in her eyes because he added in a low, silken voice, "My word is better than Coy Logan's."

Melissa had no reason to believe that. Staring at him and then the bed, she clutched Jenny to her. "I promise that somehow I'll earn enough money to repay every penny of Coy's debt to you."

His green gaze shifted away from hers for a moment. "Well, settle in," he mumbled and pointed a thumb over his shoulder. "I'm going back to work."

He gave her a lingering look and then turned to leave.

Not only would Melissa pay him back, she'd make enough to leave this wild, crowded place and the savage man who had taken them in. She would return to Portland to make a life for herself and her daughter.

No man would ever have power over them again.

Chapter Two

The door slammed, and Melissa stood on the other side of it, listening to Dylan Harper's footfalls going down the stairs. Left alone with Jenny to survey the log-walled room and her circumstances, she struggled to grasp all that had happened to her today.

That Coy had *traded* his wife and his own child to a stranger to pay a debt— She did not feel hurt, exactly. After all, how could someone who had worked so hard to earn her loathing still hurt her? She had been his wife for just over a year, and learned early on that he was much less of a man than she had originally believed. But discovering the full extent of his selfishness and disloyalty had still left her badly shaken. She hadn't realized that he did not care for her and Jenny at all. Or maybe she simply hadn't been able to admit it to herself until this moment.

In truth, she knew that she would not miss him. Despite his big talk about the future during their very brief courtship, he had proven himself to be short-tempered and lazy, like her father and brothers.

But what about Dylan Harper? Though he claimed otherwise, and while he actually worked—at his own business, too—she had learned the hard way not to take any man at face value.

If looks alone reflected a person's character, if good people were handsome and the wicked ugly, life would be simpler. But sometimes beautiful faces hid dark hearts, she knew, and while Dylan was much better-looking than Coy, that didn't tell her much. Tall and broad and muscled, his form suggested a life spent at work on tasks more physically demanding than sitting on a tree stump, lifting nothing heavier than a whiskey bottle, or complaining about the government, as Coy had been apt to do.

She had seen a sharp, untamed intelligence in Dylan's green eyes. His hair was the color of buckskin—blond, but darker than her own. He had a wide brow and a long narrow nose that snubbed slightly at its end, and his square jaw suggested a stubborn, determined temperament. His mouth was full and sensuous. He was savage, magnetic—he could draw people as strongly as he pushed them away. She sensed a hunter in him, wild and independent. There was no question that he was attractive. In fact, she thought he was the most handsome man she had ever seen. But how would he treat her and the baby? And if he got tired of their arrangement and decided not to see it through as he'd promised, he might toss them out in the muddy street if he wanted to.

Melissa knew she had to think of some way to protect herself and her child. There were no guarantees in life—this afternoon she'd learned that not even marriage protected a woman.

Jenny began to wail then, her patience exhausted, and Melissa was dragged back from her ruminations. She took two steps deeper into the room, looking for a place to change the baby. Dirty dishes cluttered the little table and clothes were slung over the two chairs. The quarters were close up here, just as Dylan had said, with a low, timbered ceiling. In fact, with him in the room, it had seemed even smaller still. His lean male ranginess filled the whole place in a way that she found more than a little threatening. Finally, she laid the baby on the floor and unpinned her soaked diaper.

"Hushabye, little love," she crooned as she fashioned the coarse flour sacking around Jenny's bottom. Trying to keep the quiver out of her voice, she forced herself to ignore the words EMERALD MILLING stamped on the fabric in blue ink. This was not the life a mother envisioned for her child. She herself might be dressed in old, worn clothes and feel just as old and worn. But she wanted so much more for Jenny Abigail. She lifted the baby into her arms. "Everything is going to be fine. Tomorrow I'll get material for some new clothes, and I'll make you better diapers." Jenny stopped fussing and considered her with solemn eyes. "We're not off to a very good start together, are we?" Melissa whispered and rose to her knees. "But I'll get us out of this, just you wait and see."

Pushing aside the shirt that lay on one of the

chairs, Melissa unbuttoned her bodice. Jenny was too thin as it was, and she didn't want her to miss any meals. The baby rooted around until she settled down to suckle. A sense of contentment washed over Melissa, and she snuggled her child close, smoothing a hand over her silky head. The silence gave her a moment to rest and study her surroundings.

There was only enough space for her to make a little corner for herself and Jenny. Glancing around, she spotted a crate the baby could sleep in. The poor little thing had never had a cradle, a fact that bothered Melissa a great deal. A baby ought to have a cradle, even if she had nothing else.

A year ago, she had viewed Coy as her deliverer. That he was a friend of her brothers should have given her pause, but it hadn't. She had been so anxious to get away from the tiny back street rooms she grew up in, away from the drunkenness and Pa's constant angry harangue, she had ignored the nagging doubts that had nipped at her and decided to marry Coy in spite of them.

She could still see Coy sitting at the kitchen table that rainy spring afternoon with Pa and her oldest brother, James. It was before her mother had died. Melissa hadn't been included in the discussion that decided her future, but she'd eavesdropped from her place at the stove and peeked at them now and then.

"Take her if you want her, Coy Logan," her father had groused with a dismissive wave of his hand. He passed a bottle of cheap corn whiskey to Coy after taking a long swallow for himself. "She'll be one less mouth I have to feed."

Hearing that, Melissa turned to face the stove again. Jack Reed had not earned a full day's pay or put food in any of his children's mouths in more than ten years. Her mother had been the one who worked—the one who had kept food on the table, as poor as the rations had been. Melissa had stolen another glance over her shoulder.

"I don't like it, and no offense to you, Coy," James had said, idly scratching his crotch. "But who's gonna take care of us if Lissy leaves? With Ma working for the Pettigreaves in their fancy house, there won't be anyone to cook and wash. Ma don't get home except on Thursdays. We have to eat in the meantime."

This had raised a heated discussion, but in the end Coy had won her hand. And although she hadn't known it at the time, that was the day her dreams had begun to crumble.

But all of that couldn't be helped now. She had more immediate concerns. She put Jenny over her shoulder and gently patted her back. The baby's velvety temple pressed warmly against Melissa's cheek, filling her with warmth that quickly turned to an almost overpowering urge to weep. She tightened her hold on her daughter, trembling slightly with the force of her emotions. *Please, God.* Melissa had long since realized that her own dreams had drifted away like dandelion fluff on the wind. But even so, deep in her heart, she still held dreams for her baby. She wanted more for her than hunger and betrayal and the stunning impact of a man's brutal knuckles against her jaw if she so much as dared to speak her mind. Those weren't outlandish dreams. Melissa wasn't young enough or foolish enough to set her sights too high these days. But she prayed that Jenny got chances that she'd never had, and that she would somehow figure out a way to smooth the path for her daughter.

Resolutely, she lined the crate with a piece of the blanket Dylan had given her and laid Jenny inside. The baby waved her fists vigorously, apparently pleased enough to have a dry diaper, a full stomach, and a place to rest. Swallowing hard to ease her tight throat, Melissa chucked the infant under the chin.

"Well, it isn't a real crib, button, but at least you don't have to share it."

Melissa's gaze skittered to Dylan's big, rough-hewn bed. It was made from slender tree limbs, the headboard and footboard bent into arches and secured at the joints with rawhide thongs. Rustic, she thought, but oddly pleasing to the eye and considerably better than anything Coy had ever provided. A couple of animal hides that had been stitched together—wolves' hides, Melissa thought—were draped over the end and appeared to serve as a blanket. Long-legged jeans were slung over the pelts and a pair of boots sat on the floor.

Just as Dawson was basically a man's town, this room lacked any hint of a woman's touch. But at least the windows were glazed with real panes of glass, and they opened. The tiny miner's cabin she and Coy had lived in had just one window, and it had been made of empty bottles held together with dried mud. Dylan's windows even bore heavy curtains to close out the light of the midnight sun. Well, they couldn't be called curtains, exactly. They were just rectangles of canvas with raw edges—they had probably been cut with the same knife and method that had created Jenny's diapers from the sacking.

A small galvanized steel sink with a pump stood against one wall. There were homes in Portland that had real faucets with running water, but she had never seen one. This she was accustomed to, and it meant she wouldn't have to haul water to wash dishes and clothes, as she had at Coy's cabin. Beneath the jumble of dishes, an oilcloth graced the table, another step up from her last dwelling. But the place needed a good cleaning.

She rolled up her thin sleeves and put a kettle of water on the stove to heat. Then grabbing the corn broom that stood in the corner, Melissa began sweeping.

Staying out of Dylan's way would be difficult in a place this small, and tight living conditions tended to make tempers short. And he'd made it no secret that he really didn't want them there. But experience had taught her that she had to keep him in a good humor. That was the only way she knew to protect herself and Jenny.

She intended to do her best.

* * *

Downstairs at Harper's Trading Company, Dylan stood over a crate of oranges, unloading it into smaller baskets. The fruit was a little soft from the trip up here on a steamer, but the captain who had sold it to Dylan had given him a fair price.

Although it was after nine o'clock at night, the sun threw a wedge of bright light across the plank floor, and crowds still wandered the street outside as if it were the middle of the afternoon. After two years up here, he still hadn't grown accustomed to a summer sun that shone until midnight. He was glad for the light tonight, though. It gave him an excuse to work in the store and keep his mind off the footsteps he kept hearing overhead.

Unloading a crate of oranges didn't take much concentration, though. And that was the problem.

It was a rare moment that found him alone in the store, and the thoughts spinning through his head were glum.

Business was good, he couldn't complain about that. With thirty thousand stampeders surging into Dawson to strike it rich in the gold fields, he was making more money than he would have believed possible.

Initially, he'd planned to dig for gold too, just like the rest of them. *And* he'd had the advantage of being here when George Carmack made the big gold discovery on Rabbit Creek that had started all this. Good claims had still been available then. But mining was grueling work, and there were no guarantees. Despite the men who became rich, many more did not. Dylan expected to work hard, but after trying his hand at mining, he had decided that he'd rather spend his energy on a sure thing. And it was a sure thing that these men needed equipment and supplies. So he let them dig for the gold, and they brought it to him when they bought whiskey and flour and tobacco, and anything else he could find to sell them. No, it wasn't business that put him in this sour mood.

Melissa Logan had done it for him.

His thoughts were interrupted when a stampeder who looked as if he'd been a teacher or a bank clerk back home stopped in to buy pipe tobacco and one of the oranges. But Dylan wasn't distracted for long. As soon as the man left, Dylan returned to his brooding.

He'd seen a number of astounding things since coming North—moments of foolishness, greed, and great compassion. There had been the time in Joe Ladue's saloon when a lovesick miner solemnly offered to pay one of the saloon girls her weight in gold if she'd marry him. She had agreed. He'd watched two partners who had made the harrowing trip to Dawson separate in a fury after they finally arrived. While dissolving the partnership, they had gone so far as to try and split their one skillet in two with a hatchet. He had contributed money to the emaciated Jesuit missionary, Father William Judge, called "The Saint of Dawson," who worked himself to exhaustion tending those who jammed his hospital, day and night, with scurvy, dysentery and malaria.

But all of those things had involved *other* people—he'd been merely an interested spectator. Today, though, he had been right in the thick of it. Today had just about beaten them all.

Now a woman and baby were upstairs in his room, and would be there for the duration, however long that might be. He didn't want a woman and her kid. He was already kicking himself for letting Rafe talk him into taking Coy Logan's gaunt-eyed, lank-haired wife. He paused, an orange in each hand, and thought about her appearance. Well, maybe she wasn't so bad as all that. Those unsettling gray eyes were downright attractive, when she lifted her head to look at you. And while she was too thin, her recent motherhood gave her a hint of roundness that would probably bloom if she had three squares a day. But she looked worn out. Life with Logan had probably been no picnic, he conceded.

But Melissa or not, Dylan would not let anything get in the way of his goal—to make enough money to go back to Oregon and buy the land he'd yearned for, where no man could tell him how to live. He'd wanted to breed horses, but money had never meant anything to him. Not even *she* could make Dylan change his mind. Now he would prove to his father it didn't matter that he'd banished his eldest son from the Harper fold; he was doing just fine on his own, and without cheating anyone.

Dylan straightened and let his gaze run the length

of the shelves. He sure as hell had never pictured himself doing this kind of work.

At that moment Rafe Dubois walked in. Even without looking up, Dylan would have known he was there. The man's breath was so short, he sounded as if he'd run up ten flights of stairs with a horse on his back. In the midst of all the mud and rough-dressed men, his immaculate attire seemed incongruous. In fact, Dylan sometimes wondered how he had become friends with a man whose background and views on life, sardonic and lyrical by turns, were so different from his own.

"Still here?" Rafe asked, plucking an orange from a basket. "You should have closed up long ago. You wouldn't want to keep the wife waiting."

At Rafe's comment, the long-ago memory of a lithe, raven-haired beauty suddenly rose in his mind, sharply detailed, and so different from the blond waif upstairs. He frowned. "Those oranges are a dollar each," Dylan groused, not in the mood for the lawyer's wit. Then he admitted more reluctantly, "Anyway, I'm not ready to go up there."

Rafe leaned against the counter and peeled the orange, ignoring Dylan's remark about the price. "Then I believe I'll accompany you next door and let you buy me a drink. As payment, shall we say, for my legal services."

"I should charge *you* for getting me into this. Besides, you don't need me to buy you a drink." Dylan had never seen a man who could put away as much liquor as Rafe could. He drank at least a quart a day, although he never really seemed drunk and he never staggered. Rafe had not told him so, but Dylan suspected that his drinking had cost him his law practice. However, his considerable gambling skill seemed unaffected, and he made a fairly comfortable living at it.

"Stop your bellyaching, Dylan," Rafe said, popping an orange section into his mouth. "That little girl needed someone to look out for her and her baby. And you can use the company."

Dylan frowned again. "I don't need company—"

Rafe straightened and flung the orange rind out the door into the muddy street. "God, you're as cross as a grizzly bear with a boil on his ass. I think you'd better go next door with me to the saloon. Mrs. Harper doesn't need to deal with your foul mood after the day she's had."

"Oh, hell," Dylan said, cringing. *Mrs. Harper.* He tossed the last orange into a basket. Rafe was probably right, a drink didn't sound like a bad idea, especially given the circumstances. And it gave Dylan an excuse to put off the inevitable for a while longer. "All right, let's go. But just for a while—I have work to finish."

Rafe pushed himself away from the counter and smiled, all gleaming white teeth, emphasizing his pallid thinness. His skin was pulled tight across his cheekbones, and his eyes looked like hollow sockets. Sometimes, when the light was just right, his smile reminded Dylan of a grinning skull.

As they walked to the Yukon Girl, Dylan almost

suggested that they cross the street and drink at the Arctic Star instead. After all, he was trying to get his mind *off* Melissa, and returning to the scene of their "wedding" probably wouldn't do the trick. But he decided it really wouldn't matter. It sure as hell wouldn't change anything.

The Yukon Girl was noisy and crowded with a cross section of the men who had come to Dawson seeking their fortune. *Cheechakos,* the old-timers called them, newcomers. Newcomers of every stripe—buckaroos, escaped convicts, schoolteachers, ex-buffalo hunters—filled the streets and the barrooms up and down Front Street, all hoping to strike gold. Dylan knew that most of them would be disappointed.

"God, will you look at them?" Rafe drawled, gazing at the crowd. Many of the men sat with elbows on the tables, shoulders hunched, looking dispirited and apathetic. "They were expecting Paris on the Yukon River, I imagine. Too bad the poor bastards didn't know that most of the best claims were already staked before they left Seattle last fall."

"Most of them know it now," Dylan replied, pouring his own shot. "I bought an outfit from a man yesterday who said he'd camped for five days in that line outside the recorder's office. When his turn finally came up, he found out that no ground was left to claim. He sold me his gear for a fraction of what he paid for it and said he's trying to scrape up enough money for passage home—if his wife will have him."

Lounging against the bar, Rafe poured himself a full tumbler of whiskey while Dylan watched. He'd never said much about Rafe's drinking. But he couldn't resist a comment now, when just walking across room had left the man panting for breath. "I don't suppose that liquor is going to do much for your condition."

Rafe fixed him with a look so suddenly sharp and cold, Dylan lifted his brows. "Rheumatism fever sealed my fate when I was twelve years old, Dylan. As it is, my heart has lasted longer than the doctors thought it would. Now I didn't come to the Yukon to search for gold, and I sure as hell didn't come up here for my health. I came just for the fun of it. My time is short, and I intend to make the most of what's left."

Dylan shrugged and shook his head. Every man had to find his own path. That's what an old prospector had told him, and he'd come to recognize the unshakable truth of it. He had to admire the fact that Rafe spoke so casually and pragmatically of his own death.

"I don't know what fun there is in being jostled by this pack," Dylan commented. He had spent his life in the clean, misty shadow of the Cascade Mountains and wanted nothing more than to go back to it, to live on his own land, on his own terms. "All I want is to make my money and leave."

Rafe laughed shortly, his biting humor restored. "Oh, but that's where we differ, my friend. Over the years I've seen many examples of man's folly. This is the best yet, and it's been my privilege to witness it. Some of these people gave up everything to come up here. They sold prosperous businesses, they left wives and children, or as in the case of that fool, Logan, brought them along. They took their lives in their hands to make the passage, camped in tents on frozen lakes for the winter—they risked everything to race up here only to discover there's nothing left for them. And some of those who have made money have lost it to me at the gaming tables." He chuckled ruefully. "It's a damned tragedy, if only they knew it."

At the mention of Coy Logan, Dylan tossed back a second drink. He knew it was cowardly to dawdle here, and he was no coward. "I'd better get back to work," he said.

Rafe tipped him a knowing look and grinned again, that wide, white-toothed smile. "That's fine, you go on." He lifted his head to scan the card tables. "I believe I see a game that bears closer inspection."

They parted then, and Dylan elbowed his way through the horde and out to the street. Outside, the milling, aimless parade of men continued like fallen leaves caught in a stream eddy. It was a hell of a thing when a man lost his direction, Dylan thought as he glanced at their blank faces. Anything could derail him—the dream of easy money, a twist of fate, an itch for a faithless woman.

The faint rumble of dancing feet and a discordant blur of music poured out of the open saloon doors along Front Street—piano, fiddle, harmonica, even accordion strains, all jumbled together. Loud, raucous laughter and voices lifted in song added to the din. God, he wanted to get away from here.

As Dylan climbed the stairs to his room, the smell of home cooking wafted to him, and his steps slowed. At first he thought it was carried on the breeze from one of the saloons, but it grew stronger as he approached his own landing. Pushing open the door, he found the room straightened, and the little table was set with two tin plates and silver. Melissa had cooked dinner?

This was a rarity for him; he got most of his meals in the saloons in town. He didn't even keep much food up here. Looking around, he saw pans on the stove, and Melissa putting down the baby in an old crate. Seeing him, she whirled, obviously startled, and backed up a couple of paces. She watched him with wary gray eyes, as if he were a cougar that had stalked into her campsite.

Well, damn, he wasn't going to bite her, he thought, feeling out of place in his own room. She didn't have to jump away from him like that.

"I-I didn't know if you wanted dinner, but— I hope bacon and biscuits are all right." She never seemed to raise her voice above a murmur. Her apprehension was like a living thing as she hovered next to the baby. She seemed to be trying to make herself as small and unobtrusive as possible.

"Well, yeah, sure . . ." He shoved a hand through his hair, at a loss for words. He hadn't really expected her to do any cooking or cleaning for a few days, and certainly not tonight.

She had tied on an old towel for an apron, knotted at the back of her waist. Since she had nothing else to wear, she still had on the same threadbare clothes. Her hair was tidier, the loose tendrils secured again, but beneath her eyes dark smudges gave her the careworn look of a woman twice her age.

"Have you eaten?"

She shook her head.

He waved her to the table. "Come on, then, sit down."

Edging closer, she plucked the bacon and biscuit pans from the top of the stove, then served him first. It made him uncomfortable to have her wait on him. He'd grown up with that, and he'd never liked it.

Melissa sat then, taking a biscuit and a thin slice of bacon for her plate. Not enough, in Dylan's opinion, to keep even a cat going. Her nervousness was palpable, and she lowered her gaze and said nothing, opening a vast chasm of silence that only increased the tension in the little room.

Hell, she was so quiet and mousey, if the place were bigger, he could easily pretend that she wasn't there at all, and go about his business. But she was sitting right across the table from him, and it felt damned awkward. Searching for a distraction, he tried a biscuit. It was flaky and tender; at least she could cook.

"This is good," he said, staring at the top of her

lowered head. "Sorry I didn't have more up here for you to work with."

She lifted her head, and she seemed to light up for a moment. "Oh, that's all right. When I lived at home, sometimes I had to fix meals with less than this. We never had much to go around."

"Well, it's good," he repeated, trying to imagine "less than this." He'd had plenty of good food at home, including the game he had hunted to put on the table.

"Thank you," she murmured, retreating into herself again.

This situation was impossible, he thought, and swallowed the rest of his food without tasting it. He felt her gaze on him when he wasn't looking at her, but she wouldn't meet his eyes. She didn't talk; she was edgy and nervous. He didn't want her lurking in the corners, silent and fearful. Having someone to cook and clean wasn't worth that.

He glanced at the bed, straightened now, and wished that he had this afternoon to live over again. He wouldn't have allowed Rafe to talk him into this ridiculous arrangement. Yes, the woman had needed help, but cash would probably have done the trick. He sat up straighter as the idea sprang to life. Maybe it wasn't too late. He could give her money for a hotel room and get her out of here.

He sank back in his chair. No, that wasn't the answer, either. The "hotels" in Dawson were little more than tents and shacks with signs hanging over their entrances. They sure as hell were no place for a woman and a baby. Sighing, he pushed his plate away. There was nothing else to do but see this through.

"Thanks for dinner," he said, and stood to look at his pocket watch. "It's almost ten, and I have to check on the store before we go to . . . before I turn in. I'll be back in a little while."

Melissa nodded and watched him leave, her heart pounding with trepidation. He was so tall, so broad at the shoulder, he could do to her whatever he pleased and she would be powerless to resist him.

Rising from her chair, she cleared the table and washed the dishes, while the minutes slipped past like the bar of soap in her hands. She listened for the sound of his boot steps outside, but heard nothing except faint banjo music from one of the saloons down the street.

A dangerous man, they said.

A gentleman, Rafe Dubois had told her.

Which was right? Neither? Both?

She glanced at the big bed as she lifted Jenny from her makeshift cradle to feed her. For a moment she considered putting the baby in the middle of the mattress, then decided against it. Using Jenny as a shield would be wrong.

After the baby was glutted with milk and sleeping soundly, Melissa put her back in her crate and began undressing for bed. Pouring warm water into the bowl on the washstand in the corner, she splashed her face and neck. She released her hair from its knot and loosened it with her fingers, then paused, her hands suspended in the strands. A small mirror hung on the wall over the bowl, and she let one hand drop to the bruise left by Coy's fist.

Her own hand mirror had broken on the journey up here, and now and then she had caught sight of herself in a store window. But she'd not had a good look at her face for weeks, long before the last time Coy hit her.

She trailed her fingers over the mark. Purple-brown in the middle, it had faded to greenish yellow at one edge, like a rainbow of the ugliest colors. Coy had struck her twice before. Usually he'd get drunk, or angry, and he would break things, or kick something. As frightening as his violent behavior had been, she had believed herself safe from his abuse because of it, that he was satisfied to smash a bottle or put his fist through a barrel lid.

Then a month ago, when Jenny had been cranky and colicky and wouldn't be soothed, Coy had turned his impatience and anger on Melissa. Two weeks after that, he'd gotten mad because his dinner was dried out. She'd known it would only make things worse to point out that it had reached that state while he was sitting in the saloon. It was best that he'd abandoned them, she thought, straightening away from the mirror.

But now she had Dylan Harper to worry about.

Since she had no nightgown, she would have to sleep in her thin chemise and petticoat. With her pulse pounding heavily in her throat, she climbed into the big bed.

Maybe he wouldn't come back tonight, she hoped wildly as she lay there trembling. She'd had the same wish about Coy. Maybe he would never come back. He might fall in the Klondike River and drown. Or maybe a wolf would come down from the hills and—

Suddenly, she heard a low, tuneless whistling outside and the sound of a step on the bottom stair. He was coming. He'd be here in seconds. Oh, please, God—

Melissa lurched up and glanced around the room desperately. Something, anything— Her gaze fell upon a big sack of rice leaning against the wall. Springing from the bed, she struggled with the sack, dragging its dead weight across the floor. All the while the footsteps grew louder, closer. With strength she didn't know she possessed, she flung the sack up to the bare, blue-striped ticking, and rolled it to the center of the mattress. It was dumb, it wouldn't stop him, but she had to try.

Climbing in after it, she squeezed her eyes shut and tried to slow her breathing. Around the edges of the canvas curtains the sun blazed in the Arctic sky. She wished the night was dark, as it would be back home, so that she could hide her state of undress in its shadows.

Dylan lifted the latch and walked in to find Melissa lying in his bed. Something lay beside her, and it was way too big to be the baby. It took up the full center of the bed, leaving not much room on either side. He narrowed his eyes. Damn if it wasn't the sack of rice. He drew closer to the mattress to study her. Her eyes were clamped shut, and a slight frown drew her brows as if she had put all of her concentration into her charade. She clung to the edge of the mattress, but he knew she wasn't asleep. She was panting, probably from lifting the rice, and a light dew of perspiration shined her forehead. God, he knew that sack weighed seventy-five pounds. He'd carried it up here himself.

He would have laughed at the whole thing, but she was afraid of him and that bothered him. Coy Logan and maybe other men before him had made her fear Dylan, and all she had to defend herself with was a bag of rice. And there was no humor in that. Or in the bruise on her cheekbone that was beginning to turn green and yellow.

But even more disturbing to him was his body's response to seeing her in his bed. Her long, pale hair fanned out over the pillows, and the swell of her breasts strained against her flimsy chemise. She was too thin, so unlike the Eliz—

Impatiently, he turned on his heel and saw the baby. He took a step closer. She slept in her little crate, like a soft flower bud. A hint of long-forgotten tenderness brushed his soul as he looked at her. Oh, she was kind of cute, he supposed. Her hands were clenched into fists on either side of her downy head, and he stared at them, fascinated by their tiny perfection. She looked like her mother, lucky girl, and not Coy Logan.

Pushing aside one of the canvas curtains, he saw the sun resting on the horizon, as low as it would set at this time of year. In three hours it would begin to rise again, and three hours after that, his work day would begin.

Sighing, he turned his back to Melissa and sat on his side of the bed to pull off his boots. Then he stripped to his drawers and lay down between the hard rice sack and the edge of the mattress, feeling like a stranger in his own place. He stretched out on his back, with his hands under his head. The faint fragrance of soap drifted to him from the other side of the bed.

Dylan knew it would be a long night.

Chapter Three

The next morning, Melissa woke with a start, disoriented and groggy. Her bleary gaze shot from a timbered ceiling overhead to a fur-covered throw at her feet. A pair of jeans hung over the end of the bed, and she saw a belt looped over a branchlike bedpost. Where was she? Then it all came back to her. This was Dylan Harper's room.

Peeking over the hump of the rice sack, she saw that Dylan was already gone, but the scent of buckskin and man lingered in the bedding.

She must have finally drifted off during the night, she realized, but she was exhausted just the same. Lying there, vigilant and as taut as a fiddle string for hours, she'd been aware of his every breath. Her muscles had drawn even tighter whenever he moved. She couldn't forget about his reputation—everyone knew about Dylan Harper, and they walked a wide path around him.

Once, she had chanced a quick look at him. There he lay with no shirt, in his drawers, for heaven's sake, and all that long, sun-streaked hair. Certainly none of the men she had ever known, not her father or her brothers, not Coy, had ever refrained from crude behavior in front of her—and Dylan's behavior was not really crude. But it seemed to her that stripping to his underwear in her presence when they had just met was shocking. That she had also slept in her underwear wasn't the same—hers covered more. And *he* had seemed to have no trouble sleeping at all, she thought grumpily. He'd rolled toward the rice sack and had even thrown a muscled arm around the thing, as if he were embracing it. God, that could have been her, she thought, glad she'd erected the barricade between them. Asleep he'd looked different, not quite as forbidding, although a slight frown had crimped his brow even in sleep, as if some worry that he bore never let him truly rest.

At least he'd left her alone, and she was glad for that. She climbed out of the bare-ticking bed and plucked Jenny from her crate. Creaky pain shot through her arms and shoulders, reminding her of last night's exertion with the heavy sack. Melissa had given little thought to its weight at the time, but now her arms and shoulders ached from dragging it up to the bed.

"How's my button?" she whispered with a smile. The baby waved her fists sleepily. No matter how tired or discouraged Melissa might be, Jenny never failed to lighten her heart. In her mind the baby was her reward for enduring Coy, and for that single reason she did not entirely regret marrying him.

Jenny gurgled at her and smiled back. Thank God

she slept through most nights and wasn't a fussy baby. Whenever she had cried around her father, and it hadn't been often, he'd threatened to smack both her and Melissa if she couldn't quiet her, "and right now, damn it." Although he had never hit the baby, Melissa had feared it was only a matter of time. She had never struck anyone herself, but if that day had come, if Coy had once raised a hand to her Jenny, she believed she would have killed him.

After she fed Jenny and gave her a clean diaper, Melissa washed, this time avoiding her reflection, and put her old clothes back on. Between bites of a cold biscuit from last night's dinner, she spread her carefully mended skirt between her hands and looked at it. The gray muslin was so thin in some places she could see her white petticoat showing through the sheer spots. She dropped the folds and sighed. Melissa had never owned fine things; no one in Slabtown did. People like the Pettigreaves, the family her mother had worked for, had indoor plumbing and electric lights, and even an automobile with a man to drive it for them. Her mother had told her about their wonderful hillside house on Park Place—it even had an *elevator*—and the lavish parties they gave with such exotic foods as lobster and oysters and goose liver paste. Once, Melissa had even gotten to taste a bit of lobster when her mother brought it home, wrapped in clean waxed paper. The paper was another luxurious convenience that she had only seen before on blocks of butter.

No, Melissa had not grown up with fine things;

most of her life had been one of want and making do. But she'd always had sheets on her bed, even if they had been as thin and translucent as onionskin. And never had she faced having no other clothes to put on her back until now. She glanced down again to her shabby skirt. Dylan had said he'd take her out to buy things for herself and the baby, and it bothered her to accept them. Yet just as she was without clothes, she was also without choice. For Jenny, she thought; she had to do it for her.

The door opened suddenly, startling her, and Dylan Harper walked in. This time she hadn't heard his approach on the stairs. He had to duck under the top of the door frame, she noticed. His tall, lean-muscled form dominated the room, dwarfing everything else in it, and his intense green eyes swept the room, resting briefly on the rice sack in his bed. Finally, he shot her a probing look before she dropped her gaze. She retreated a step.

"Ready to go down to Wall Street?" he asked, as if he had read her mind.

She nodded, and with obvious stiffness, picked up Jenny who slept on unconcernedly. She felt his eyes on her, but didn't look up. Dylan stood aside to let them pass, then followed her down the narrow staircase. With each step she took, Melissa was aware of him behind her, his physical presence and the strength he emanated was a force to be reckoned with. She just prayed she could reckon with it later.

Below, the crowd continued to wander the knee-deep morass that was the street. The morning sun was warm, and a breeze blew in from the rivers, but the mud was slow to dry out. Dylan walked between her and the busy, jostling herd, sheltering her from a careless elbow and the pack animals that slogged by.

"Did you sleep all right last night?" he asked, breaking the silence between them. She felt his boot heels reverberating on the boards under her own feet.

"Yes, thank you," she said.

"And did the rice help?"

Melissa glanced up quickly; was that anger she heard in his voice? But his handsome face wore a faintly amused expression. "Well, um, I thought—it seemed like the right thing to do, I guess."

He lifted his hat and resettled it. "You must be stronger than you look—that sack weighs seventy-five pounds. And it takes up a lot of room. I never had the urge for more than two in my bed."

His insinuation brought heat to Melissa's cheeks. A man with his good looks certainly wouldn't suffer for female company. But the range of this man's reputation that Melissa had heard about did not extend to women, she realized. He was known only to have a drink or two in the saloon with Rafe Dubois, or by himself, and then go on his way. The few saloon girls and camp followers who approached him were given a smile and sometimes a tip, and nothing more, it was said. If he had dalliances with women, he kept it very quiet. But as she walked beside him on the duckboards, she sensed a raw, restless energy that was so powerful, she quailed a bit. And whenever her arm brushed his on the narrow walkway, she felt a peculiar quickening in her chest.

But she forgot about Dylan Harper and everything else on her mind when they turned the corner toward the waterfront. Laid out before them was Wall Street, and beyond that, Broadway Avenue. Thinking they would have escaped the crowd down here, Melissa halted, amazed at the display that stretched for blocks. Lining these streets were people selling all manner of goods, and the throng swarming Front Street surged down here to see the marketplace. It had the air of a bazaar, as vendors told of their wares from every booth and tent. Patrolling the proceedings were a few scarlet-coated Mounties.

Although Melissa had been in Dawson nearly two months, she had seen none of this up close. Everyone wanted cash down here, Coy had said, and saw no point in going. The display was astounding.

"Lady, gentleman," a young man called to them, "I have fresh grapes here, and tomatoes. Sir, how about a glass of pink lemonade to refresh yourself and your wife?"

"Oxen! Look at these fine beasts!" A gap-toothed man pointed to a pair of sharp-horned bovines in a small pen. "No hard overland passage for them, no, sir and no, ma'am. They made the trip on a steamship and are ready for work in the gold fields—"

"Rifles, friends, and good ones, too! A gross of them—one hundred and forty-four rifles for a dollar! Just a token payment, they're almost free!" Of course they were cheap. It was illegal to carry a gun in Dawson.

"What price would you pay to save your immortal soul from this greedy, godless place in the Arctic?" thundered a man dressed in ministerial black. "I bring you Bibles, God's own word right here, on sale for coin or gold dust—"

Dylan took Melissa's elbow to guide her past the displays of clothes, furs, jewels, opera glasses, patent-leather shoes, dime novels, ostrich feathers, and complete sets of Shakespeare with gilt edges. Against the blue sky, signs flapped in the breeze over tents, advertising dentistry and medical doctors, palmistry, and massage. There were dry goods and music, fresh-baked bread and ice cream made from condensed milk—as of yet, no dairy cows had arrived in town. There were seventeen-dollar brooms and twenty-five-cent slickers. One man offered a rare, recent copy of the *Seattle Post-Intelligencer* for fifty dollars—and got it. Newspapers and reading material were scarce.

And everyone called out about their goods at the same time.

"Mercy," she said, left nearly breathless by the noisy commotion around her. Across the way a particularly loud man's voice made her flinch. She had never learned to ignore a man yelling.

"Yeah, I hate crowds too," Dylan said, his expression grim. "We'll find what you need and get out of here."

She clutched Jenny to her, and Dylan took her

elbow to guide her. Coy had always walked ahead of her and left her to manage on her own. Although she could not ignore Dylan's size and height as he towered over her, she appreciated his help.

But she was still wary of him.

"What are these people doing here? Are they here because it's Saturday?" she asked, puzzled by the display. Back home in the summer, she saw farmers come to town to sell their crops on Saturdays. "They can't have come all the way up here to do *this*."

He gave a hard push to a mule that came too close. "No, most of them made the same trip you did, to search for gold. They dragged tons of this stuff over the mountains and down rivers. And most of them found out there are no claims left to stake." He scanned the vast emporium. "But I get the feeling that for a lot of these people, the main goal was just to get here. Now that they've done that, they don't know what else to do. They're sort of lost." He lifted a hand and made a sweeping gesture at the crowd. "They're selling everything they can to raise enough money to go home. Rafe is right—this is folly."

Aside from the brooms and newspaper, most of the things here were inexpensive. Melissa chose two serviceable dresses, two nightgowns, and a pair of shoes for herself. They were the first clothes she'd ever owned that weren't hand-me-downs. She bought some white-muslin to make dresses for Jenny, and a ten-yard length of real diaper fabric folded in a paper wrapper that read Sears, Roebuck. She also bought two sets of ready-made sheets for the bed. Dylan paid for the purchases as they went.

"Thank you," she said. "I don't want to keep you from your store, and I-I'm going to need to feed the baby pretty soon."

Dylan stared at her, and she worried that she had spent too much or said the wrong thing. "Is that all you're going to get?" Dylan asked. "Don't you want some other things, you know, female doodads?"

"Like what?" she asked, surprised.

"Well, like—" He strode ahead of her and stopped at a booth that had women's silver-backed mirrors, combs, and brushes displayed on a plaid wool blanket. A few cut-crystal perfume atomizers dotted the presentation. He gestured at the assortment. "Like this."

The man selling the vanity sets brightened. "Step right over here, ma'am, and see. These fine brushes and mirrors were made for Queen Victoria herself—" Dylan gave him a skeptical look. "Well, they come a far piece to get here."

Melissa shifted Jenny in her arms and approached the booth. She did not want to be any more indentured to Dylan Harper than she already was. How on earth would she ever pay him back if she kept digging a deeper hole of debt? Reaching out her free hand, she let her fingertips trace over the intricate designs on the silver handles that gleamed with the blue sky overhead. Still, she supposed a body had to have a hairbrush and comb. They were such basic possessions.

"Yes, they're very nice," she agreed with the merchant. Glancing up, she noticed the man studying the bruise on her cheek. Then he looked Dylan up and down with obvious censure.

Dylan saw it too, and he felt his own face flush. Clearly, the peddler held the same low opinion as did Dylan about a man who would raise a hand to a woman.

Damn it, he hadn't wanted to get involved with this washed-out female to begin with. But his sense of honor—and Rafe's noble prodding—had put him in the role of her protector. He wasn't the one who had hit her, and it irked him that anyone would think he had. But what could he say about it? Nothing. He picked up the most expensive vanity set and an atomizer, and paid the man quickly to escape his silent criticism. Dylan wasn't in the mood for it. Taking Melissa's elbow, he steered her onward to a rack of dresses.

Last night had been long and mostly sleepless, although he thought he'd dozed for a while. Feeling like the second biggest heel in Dawson—after all, he wasn't *worse* than Coy Logan—Dylan had had trouble keeping his mind from straying to the other side of his bed where Melissa lay. It was hard not to; aside from a saloon girl or two, he hadn't slept with a woman since Eliz— Here it was, two years later, and he couldn't say her name aloud, or even think it without feeling a twisting viper of betrayal gnaw at his gut. Even now, after everything that had happened, in those twilight moments between wakefulness and sleep, he still saw her face play across his eyelids, the sweet lushness of her body, her ink-black hair. She had tried to change him, bend him to her way of doing things. And when he would not yield—

"Go ahead and find a couple more frocks," he told Melissa gruffly. Whether he liked it or not, he felt responsible for her, and he couldn't very well let her and the baby go around in rags and flour sacking.

She lifted her face to his, and he got another dose of her eyes, gray and clear. What was it he saw in them? He sensed that there was another woman behind them, a completely different one from the skittish, colorless female the world saw.

"Oh, but you've already spent too much," she said, pushing at the strands of hair that had again come loose from the knot at the back of her head. "As it is, I owe you money for today, and for Coy. I don't want anything I can't pay for."

"Never mind about that for now," he said, annoyed at her mention of Logan. Even though he'd dumped her on Dylan's front step, she still wanted to shoulder his obligation. He had to admire her pride, but if he ever saw that money again, and he certainly didn't expect to, it would not come from her. "You'll work for me, just like I told you yesterday. But you can't wear the same thing day after day. You should probably have a shawl, too. It gets cold here at night sometimes, even in summer."

"Of course, whatever you think best—" She looked

as though she would have said more, but apparently changed her mind and dropped her gaze again.

Dylan sighed. She had probably learned her meekness just to get by in life. He supposed that a lot of men would be more than pleased with her cowed, docile obedience.

But Dylan Harper was not most men.

Dylan carried Melissa's purchases for her as they made their way back through town to the store. Walking next to him, she could not help but notice the wickedly long knife sheathed in leather and resting against his thigh. That he might actually use it was a frightening prospect, and yet she thought it suited him. She knew nothing about him, but he seemed as though he might have lived much closer to nature than she had. His long, sun-streaked hair and easy, graceful gait did not suggest a man who had spent his days behind a desk or even a counter. Yet his wildness was tempered, and he possessed better manners than the few men of her acquaintance. With his long legs, he'd be able to walk much faster than she, but she thought that he made an effort to keep from getting too far ahead of her.

When he did gain the lead, she found herself studying his wide shoulders and straight back. Then her gaze drifted down to his lean hips and backside, which were highlighted by the snug black pants he wore today. Melissa didn't really know much about men; her marriage to Coy had not been very enlightening, and what little she had learned at Coy's hands wasn't good. But Dylan bore a magnetic sensuality that she detected, even in her ignorance. He was powerfully and cleanly built, and she supposed that *some* women might find him appealing.

As for herself, Melissa felt certain that she would never want a husband again. But what people wanted and what they got did not always agree.

Returning to Front Street, she found it quiet for now. The carnival atmosphere that poured out of every saloon and dance hall along the wide, muddy thoroughfare each night wouldn't get started again until mid-afternoon.

"God, just look at what they've done to this place," Dylan said, more to himself than to her. He pointed at the surrounding hills, logged nearly bare. What didn't go for firewood, and to build sluice boxes and pilings for mining operations, was used in the explosion of new construction aided by the twenty hours of daylight. Skeletons of half-raised buildings added to the wildly contrasted landscape, and sawmills were kept running around the clock. In place of the trees were white orchards of ragged tents that housed ragged men, crowding the hilltops and spilling down their sides. "When I came up here two years ago, it was nothing more than a some tents and a moose pasture. A few hundred people lived here. It was hardly a paradise to begin with—it's pretty swampy and the mosquitoes are so thick they'll eat a man alive. But at least at night you could hear the wolves howling in the hills, or maybe a moose calling for his mate. Now a man can barely hear himself think."

"You don't believe the gold rush is a good thing?" she asked, stepping around a deep puddle.

He shrugged. "I'm not saying it is or isn't—I didn't come to Dawson for that. I just drifted up here with no particular plan. It was a good place for a man who had nowhere to—" He broke off for a moment. "But then Carmack found that gold on Rabbit Creek, and the rush was on. Now this town only has a little peace and quiet on Sundays." By order of the North West Mounted Police, all business and work in Dawson ceased every Saturday night from midnight till two A.M. on Monday morning. So unforgiving was the blue law that anyone caught working, even fishing for his dinner or chopping wood for his own fire, was sentenced to the woodpile, where he could chop all he liked.

"I've never seen anything like Dawson," she said, staring in amazement as four men hoisted a crystal chandelier from a wagon bed.

"Do you like it?" he asked, watching her with those probing green eyes.

"No. I'll be happy to go back to Portland. It wasn't my idea to come up here to begin with."

"I didn't suppose it was. There are women here who wanted to dig for gold beside their husbands, or to even work claims of their own." He studied her with a questioning expression that was almost gentle. "But they came mostly because they wanted to, not because someone dragged them up here."

She lowered her eyes to the top of the baby's head, but not before she noticed how striking he looked with the clear blue Yukon sky behind him. The sun highlighted the blond streaks in his hair that blew back from his shoulders in the light wind. He seemed completely unaware of his elemental handsomeness, but Melissa was not. She didn't want to notice his looks. She had known women on her street who waved farewell to their good judgment and had believed some man with a pretty face or smooth words, all to no good end. At least she could say that desperation had driven her to marry Coy, not the loss of her sense.

They reached Harper's Trading, and she was glad. Small though Jenny was, she was getting heavy in her already aching arms. Added to that, Melissa's breasts were growing firm with milk. Dylan followed her upstairs with the things she had bought, but she was grateful when he turned to go back to work. He treated her well enough, but she felt that odd quickening in her chest when he looked at her.

"Come by the store later and choose whatever provisions you need," he said, standing by the door. "I'd like to see what you can do with more than bacon and biscuits."

Chapter Four

When Dylan walked into the store, he saw Rafe tipped back in the rocking chair beside the cold stove, flipping cards into a chamber pot that he'd taken from a shelf. His feet were propped up on a keg, and a whiskey bottle and a half-empty glass stood on the plank flooring next to him.

"I wondered where you got off to. I've been languishing here for the better part of an hour. Between card games, drinking in the saloon without intelligent conversation sometimes loses its allure." He grinned at Dylan and gestured at the strongbox. "I did manage to sell a pair of rubber boots and some matches to one of your adventurous customers in your absence. I put the dust in your box."

Dylan laughed, highly amused at the idea of Rafe Dubois, a high-born Southern gentleman with silk handkerchiefs and French-laundered shirts, working behind his counter. "Maybe you should think about a job in trade. I could use the help here. You already have a key to the place."

"That is an offer that I'll believe I'll pass on, thank

you. I did you the favor since you'd wandered away from your business."

Dylan shrugged and hung his hat on a peg near the now cold stove. "I took Melissa down to the waterfront to, you know, buy her a few things." He mumbled the last part of the sentence, but Rafe heard him perfectly well.

The other man recrossed his ankles and pitched another card at the chamber pot. So far he'd missed only twice. "A shopping expedition? What a picture of domestic delight."

Dylan knew Rafe was teasing him, but he felt defensive. "Hell, Logan abandoned her here with just the clothes on her back. The baby didn't even have a diaper."

A card pinged off the inside rim of the enamal pot. "So I gathered," Rafe said, keeping his eyes on his game. "And how is Melissa and her child faring?"

"All right, I guess." Dylan hoisted a crate of beans to the counter and began putting the cans on the shelf.

"And you? How are you doing with your new arrangements?"

"This is a great time to ask, considering that you got me into this."

"I'm guessing there's a fine woman hiding beneath Melissa's timid exterior. You make a nice-looking little family."

The word *family* made Dylan wince. "The hell we do. That's not why I agreed to this. Logan would have sold her to the highest bidder. I couldn't let that happen." He had the feeling that Rafe was enjoying this enormously.

"You'll thank me later."

"For what?"

Rafe looked up. "For giving you something more to care about than proving a perfidious woman wrong."

As if summoned by his comment, Elizabeth's face rose in Dylan's memory. Raven-haired. Beautiful. Treacherous. He swung around, frowning. "Is that what you think I—" he began.

Just then, though, a couple of stampeders came in for supplies, and his attention was forced away from the subject of fickle women.

The two miners both smelled like cow flops on a riverbank at low tide—not a lot of washing went on at the claims. In fact, not a lot of anything but digging and sluicing went on. Frantic to make good on the claims they'd filed, the miners often worked twenty hours a day, especially during these periods of almost total daylight. Thinking about that reminded Dylan why he'd chosen to open this store.

"How's it going out there?" he asked them, not really wanting an answer.

One of the miners, a rough cob with a grizzled beard and a battered hat, replied, "Me and my pard over there, we've been digging night and day for a little color." He indicated the other man, a mild, simple-looking sort who stared at the bushel basket of oranges serving as a doorstop. The first man eyed Rafe suspiciously, who appeared not to notice anything beyond his cards. But Dylan knew he was listening avidly. These two were probably prime examples of what Rafe called man's greatest folly. Then the miner leaned closer to Dylan and whispered confidentially, "I just know I'm gonna strike it rich, but I have to keep an eye on old Jim. He tries to pretend that he's simple, and he does a good job of it. But given half a chance, I know he'd stick a knife in my gullet while I'm asleep and steal my poke." He squinted one eye venomously.

"Is that a fact?" Dylan backed away from the stench of his foul breath and unwashed body. He sensed Rafe's suppressed laughter as he continued to pitch cards at the chamber pot.

The gold rush had brought all kinds of people to the Yukon, and funny things happened to some men's minds in the face of such great potential wealth. He knew of one stampeder who had come up in '97 and mined thirty thousand dollars. But the money had given him no pleasure. Anxiety about being robbed had driven him to the edge of reason, until he was overcome by worry and shot himself. Another one, rotting with scurvy and almost lame, grew so obsessed with finding gold that he wouldn't take the time to be treated. Gold wouldn't buy much in the grave, Dylan thought.

A sizable pile of beans, coffee, nails, tobacco, and other supplies was assembled on the counter, and the men handed over their pokes to Dylan to weigh the payment.

Gold dust was the common legal tender in Dawson, and gold scales were as much a part of everyone's possessions as shovels and whiskey. Except for those rare occasions when he received coins or paper money, all of Dylan's transactions involved weighing raw gold. As he sprinkled dust onto the one pan, the rough cob suddenly grabbed his wrist.

"I seen what you're up to," the miner erupted angrily, revealing blackened teeth. He reached for a knife from his belt. "I never seen such a place—there ain't an honest man up here. Well, nobody's going to cheat *me*, by God! I wish to hell the Mounties would let a man carry a gun. I'd—"

Stunned, Dylan jerked his hand away and grabbed the meat cleaver beneath the counter. The miner yelped. "You'd be on the floor now, bleeding your guts out because I would have shot you. I don't cheat *anyone*," he said in a low, clear voice. He swung the cleaver down, narrowly and purposely missing the man's hand. It caught the corner of his grimy shirt cuff beneath its blade and drove it deep into the planks, trapping his arm. From the corner of his eye, Dylan saw Rafe rise from his chair and edge closer.

The miner's eyes looked as big as flapjacks, and his mouth opened and closed like a fish's. But no sound came out. His dim-witted sidekick, Jim, merely looked puzzled.

"You should be glad the MP don't allow firearms in Dawson, mister," Dylan said in the same low voice. "Where I come from, you falsely accuse a man of cheating and you find yourself in a world of hurt. But this is your lucky day, and I'm going to let you keep your hand. Now you take Jim and get out of here. And don't come back."

Dylan left the cleaver in the counter, and the miner yanked and yanked on his shirtsleeve, like an animal with its leg caught in a trap, until the fabric finally gave way.

"You're a crazy son of a bitch!" the man panted. He scrambled out of the store, pushing Jim ahead of him, and Dylan watched them go.

It was then that he saw Melissa standing there in a new dress, her eyes filled with fear.

Melissa gaped at Dylan, her heart pounding against her ribs like a hammer on a rock. She had walked in just in time to see Dylan produce the legendary meat cleaver and sink it into the miner's arm, pinning it to the counter. At least from where she stood, it had looked like the blade had impaled flesh.

Dylan turned his gaze on her, and the frightening blank fury on his face nearly froze the blood in her veins. His eyes seemed as hard as green bottle glass, and his jaw was so tight, she could see the muscles working in his cheek. This was the man she'd heard about, the man with an icy rage that most knew better than to cross. Dear God, she had to live with him, *sleep* with him in the same bed.

Dylan stepped out from behind the counter. "What are you doing here, Melissa?" His fists were clenched.

He seemed enormous, as big as a mountain, and tension radiated from him in waves. She could hear the anger in his voice, and her eyes fell to the tendon and muscle in his forearms.

She cast a panicky look at Rafe Dubois, but he merely nodded and smiled. "Mrs. Harper," he acknowledged pleasantly, "you look very nice this afternoon." Then he sat down in a chair and began fiddling with a deck of cards. She took a step backward and laced her fingers together to make one tight fist over her heart.

"Thank you. I-I just came for some flour and the other things . . . like-like we talked about earlier." She heard the quiver in her own voice and hated it. "But I can come back—this is a bad time."

Dylan came closer and reached for her, closing his big, warm hand around her upper arm. His long fingers encircled it easily. She uttered a little squeak and tried to pull away, but his grip was sure.

"No, it's not a bad time." He exhaled, as if discharging a bit of the rage that was percolating inside. "Now and then I get a surly customer, or one who's not quite right in the head."

And it was sane to nearly chop off a man's hand? she wondered foolishly, feeling a swell of hysterical laughter fill her chest. Realizing that he wasn't going to let her leave, she said, "I just need one or two things to cook dinner." Maybe she could make a quick escape, she thought, and leave him down here with his temper.

He released her arm with seeming reluctance, and she immediately stepped back. "All right, take whatever you want to make a good meal. You might as well look through this stuff, too, before I put it back on the shelves." He gestured at the supplies still heaped on the counter. "If you need help taking anything upstairs, I'll carry it for—"

"Oh, no, I don't want to trouble you," she said quickly, avoiding his intense gaze. "If you'll just give me a gunnysack, I can manage." She glanced up, and he watched her for a moment longer. Then he nodded and walked away.

Melissa had trouble keeping her mind on her task; she picked up and put down the same tin of baking soda three times before she realized what she'd done. In the end, she'd collected a few potatoes, coffee, sugar, a piece of ham, some dried apples, and a couple of other staples. It hadn't seemed like much. When she filled the burlap sack Dylan gave her, it turned out to be heavier than she'd expected. She gripped it tightly, but when she dragged it from the counter to lift it, the sack dropped to the rough floor with a thud, bending her with it.

"Melissa, let me bring this upstairs for you," Dylan said. His frown dipped to the bridge of his nose, giving her no confidence.

Worried that he would simply grab it away from her and take it himself, from her bowed position she protested, "No, please don't bother. I just lost my grip on it." With supreme effort she lifted the sack and stood upright, then dragged it toward the door. Her arms and shoulders, already stiff from lifting the rice last night, flared with pain, but she refused to let him see that.

"I'll have dinner ready in an hour or so," she panted and hauled her groceries through the open door, glad to have made her escape.

Dylan stared at the outside wall as he listened to the sound of her slow steps going up the stairs on the side of the building. It sounded as if she were dragging the weight of the world with her.

From his post by the chamber pot, Rafe Dubois looked first at the now empty doorway, and then at Dylan. "Hell, that girl is scared to death of you. She probably fears you more than she does the devil himself," he remarked with casual surprise.

Dylan shrugged, wishing Rafe hadn't noticed. "She's got a safe place to live here and more food than she's probably seen in three months. I can't help it if I scare her—that's her problem."

But he knew that was a lie, and Rafe's quirked eyebrow told him that he knew it, too.

Upstairs, Melissa's cooking efforts were hampered by Jenny. She had fed and changed the baby, but for some reason her usually quiet and happy child would not settle down. In fact, she had started getting fussy as soon as Melissa had fed her. It was as if her own nervousness had telegraphed to Jenny. She put the baby in her makeshift bed, but after a few minutes she started crying, and Melissa picked her up and walked with her, anxious to quiet her. She checked the little girl's diaper for open safety pins and felt her for fever. She found nothing. But when she tried to lay Jenny in her crate again, the baby recommenced her howling, forcing Melissa to pace the room with her.

"Hush, now, button, hush," she urged feverishly. "We have to be quiet, just like before when your father was with us, remember? He's gone, but we still have to be quiet."

Between moments of walking with the baby, Melissa managed to put together a meal of boiled ham, mashed potatoes, and apple pie. There was no butter, and only canned milk for the potatoes, but then she hadn't tasted fresh milk since she passed through Seattle, months earlier. Butter was something she had not often seen in her life.

She caught herself listening for the slam of the door downstairs in the store, for Dylan's footfalls on the stairs. The sight of him with the meat cleaver in his fist wouldn't leave her mind. How far would that rage go?

The most frightening part of his anger had been the deadly cold of it. Coy would rant and swear and carry on, yelling and throwing things. A lot of noise had accompanied his fits of anger. Coy's outbursts had been no less frightening, but they hadn't sneaked up on her. Dylan's fury made her think of a cool and deadly snake, sliding up from nowhere.

Dylan was so different in every way from Coy, or her father and brothers. At least he seemed so in her few dealings with him.

But a temper was a temper, and she imagined that one slap or punch hurt just as much as another.

Her heart, though . . . she had learned to keep it

safely out of reach. The bruises healed, but a broken heart would not fare as well.

After Rafe left Harper's to search out a card game at the saloon, Dylan decided to lock up for an hour or so and go eat dinner. He thought he detected the aroma of ham and hot apple pie drifting down through the ceiling. It smelled better than any saloon food he'd tasted in Dawson, maybe better than anything he'd eaten since he left The Dalles, his hometown in Oregon.

He stood outside on the duckboard and flipped the hasp over the door, then secured it with a padlock. Despite the hundreds of thousands of dollars in gold dust deposited here in Dawson, he knew a lot of business owners didn't bother to lock their doors. The Mounties' presence was so respected, and the threat of banishment from Dawson so real, genuine crime was a rarity here. No one wanted to be forced to leave town and forfeit his one big chance to strike it rich. Men were arrested for using obscene language, or cheating at cards, or for selling whiskey to saloon girls. Theft, robbery, and assault were surprisingly rare; towns with far fewer people living under calmer circumstances experienced much worse. But Dylan had been burned by tempting fate, and he kept his place locked.

Dawson's low instance of crime wasn't the chief subject on his mind, though. His thoughts kept drifting back to Melissa. It wasn't difficult for him to picture her standing at the stove in that new dress he'd seen her wearing when she came into the store. It had looked nice on her, with its narrow blue-and-white stripe, and high white collar that made her neck look like a swan's.

More than her dress, though, he remembered her expression of pure, ashen terror when he'd glanced up to find her standing over there by the basket of oranges. Fierce annoyance had been his first reaction; why the hell had she chosen that moment of all moments to walk in? If the miner had decided to make the situation uglier than it was, having a woman in the mix could have complicated things considerably.

But he knew that Rafe was right. She feared Dylan more than anybody else. He felt certain that she'd seen her share of violence in her life. And in a town like Dawson, where everyone was struck with gold fever, scrapes like the one with the miner were bound to occur. Still, he didn't want her to be afraid of him; how would she share that small living space upstairs—how would she even work for him—if she feared him?

Settling his hat, he recalled that Elizabeth had been afraid of him sometimes, but she had seemed to relish the fear. It had excited her. In turn, she had aroused in him a dark, hot desire that gave him no peace, not even after their clandestine moments in his bed over the stables. He paused, his gaze fixed unseeing on the milling crowd. How did she like her life now? he wondered bitterly, with her wealthy, dull husband—

As he climbed the stairs, he heard the muffled

sound of the baby squalling and it shook him from his thoughts. None of his past mattered now, he knew, and looking back to review regrets was one of the biggest mistakes a man could make.

When he opened the door, he saw steaming food on the stove, and Melissa pacing back and forth with the baby in her arms. Hearing him, she whirled and her expression made him think of a doe he'd once startled in the woods. Their eyes had locked for just a moment, and he had seen her terror before she bolted off through the brush.

"Oh! I'll have your dinner for you in just a minute." She put the baby in her crate, and the child began howling again. In a rush she slapped the potatoes, ham, and some biscuits on the table, all the while shifting her gaze between him and Jenny. Then she hurried to the crate and picked up the baby again.

Baffled, Dylan threw his hat on the bed and sat down at the place she'd set for him. "Aren't you going to eat?"

Melissa paced the small floor, jogging Jenny in her arms. "No, not now. Not until—" The baby's wails climbed to ear-piercing shrieks. "Oh, please, button, please don't cry," she begged. With her cheek pressed to Jenny's head, plainly she was beside herself with worry.

Dylan took a bite of the ham. It tasted good, but he couldn't really enjoy it while the agitated woman paced with her screaming child in this little room. Her pale hair had come loose from its knot again and hung beside her face in damp tendrils. He pushed the other chair out with his foot. "Maybe if you stop pacing and sit down?" he suggested. He didn't know much about kids but he thought that Melissa was making things worse.

She eyed him warily.

"Come on," he urged.

Melissa edged closer, feeling as if she were approaching a wild dog, and perched on the edge of the chair.

"What's the matter with her? Is she sick?" Dylan asked over the bawling.

"No, I don't think so," she said, hearing the overwrought edge in her own voice. "She usually isn't like this—I just don't know what it is." She continued to jog Jenny frantically in her arms, all to no avail. The baby turned the color of a ripe plum with her screeching. "Jenny, Jenny, don't carry on so, sweetheart, please."

Melissa glanced up at Dylan's stern face, and her heart thundered inside her rib cage. She was familiar with that kind of expression—he looked angry and impatient, while he fixed her and the baby with that hard, green glare. On top of that, his dinner was growing cold in front of him, and she knew how men hated that. Oh, God, please make Jenny be quiet, please, please, please—

Suddenly, Dylan reached out to touch the baby's forehead. Melissa pulled back and clutched Jenny to her chest, unable to completely bite back a scream of her own.

He withdrew his hand and stared at her. "Does she have a fever?" he asked in that quiet, deadly serious voice she'd heard him use on the miner.

She shook her head and kept her eyes down, resenting him in that moment because she feared him, and hating the way it crippled her.

Melissa heard the legs of his chair scrape across the floor, and she held her breath. Now she would hear his boot heels on the plank flooring as he came around to her side of the table. She waited for the sharp, heavy impact of his fist, or the fiery burn of a slap. Either, she knew from experience, would make her head feel as if it were going to come off with the blow. Lights would flash behind her eyes, like a thousand candle flames bursting into stars. She bent farther over Jenny, shielding her as best she could, and drew in a deep, sobbing breath.

But instead of coming toward her, she heard the boot heels walk away, and then the door opened and closed. His footsteps rumbled down the stairs and glancing up, she found she was alone with Jenny. Dylan's plate still held most of his dinner, and his coffee was untouched.

She and the baby had driven him out of his own place. No man would tolerate that, and it wouldn't surprise her if he went to the saloon. Now she had to worry about when he would come back, and in what condition. For a wild moment Melissa considered piling everything in the room against the door to keep him out. Or maybe she could pack up Jenny and leave before he got back.

And go where? she asked herself, trying to hear her own thoughts over the baby's crying. Could she find some kind of work? She wished she could dissolve into tears like Jenny, but she had to keep her wits about her or she would be utterly and irretrievably lost.

But before she could formulate any other ideas, she heard Dylan coming up the stairs again. He'd been gone only a moment—strange that she had already learned the sound of his steps.

He flung open the door, then maneuvered an oak rocking chair through the narrow doorway. His sun-streaked hair fell forward, obscuring his face as he wrestled it into the room. "I had this downstairs," he said, straightening. He carried it to the window and angled it so that it faced the street. A mild breeze drifted in. "Rafe will probably miss it, but I thought it might help."

Melissa gaped at him, taken by complete surprise. She sat motionless, still perched where he'd left her, and stared at Dylan's handsome face. She saw no anger there, no threat.

He came closer, slowly and carefully. Then he held out his hand. "Come and sit by the window for a few minutes. It might make both of you feel better." He didn't raise his voice over Jenny's squalling, but Melissa heard him perfectly.

"I'm sorry your dinner got cold," she babbled. "I can put it back in the—"

"It doesn't matter, Melissa. I'll take care of it." He pushed his open hand closer to her. She hesitated, then shifting Jenny to one arm, put her own hand in his palm. His fingers closed around hers, and he helped her to her feet.

"Thank you," she murmured as she settled in the rocker. Giving a push with the heel of her shoe, she set the chair in motion. It felt welcoming and soothing, and even Jenny began to quiet.

He turned to walk to the table, then stopped and fixed her with a direct look. "I've *never* hit a woman in my life. I sure as hell don't plan to start now."

Dylan sat down at the table and poked a fork into his cold dinner. It tasted good, but he wasn't very hungry. The sight of Melissa huddling over her child, obviously trying to protect them both, had stolen his appetite. And the naked gratitude and relief he'd seen in her eyes when he brought in the rocker had startled him. Did she really believe that all men were like Logan? Was that the only way of life she had known?

His gaze fell on her again. She sat in a shaft of sunlight that slanted through the open window. It cast a bright halo over her blond hair as she looked down at the baby and rocked her, stroking her silken head with her hand. For just an instant, he wondered what it would feel like if her hand stroked his hair. Would it heal? Would it bring forgetfulness?

Presently, he heard Melissa humming softly in a voice so sweet that he put down his fork to listen. The picture of mother and child was perfect in that moment, and Dylan felt a stirring in his soul.

Once, a long time ago it now seemed, he'd envisioned his own wife holding their baby like this. He dragged his gaze back to his food. Once, a long time ago, Dylan had let his love for a woman drive him to distraction.

It was a mistake he swore he would not repeat.

That night Melissa lay in Dylan's bed, made with the clean new sheets she'd bought. The quiet, semi-dusk of midnight gave the room a mellow pink glow. Jenny slept. She had at last exhausted herself when Melissa had calmed down too.

The sack of rice still separated her from the fierce, sun-blond man on the other side of the mattress. But he didn't seem quite as frightening now, and she didn't cling so tightly to the edge of the bed. She heard his slow, even breathing and knew he slept, too.

There were no guarantees in life, but tonight the agreement into which they'd entered at the Yukon Girl Saloon had been sealed.

And it had been accomplished with the gift of a rocking chair.

Chapter Five

Over the next few days, with decent food and a little peace, Melissa began to regain her strength. She still jumped at loud voices and noises, but not every time, and the bruise on her face had finally faded.

The rocking chair had proved to be a godsend. After that one horrible night, Jenny had settled down again into her sweet-tempered disposition, but Melissa loved to rock the baby while she fed her or put her to sleep. Sometimes they just sat by the window and rocked while Melissa sang to her. Jenny would stare up at her with wide eyes and a half smile, captivated. Although the noise from the street below was nearly continuous, it was the quietest, most tranquil time that Melissa had known as a mother—in fact, in her whole life.

No loud voice assaulted her ears, no drunken man demanded intimate access to her body, slobbering kisses on her and using her until he passed out.

Though she viewed Dylan as an intimidating man, now she didn't *always* flinch when she heard his footsteps on the stairs. And, true to his word, he had not made one attempt to touch her in any way beyond the night he offered her his hand. Except for meals, though, she hardly saw him. They settled into a routine—he spent most of his time downstairs in his store, and Melissa kept to this room, cleaning and cooking and taking care of Jenny.

She was in a peculiar position. She knew that she and Jenny were invading his privacy, and that he felt stuck with them, as if they were a pair of charity cases. Which, she supposed, they were. She wasn't really Mrs. Harper; she worked for him, he said. And he had given her money last Saturday, telling her it was a week's wages. But her job was not like a shop girl's, or a factory worker's, or even a domestic's, at least not like her mother's had been at the Pettigreaves. In order to earn her keep and pay back Coy's debt, she would have to do more than just sweep this room and cook. At any rate, it wasn't enough to keep her busy.

Dawson was like a giant carnival, and Melissa knew that a lot of gold dust changed hands in this town, more money than she had ever seen in her life. A lot of people were growing wealthy just by catering to miners and free-spending Klondike kings. Dylan himself was making his money that way. There had to be some way she could do that, too. Having cash would give her independence and security, and the ability to safeguard Jenny's future. Nothing seemed more important to her—not nice clothes, not a husband, not even love.

Her budding desire to improve her lot was reinforced early one morning shortly after the incident with the rocker, when she and Dylan were standing under the side stairs. There Melissa had set up a washtub and scrub board to do their laundry, and Dylan had carried down some of the wash for her.

From the milling crowd, a petite, well-dressed woman with a plain face hailed them. "Dylan Harper! I haven't seen you in weeks."

Melissa recognized Belinda Mulrooney, one of the most successful entrepreneurs, man or woman, to come to the Yukon. She was highly respected and admired for her business savvy; Melissa wished that she possessed one quarter of her shrewdness.

"I'm here at the store every day, Belinda. You keep yourself pretty busy," Dylan replied, chuckling.

Everything about the woman, even her bearing, seemed energetic, Melissa thought.

"That I do. There are too many opportunities in this town to let one get past me. You should've taken advantage of that lay I told you about. The first one I took out measured five hundred feet square, and I got a thousand dollars a day for the month that I had it."

A lay, Melissa knew, was a short-term, temporary arrangement, whereby a claim owner allowed another person to mine the property in exchange for a percentage of the gold found there. A few people had suggested this kind of enterprise to Coy. He'd rejected the idea outright, saying he was no sharecropper. The truth, of course, was that such an arrangement would have required him to work.

Dylan shifted his weight to one hip and rubbed the back of his neck, giving the impression of mock regret. "Well, I know about horses, not mining. Besides, I didn't have any interest in digging around in the dirt."

Belinda grinned archly. "When that kind of money is involved, I'd dig in a hog wallow." She looked Melissa up and down, although not unkindly. "Are you going to introduce me to this lady, Dylan?"

Melissa shifted Jenny in her arms, feeling awkward, and waited to see what he would say.

He straightened. "Oh, uh, this is Melissa Lo— Harper. Melissa, this is Belinda Mulrooney. She's got her finger in just about every successful business venture in Dawson."

"Flatterer," Belinda said, then echoed, "Did you say Melissa *Harper*?" She glanced at Jenny.

"Well, it's a long—" Melissa began.

"Melissa is my . . . wife."

Belinda considered them both with a perceptive look, then glanced at Melissa's left hand. She didn't have a wedding ring—Coy had sold it long ago, and Dylan hadn't given her one. Surprised by Dylan's comment, Melissa waited for her to say something about the baby, or their obviously hasty marriage, but she only smiled.

"Congratulations, Dylan, I hadn't heard. How very nice to meet you Mrs. Harper. I've known Dylan, here, for a couple of years. He was one of the first people I met when I came up."

"Oh," Melissa replied faintly.

"You two must come by when I open my hotel. It should be ready in another couple of weeks. I'm calling it the Fairview, and it'll be the grandest place in Dawson." She began listing the hotel's attributes, ticking them off on her fingers. "I'll have twenty-two rooms with electric lights and steam heat. There'll be an orchestra in the lobby, and bone china and sterling in the dining room." She reached up to readjust her black straw hat in the stiff breeze that blew under the cloudy sky. "I've got brass beds and crystal chandeliers coming in over White Pass, so I'm leaving for Skagway tomorrow to oversee the whole thing."

"Are you going alone?" Melissa asked. It seemed like a fearsome thing for a woman to do. Skagway was a raw, wild place, far more so than Dawson.

Belinda waved her hand dismissively. "Absolutely. I have to make sure the packers I hired don't break those chandeliers, or cheat me."

She bade them good-bye then, and bustled down the street like a whirlwind through the crowd toward the site of the Fairview to harass her construction workers.

Dylan chuckled again and shook his head as he watched her go. "She's a real piece of work, that Belinda."

He took her arm as they walked toward the store for soap. Melissa had to admit that she liked the feel of his hand under her elbow.

"Thank you for, well, for not embarrassing me in front of her." She looked up at him, at the way his streaked hair caught in the wind and blew back behind his shoulders. Had she noticed the curve of his full mouth before?

"Oh, you mean I didn't belch or scratch where I shouldn't?" He grinned, showing her dimples and white, straight teeth.

The joke was so completely unexpected, Melissa burst into laughter. The Dylan Harper she knew didn't make jokes. Or so she had thought.

"No, that's not what I meant. You didn't have to tell her that I'm your wife."

"What else could I have said?" His smile faded. Releasing her arm, he shoved his hands into his front pockets, as if suddenly self-conscious. "I don't think she believed it, anyway."

"Maybe not," Melissa said softly, almost wishing he still held her elbow. But his deed counted for more than his credibility. When he had told her that she could use his name, she never once expected that he would go out of his way to introduce her as his wife.

Perhaps, just perhaps, Rafe Dubois had told her the truth when he said that Dylan Harper was a gentleman.

"You want to work? Our agreement was that you would work here for me. What more do you think you can do when you have a baby to watch?" Dylan asked when they went back upstairs.

She had broached the subject of her working with trepidation. If he'd planned on her looking after only his own wants, he might forbid her from doing anything else, and be angry besides. But after meeting Belinda Mulrooney, Melissa had given more and more thought to making some money of her own.

Dylan stood at the mirror over the washstand, barefoot and wearing only a pair of jeans while he shaved. The sun, up since three-thirty, was bright beyond the canvas curtains and fell across his bare back, outlining the plane of his shoulders with light and shadow. Melissa tried not to stare at the ridges of muscles that flanked the long hollow of his spine, or the way his jeans seemed to hang suspended below his narrow waist and follow the curve of his backside. She didn't want to notice any of those things—he wasn't her husband and she didn't want another one after Coy. But she found the sight hard to ignore.

"Coy told me that saloon girls make a hundred dollars a night just for peddling drinks and dancing with miners," she replied, shifting her attention to the sink full of breakfast dishes that she was washing.

He looked at her over his shoulder, his razor stilled in his hand, and the lower half of his face hidden by shaving soap. "Jesus, you want to work in a *saloon*?"

"No, of course I don't. But I've heard about women running roadhouses and dressmaking shops, and making a lot of money at it."

"How much money do you need?" His tone turned oddly brittle. "I'm not charging you for room and board."

She took a quiet breath before answering. "I mean

no offense, but you said yourself that this is temporary. That when you decide you've had enough you're going back to Oregon. I have to be ready for that day."

He turned back toward the mirror. "I told you that I'll give you enough to make a new start somewhere else," he mumbled.

"I really want to have money of my own, as much as I can make. Anyway, I still intend to pay you the twelve hundred dollars Coy owed you, and any other money it's cost you to take in Jenny and me."

"I don't expect you to cover Logan's debt. I told you that was between him and me, and you're not responsible for it."

He almost sounded irritated, but she couldn't imagine why. She'd expect him to be glad to get his money back. "Just the same, I will pay you in Coy's place."

Dylan drew a deep breath and swallowed the surge of bitter annoyance that rose abruptly within him. *Coy Logan.* He thought that if she mentioned him one more time, he'd search out the bastard and give him the beating he so richly deserved. And she wanted a lot of money? Elizabeth had wanted lots of money too, badly enough to reveal the object of her true love—herself. Why did it seem that the women he'd known in his life put a higher value on cash than anything else?

He spoke to her reflection in his shaving mirror. "What do you know how to do? Have you got goods to sell, or a skill people will pay for?" He tipped his head back to shave his throat.

She thought for a moment. "I can't dance or sing if that's what you mean."

Dylan would dispute that. He didn't know if she could dance, but she had the sweetest voice he'd ever heard. The few times he'd been around when she sang to Jenny, he would sit at the table and pretend to be busy with some task just for the pleasure of listening to her. But for such a timid woman, she was as stubborn as a mule.

He stole another glance at her as she scrubbed the frying pan. Apparently she had given up trying to keep her hair in a knot and now wore it in long, heavy braid that swung back and forth behind her when she moved.

In the brief gap of silence, he heard her sigh.

"I guess I don't know how to do much of anything besides cook and clean. That was all I ever did at home in Portland." She sounded defeated. "I never earned anything for it."

"Yeah? Why did you get stuck with it?"

She paused a long moment before answering. "My mother worked as a maid for a wealthy family, so she only came home one day a week. The rest of the time I took care of my brothers and my father." He heard a sharp edge of resentment in her voice.

"Things weren't so good there, huh?"

She paused on her way to the landing to throw out the dishwater. "No, they weren't."

She didn't elaborate, and Dylan didn't ask her to.

He knew the story wouldn't be a happy one, and hearing the details would just make it harder to keep his distance.

And he was having some trouble with that as it was. Sometimes her image rose in his mind when he least wanted to see it. Hell, he was just a man, and having her in his bed, even with that damned rice sack between them, gave him all sorts of notions. He kept telling himself that it was because he hadn't had a woman in months. It *had* to be that—it had to be the reason he sometimes woke in the middle of the night and propped up on his elbow to watch her sleep.

Let her find work, he decided, shrugging off the picture in his head. So much the better for him—he wouldn't try to stop her. If she learned a way to make a living, he'd be able to send her on her way without a twinge of conscience over how she would fare alone in the world with an infant. And he could go back home to The Dalles, buy the land he longed for, and get on with his own life.

He wiped the rest of the soap off his face and put on his shirt. It was nicely ironed. The collar and cuffs bore just a touch of starch, and all the buttons were sewn on. Until Melissa had moved in, he'd usually washed his clothes in a bucket and draped them over the chairs to dry. Then he'd put them on as they'd dried, wrinkled and stiff as boards. This was a luxury. A man could get used to sweet singing and good meals and ironed shirts.

He stopped himself. Yeah, a man could get used

to a lot of things—the scent of a woman's hair, the lure of her body, the teasing softness of her voice.

And that was when his troubles would begin.

After dragging the rest of the wash downstairs, Melissa put Jenny in her crate and set the box on a chair next to the washtub. The morning clouds had burned off, and the sun began to emerge. Dylan had put up an awning to create a roomy shelter, and strung rope between two pairs of poles to give her a clothesline. A little stove that he'd set up just behind the building provided her with a place to heat water.

It wasn't the best arrangement—she didn't know what she'd do come fall when the weather began to grow cold. And it felt strange to do wash in full view of the passing throng, who had only to look down the side street to see her working here. For now, though, the days were mild and this spot would have to serve.

Up and down Front Street the incessant racket of hammers and saws echoed as new three- and four-story buildings rose from the place that, until a little over a year ago as Dylan had pointed out, had been nothing more than a few tents and a moose pasture. At least the muddy streets had finally begun to dry out under the June sun.

Jenny gurgled and waved her fists, apparently pleased with her change of location. Looking at her, Melissa felt her heart swell with love. She was such a beautiful child, so full of promise, her future bright with whatever possibilities Melissa would be able to give her.

"Would you like to hear a song, button?" Melissa asked as she plunged her hands into the soapy tub to scrub a diaper. She took up Stephen Foster's ode to Jeannie, but changed her name to Jenny, and her light brown hair to pale blond. The little girl smiled and watched her, fascinated, as though she understood the words.

After she washed her own things, she began Dylan's clothes. They carried the scent of him, not an unpleasant smell, and one that Melissa had come to recognize, just as she knew the sound of his footsteps on the plank flooring in the store. While she worked, she sang softly, as much to amuse herself as to keep the baby happy. Melissa was in the middle of "Shenandoah" when she looked up and saw a man standing just at the edge of the awning.

She sprang up straight from the washtub, her heart lurching around in her chest. "Wh-what do you want?"

He looked like any of the other grimy, tired men she saw on Front Street, bearded and wearing a battered hat. He was about thirty, she thought, perhaps a few years older than Dylan.

" 'Scuse me, ma'am, I don't mean no harm. I was just passing by"—he pointed his thumb over his shoulder toward the duckboards—"and I thought I heard singing."

Melissa put herself between the stranger and Jenny. "I was singing to the baby," she said while mentally calculating the distance to the front door of Harper's Trading.

He nodded, his face shadowed by a trace of melancholy. The clearing sky behind him contrasted with his expression. "It sounded so sweet, I just wanted to listen for a minute. Sort of reminded me of home, that's all."

Melissa relaxed slightly. "Have you been gone long?" She didn't bother to ask if he'd come from far away. Everyone had traveled a long distance to get to this place.

He nodded. "Yes, ma'am, I left Sacramento just about a year ago now, but it seems ten times that. The missus and my two girls are waiting there for me. I promised I'd come home a rich man." He chuckled humorlessly. "I guess I can't go yet, but I sure miss them."

"I imagine they'd rather that you were there with them, rich or not."

"Oh . . . after I talked so big about what a grand life we'd have, and all the fine things we could buy, I don't feel like I can go home a failure." His rueful smile all but admitted the foolishness of his logic.

He sounded determined and yet hopeless at the same time, and Melissa could think of nothing else to tell him. "Well, good luck to you. I hope you don't have to be away from your family much longer."

"Thank you for the singing, ma'am. And good luck with your business, too." He gestured at her washtub.

"Oh, no, not a business. This is just my family's

wash. My baby's." She glanced at Dylan's wet shirt in her hands. "And my husband's."

The stranger looked down at his own muddy clothes, and then at her. "Ma'am, forgive me if I seem like I'm getting above myself, but— Being out in the gold fields most of the time, I don't get any clothes washed regular-like. Generally, I wear them till I can't stand them no more, then I buy new duds and throw the old ones away. I guess it seems like a waste of money. Would you consider— Well, ma'am, could you be persuaded to do laundry for me if I paid you?"

Someone wanted to *pay* her to wash clothes? All these years she had performed such work in exchange for nothing more than a roof over her head.

"I should probably ask my husband," she said. Melissa was unaccustomed to being permitted to think for herself. In fact, none of the men she had known believed a woman capable of intelligent thought.

Then she remembered Belinda Mulrooney and her enterprising spirit, and the germ of the idea she'd discussed with Dylan began to take hold. Melissa could probably do very well in a town with thousands of men who were far away from the domestic services of home. This might be just the chance she was looking for.

"On second thought, I'll do your wash, Mr. . . ."

"Willis, ma'am, John Willis."

"I'm . . ." She faltered a moment. "I'm Mrs. Harper, Mr. Willis. Bring your clothes." In one of the most daring decisions Melissa had ever made, she added, "And tell your friends to bring theirs, too."

"I'm going to need a lot of soap, I guess, and starch, and a couple more washtubs." Melissa ticked the items off on her fingers as she paced in front of Dylan's counter. She'd hurried into the store with Jenny, anxious to get her new venture under way. The prospect of planning for her own destiny was terrifying but exciting, too. "Oh, and I'll need to string more clothesline. I guess I'll have to get a pair of those gold scales too, since I'm starting tomorrow." She stopped then and considered both Rafe and Dylan. She realized that she was the only one talking, and an alarm sounded in her mind. In making her grand plans she'd forgotten how much men disliked women to think for themselves. "That is, if it's all right with you. I'll still take care of the chores upstairs."

Dylan shrugged indifferently, shifting his sun-blond hair. "I don't care what you do with your time as long as you keep your end of your bargain with me." He took a sip from a thick-lipped white coffee mug, then began piling bars of yellow soap in front of her on the counter.

"I can do both," she hurried to assure him. "I can still cook and clean for you, and do this, too."

"Then do what you want."

She shifted Jenny to her shoulder. "Maybe I should have a sign painted. You know, so people will know I'm here. MRS. HARPER'S LAUNDRY, or something like that. Are signs expensive?" It was a silly question, she realized—everything in the Yukon was expensive.

Dylan hoisted a forty-pound crate of Kingford's Silver Gloss Starch to the counter. "You don't need a sign. I can promise that you won't lack for business. Once the word gets out, you'll be buried under a pile of dirty clothes." His tone had that funny brittle edge that she'd heard once or twice before.

He didn't like the idea. She could tell by his voice and the flinty expression in his green eyes. She didn't even think that Rafe liked it—he sent Dylan a look that was even more forbidding than his friend's hard, blank expression. But at least Dylan didn't object outright, and she had gained enough wary confidence in him to believe that he wasn't simply waiting until they were alone to explode in a boiling fury.

About that time Jenny started fussing for her afternoon meal, and Melissa welcomed the chance to escape. "Oh, dear, I'll have to come back for everything."

"I'll put it under the stairs for you," Dylan said, and her last thought of him was that he was the most complex man she had ever known.

Dylan watched Melissa leave, and heard the swish of her calico skirt as it brushed around the door frame. This was a hell of a change from the silent, terrified rag doll he'd met three weeks ago. She was still too thin, but her new clothes helped to hide that.

With no little effort, Rafe unfolded his long cadaverous frame from the straight-backed chair that now took the place of the rocker. Dylan could hear his breathing again today. "I'd almost believed that I made the right decision in giving Melissa and her child over to your protection." Walking to the counter, he removed a small silver flask from the inside pocket in his coat and took a drink from it. "I admit that I'm wondering if I did the right thing."

Dylan stared at him. "Why?"

"I'd hoped that you'd make her life a little easier—obviously that woman has been sorely abused. But now I find that she feels she has to wash clothes in the street to earn her own way. She'll be prey to every unsavory opportunist in Dawson. What did you say to give her the impression that she has to work?" Rafe's slow, melodic drawl could cut like a whip when he was peeved.

"Not a goddamned thing! And she won't be in the street," Dylan retorted, surprised that Rafe would care about his relationship with Melissa. "This was *her* idea, not mine. She told me she wants to earn as much money as she can."

The lawyer coughed, then drew a gasping breath that sounded like his last. "Have you wondered why that is?" he asked when the fit had passed.

Dylan knew perfectly well why, and the reason made him feel guilty somehow. But he wasn't of a mind to discuss his earlier conversation with Melissa. He shrugged. "Well, what woman doesn't want money?" he asked. "At least she's willing to work for it."

Rafe shrugged and took another drink. "I wouldn't subject my wife to that."

Feeling beleaguered by the interrogation, Dylan snapped, "She's not my wife!" From the first day he'd agreed to this temporary alliance with Melissa, he'd had the uneasy suspicion that his friend viewed the arrangement as permanent. "And I don't want one."

Rafe gazed at the street through the open door, as though another voice called to him. "Dylan, do you ever think about your own death?" The anger had left his voice.

Puzzled by the change of subject, he replied, "Sure, once in a while."

"Probably on those nights that seem to have no end, when the rest of the world sleeps but you can't? All kinds of thoughts are apt to cross a person's mind in the hours that should belong to Morpheus."

Dylan had to admire his friend's classical education. "True, but it isn't a subject that I dwell on."

Rafe nodded. "Probably not. Nearly every man dies with regrets, though." He tapped his thin chest. "Keeping this heart, faulty though it is, all to myself is one of mine." It was as frank a comment as he'd ever made. He considered Dylan with dark, deep-set eyes. "Don't let it be one of yours."

Chapter Six

Dylan proved to be right. The first morning that Melissa stepped outside to begin her business, a swarm of helpless masculinity with dirty clothes beat a path to her washtubs as if called by a siren's song. How word got around so quickly she didn't know. John Willis, her first customer, could not have been responsible for all of it.

Certainly, any woman with a washtub and soap could go into the laundry business, and several had. But with thirty thousand people, mostly men, in and around Dawson, there was more than enough work for all.

Even when Melissa had lived in Portland with her father and four brothers, she had never seen so much filthy, mud-caked laundry in her life. The long, sweltering day was an endless cycle of heating water, scrubbing, rinsing, and hanging wet wash. The area surrounding the back stairs became a cat's cradle of clothesline strung in every possible place, with clean shirts, pants, and underwear flapping in the breeze.

To make things a bit easier for her, Dylan had broken down the sides of a tea crate to make flooring so she wouldn't have to stand in the mud. From another box he'd fashioned a little nook for Jenny that kept the baby within easy sight and reach. These were small blessings when she discovered how hard the work would be.

To lessen the drudgery, and because Jenny seemed to like it so much, Melissa sang through most of her day. Although she kept her voice low, now and then miners would straggle down the side street to find its source, as had John Willis.

It was in the middle of "Lorena," however, that she looked up to see three men standing in a triangle of shade near the building on the other side of the narrow street. Two of them brushed at their damp eyes self-consciously. The third blew his nose with a resounding *honk* on a large red handkerchief.

Melissa cut off Lorena's sad lament in mid-verse, baffled.

The man with the red hankie stepped forward. "You'll have to excuse us, ma'am. That song has made many a soldier and weary traveler homesick. I 'spect we're no different."

She straightened and put her hands to her stiff back. "Oh, dear, I'm sorry. Really, I'm just singing to my little girl. She doesn't know the song is sad."

"But I bet she knows what an angel's singin' sounds like now," one of the other men said, his voice breaking slightly.

At the extravagant compliment, Melissa felt herself

blush and dropped her gaze back to the washtub. Heavens, what a fuss Dawson miners made over her little songs. She had lived her whole life trying to make herself as inconspicuous as possible and didn't care for being the center of attention. The men moved along after that, but returned two hours later with their wash.

Curious, despite his resolve that Melissa's laundry business didn't concern him, Dylan found all kinds of reasons to walk by the side window in the store. He had a few dozen parade-size American flags nailed to sticks that he'd bought in time for the coming Independence Day—they'd make a good display right here in this empty keg near the window. Was it going to rain? he wondered a few minutes later, and ambled back to the glass to look out at the bright, cloudless sky. Shortly after checking on the weather, Dylan saw Sailor Bill Partridge walking by and was drawn to the window yet again. It was said that the man spent all of his money on clothes and that he never wore the same suit twice.

Dylan could tell himself that he wasn't paying a whit of attention to Melissa, but in his trips to the window if he leaned against the right side of the frame he could see her working there. And he did that often. Her back was to him as she hung shirts on a clothesline, showing off her slim waist and back. Her long braid swung like a hypnotic pendulum over her gently rounded hips. He imagined his hands on those hips, warm beneath his touch while she arched her back against his chest. With the thought came swift, hot arousal that carried his imagination further. He inhaled the sweet scent of her hair and grazed her neck with soft, slow kisses that made her sigh and realize she need not fear him—

"Dylan, have you gone deef or what?"

Jolted out of his daydream, Dylan swung around to see Ned Tanner standing at his counter.

"Sorry, Ned, I didn't hear you come in," he said and left the window, hoping his face didn't look as red as it felt.

"I came by for more nails. How much are they today?" Ned Tanner had come to Dawson with the first wave of people last fall, arriving just as winter descended upon the North, closing the rivers with ice. He'd opened his restaurant in a tent and had done so well that he now was expanding to a new building on Front Street. Homely, with a pronounced overbite, oiled hair, and a personality to match, he fancied himself to be something of a ladies' man, a notion that gave Rafe Dubois no end of amusement.

"Same as last time, seven dollars a pound," Dylan said on his way to the storeroom to fetch a fifty-pound keg.

"That's what I like about you, Dylan," Ned called. "You keep your prices the same even though other folks are raising theirs. Competition, they call it. I call it thievery."

Dylan carried the nail keg out on his shoulder and set it down next to Ned. "That works for them,

I guess. But I paid the same for this keg as the last one I sold you, so I'm charging you the same. I do well enough in this store without getting greedy."

Ned pointed at the side window. "Say, it looks like you've branched out some, though. Who's that little gal you got running your laundry business for you outside?"

Dylan stepped behind the counter and put weights in one pan of his gold scales. "It's not my business, it's hers. That'll be three hundred and fifty dollars for the nails."

Ned brightened up. "Well, a woman of enterprise. She sure is a pretty little thing, and she sings nice, too." He handed Dylan his poke, the same kind of leather pouch that everyone in Dawson used to carry their gold.

"Yeah, I guess," Dylan muttered, not certain he liked the eager gleam he saw in the man's eye.

Ned reached up to straighten his tie, then ran a finger over his enormous mustache to smooth it. "There aren't many females up here that look so nice. And she's an ambitious one, too. I might be interested in making the acquaintance of a woman like her."

"Go talk to Belinda Mulrooney. She's plenty ambitious."

Ned shuddered. "Naw, Belinda is too danged outspoken and too smart for her own good. She'll never catch a husband—a man doesn't like to feel as if his wife knows more than him."

Dylan laughed. Ned might have a hard time finding one who didn't. "I guess it would depend on how smart the man is. It sounds like you want a woman who'll work hard, hand her money over to you, and keep her mouth shut."

Ned grinned. "The idea sure has its charm, doesn't it? Now what did you say that little gal's name was?"

Dylan pictured Melissa out there, scrubbing clothes and talking to every damned miner in Dawson. "Her name is Mrs. Harper." He told himself that he was only protecting her from pests like Ned Tanner, but the truth of it was that a surge of unaccountable jealousy boiled up inside him. He didn't like the feeling, but there it was. "And I'd advise you to forget about 'making her acquaintance.' "

"She's married?"

"Yeah." Dylan leaned across the counter. "To me."

The man laughed. "That's a good one, Dylan."

"I'm not joking."

Ned stared at him, mouth agape and buckteeth well displayed. "N-no, I see that. No disrespect intended, Dylan," he mumbled, his face tomato red. "Hell, nobody around here heard that you took a wife."

"Now you know."

In that moment Dylan thought that maybe everyone else should know it, too. Melissa might get the sign she had talked about, after all. It would put a damned quick end to notions like Ned Tanner's.

MRS. HARPER'S LAUNDRY

* * *

"Good afternoon, Mrs. Harper."

Melissa looked up from the blue work shirt on her scrub board to find Rafe Dubois standing there.

"Mr. Dubois, how nice to see you." She had a special fondness for the lawyer, especially since he'd liberated her from Coy. Further, she enjoyed his elegant manners and turn of phrase. They were so different from what she was accustomed to. Coy would have made some derisive remark about his "ten-dollar words," given the chance to express his opinion.

"I must admit that I'm a bit surprised you've undertaken this venture."

"I'm not sure you should be," she replied, taking up the shirt again. "Women have always worked. *I've* always worked. This time I'd like to be paid for it."

Rafe lowered himself to an upended packing crate that served as her guest chair, moving as if his every joint ached. Then considering her for a moment, he nodded and chuckled. "I suppose you're right. You must forgive me—I'm from a part of the world where women do indeed work hard, sometimes from morning until long after sunset. But custom prevents them from allowing it to show. In fact, they would be considered unladylike if they did. Rather, they are to be viewed as delicate flowers who tire easily, faint with little provocation, and must be sheltered from the world. They retire to shuttered porches and sitting rooms in the heat of the day, to do fine needlework or sip tea." He laughed again. "I was stunned to discover just how strong many of the fair gender can be."

She wasn't surprised by his veiled objection to her laundry business. She'd sensed his disapproval yesterday. Plunging the shirt into clear rinse water, she laughed. "Mr. Dubois, if women sat on their tuffets like Miss Muffett, sewing a fine seam and drinking tea, not much would get done. There would be no clothes washed or meals cooked or children reared." Wringing out the shirt, she flung it over the clothesline and groped in her pocket for clothespins.

Rafe gestured at the crowd moving in both directions on Front Street. "But in a frontier mining town, the public location of your business might create a problem for you."

She took a clothespin out of her mouth. "Mr. Dubois, I hope you know how much I appreciate everything you and Dylan have done for Jenny and me. I don't know what might have happened to us if not for you both. But I don't want to have to depend on anyone except myself." She faltered a moment, hating the little catch she heard in her voice. "Dylan has plans for his future that don't have anything to do with us. He's told me that he'll leave here when he's had enough of it. Where will that leave us if I don't do something now? To be alone in the world with a child to care for, and no way to do it . . ." She couldn't finish the sentence.

Rafe glanced at Jenny, sleeping in her little nook, then rose stiffly from his seat. "I certainly see your point, dear madam." He patted her arm, then turned to leave. "I see your point."

By the end of the day the front of Melissa's dress was wet from waist to knees, her back ached as if it would snap, and her hands were chapped. Except for quick breaks to tend the baby and have lunch herself, she had worked twelve hours.

At seven in the evening, under a sun as bright as midafternoon back home, she trudged upstairs with Dylan's clothes and a bundle of ironing in one arm, and Jenny in the other. She felt almost as weary as she had the day she'd crossed Chilkoot Pass on the journey up here. The muscles in her shoulders and arms ached from the scrubbing and wringing, and her hands shook a bit from the strain.

But even in her exhaustion she smiled to herself. Inside her apron pocket was a small leather pouch that contained nearly forty dollars in gold dust. And that was something she hadn't gotten for crossing the pass. *Forty dollars!* Back home, laborers received about a dollar and a quarter a day.

In her whole life Melissa had never had more than a dollar she could call her own. This gold dust she had earned herself, and no one would drink it up or take it from her.

Unless, of course, Dylan Harper took a mind to do just that. At the thought, Melissa pressed a protective hand over the bulge in her pocket, knowing even as she did that she wouldn't stand a prayer against him if he decided to take her money. Or anything else, for that matter. He was a big, strapping man—every inch of him hardened to lean muscle by hard work. She would do well to remember that he held the upper hand in their arrangement, and that he could change the rules to suit him anytime he wanted.

It wasn't a pleasant thought. Yet, even so, Melissa couldn't help but recall how kind he'd been to her thus far. Until fate had flung her into Dylan's path, she'd believed that the years of grinding poverty had nearly smothered out all the hope in her, and that her marriage to Coy had finished the job. But she felt hope stirring again, coming to life after years of silence. Maybe today was just the beginning of something a bit better.

"We're going to be all right, little Jenny," she whispered to the sleeping baby, then kissed her silky cheek. "I think we might be all right."

Apparently all the activity and new sights had worn out the little girl, because she slept the deep, untroubled sleep of childhood. Melissa couldn't help but smile. The baby's tender mouth made suckling motions, but otherwise she was far away in a dreamy landscape.

Inside the small room Melissa dumped the load of dry wash on the bed and put Jenny down in her crate. Dylan hadn't come upstairs yet, and she was relieved he hadn't. With all the goings on, she hadn't given a thought to dinner yet. Heavens, she hadn't even stoked the fire in the stove.

Eyeing the kitchen chair with yearning, she decided to sit for a moment, just to take the ache out of her back. But she didn't have time to dawdle—if Dylan's meals weren't ready when he wanted them, or if she didn't do the other chores he expected of her, she worried that he'd put an end to her business. She couldn't risk that.

After a brief rest Melissa hurried to the bed to sort out and fold Dylan's clothes. Holding up one of his shirts, she paused to study it. She let her hand skim over the fabric and envisioned the span of his shoulders, the length of his torso. Putting the shirt aside to be ironed, she picked up a pair of his denims, lean-waisted and long-legged.

She knew so little about the man who wore these clothes. Outwardly, he was handsome, rugged, and tall. His features were even and well proportioned. But what life he'd come from and why he was here were mysteries to her. He'd been in Dawson before the gold rush began, so Klondike fever hadn't been what brought him North.

He was by turns, gentle and savage. He had taken her in when he didn't have to, and in doing so had let Coy, a worthless deadbeat, wriggle out of a large debt that Dylan didn't expect to be repaid. Yet when a man in his store had attacked his integrity, his reaction had been swift, violent, and frightening.

But the one thing Melissa found the most troubling was her growing attraction to Dylan. She told herself it was only a silly, girlish infatuation for the man because he'd been kind to her and Jenny. That he was almost as fearsome as he'd been the first day she met him. And the arguments nearly worked.

But not quite.

Something in her made her breath catch when Dylan was near. And it wasn't giggling or girlish at all.

Impatiently, Melissa shook off the thoughts and hastily folded his shirts and jeans. Her most important task was to keep her mind on her own business and her future—a tall, blond man was not part of either. Nor were she and Jenny part of his plans. He'd made that clear from the beginning, and after all, legally she was still bound to Coy.

She carried Dylan's clothes to the big trunk at the end of the bed, where he stowed his belongings. Lifting the lid released the heavily masculine scents of buckskin and shaving soap that she found alluring. It was like sniffing freshly ground coffee, or the sweet odor of pipe tobacco. Inside, she discovered the usually neat contents in a tangled hodgepodge of drawers, socks, pants, shirts, and long johns. She remembered his plowing through the trunk early this morning. He'd dressed in a hurry to meet a steamer captain down at the waterfront.

She was tempted to leave this mess as she'd found it. She had worked hard all day, and this was an extra chore she didn't want. But she couldn't very well throw tidy things on top of the jumble and slam the lid closed. Sighing, she knelt in front of the trunk and began repacking everything. When she pulled out a pair of buckskins, something metallic fell out of their folds and clattered to the floor.

Glancing down, she saw a small oval picture frame

lying on the planking. It held a photograph of a beautiful dark-haired young woman. Slowly, Melissa picked it up to study it. The woman wore her hair up, but the style couldn't disguise its rich, heavy waves. The low-cut neckline of her gown revealed a long, slim throat graced with a strand of pearls. Matching pearl eardrops hung from her small lobes, and in her face, captured for all time by the photographer, Melissa saw supreme self-confidence. She looked like a woman who had never asked for a man's permission in her life, and was accustomed to having her own way.

Melissa sat back on her heels. A sweetheart? she wondered. *A wife?* That was an unsettling thought, but of course, it was possible. Many of the men up here had left behind wives and families. The picture frame itself was silver, wrought with intricate detail that bespoke the photograph's importance. But as Melissa considered the woman's image, she thought that something about her seemed slightly off kilter. Beautiful though she was, she didn't look as if she were the type to attract Dylan Harper. She didn't know why; if she'd thought she knew little about Dylan before, now she felt even more ignorant.

Melissa wiped the glass with the hem of her apron and examined the picture again. Had he held this woman's hand? Stroked the curve of her cheek with a gentle touch? Almost unconsciously, Melissa reached up to graze her fingertips over the nearly healed bruise on her own cheek.

Had he held her in his arms and kissed her?

Suddenly, the door opened and Melissa, still kneeling before the trunk with the photograph clutched in her hand, looked up to find Dylan towering over her. She'd been so engrossed with her own thoughts, she hadn't heard him come up the stairs. Flooded with guilt and frozen by spontaneous terror, she felt the hot blood of embarrassment fill her cheeks.

He was a giant glaring down at her—a wild, frowning man with a long torso set upon longer legs. "Did you find what you were looking for, Melissa?"

She glanced at the pile of clothes, and then at the photograph as if seeing it for the first time. She realized how this must look—as if she were snooping through his belongings, and, oh, God, maybe even stealing something. Hastily, she dropped the picture frame back into the trunk as though it were a burning coal.

"I—" she began, but her voice was just a dry croak. Her throat felt as if it were closing. She gripped one of his shirts that she'd washed earlier and held it out. "I was just folding your things. Th-they were all— I wasn't prying! Truly I wasn't. The photograph was tangled in your clothes and it fell out." To her horror, she felt her eyes begin to sting with rising tears. She was so tired, she didn't have much strength to completely stop them, so she turned her head and quickly brushed them away.

He took the shirt from her and stuffed it into the trunk along with everything else, then dropped the lid. "From now on, leave my clothes out. I'll put them away," he said, his voice deadly quiet.

She looked at his set, blank face, but could see nothing there, not accusation, not clemency. It was as if his thoughts were far away. Miserable, she nodded and rose from her knees to begin dinner.

Dylan flopped on the bed and sighed, his stomach drawing into a knot. Plainly, she was still afraid of him, but he hadn't meant to scare her.

She wasn't being nosy, he supposed, but he didn't like her poking around in his gear. He might not have minded so much if she hadn't dug up that photograph.

He hadn't looked at Elizabeth's picture since the night he threw it in his with his clothes almost three years ago, and he wished he hadn't seen it just now. He still remembered that night so clearly—Griff Harper ordering him off the property, the hired hands scurrying for the bunkhouse in the face of that final, and ugliest, explosive family battle. After gathering up his belongings in a fit of white-hot fury, Dylan had gotten on his horse and galloped through the moonlight down to the dock in town to wait for the steamboat that would carry him downriver and away from The Dalles. Before he'd left, he paid a kid to take his gelding back to the house; he'd wanted nothing that Griff Harper thought belonged to him.

Dylan had managed to bury most of the memories, but not the one of beautiful, scheming Elizabeth. It was dumb, he supposed, to hang onto her photograph. It only reminded him of what a damned fool he'd been to let himself fall prey to her manipulating.

But she had been so good at it, so accomplished, he never once suspected that she didn't care about him.

Ned Tanner didn't want a woman who was smarter than he was? He had news for Ned—there were far worse trials a woman could heap upon a man, and no one knew that better than Dylan.

He glanced up at Melissa as she peeled potatoes. "How did your first day go?" he asked, breaking the silence.

Keeping her back to him, she pumped water into the pot holding the quartered potatoes. Her movements were guarded, as if her arms were stiff. He wondered if she might be sore from the unaccustomed work.

"I washed a lot of clothes."

Dylan already knew that. He tried to imagine Elizabeth standing over a washtub for hours, doing laundry for less-than-fastidious miners, but the picture wouldn't even form in his mind.

He hoisted himself from the bed and walked over to Jenny's crate. She was just waking from her nap and still had one thumb fixed firmly in her mouth. He didn't know anything about kids, but he had to admit that she captivated him. Sometimes he was almost curious enough to pick her up and hold her to his shoulder. But what if he dropped her? Even if he didn't, she was so little, he might hurt her somehow.

So he settled for brushing her velvet cheek with the back of his finger. Compared to her head, his hand looked enormous. When she saw him, *she* didn't flinch in fear. She waved her arms and kicked, and gave him a big grin, showing off her toothless gums. He couldn't help but smile back at her. "Hey, little Jenny," he whispered. Then louder he asked, "And the baby? Did she get along all right?"

"I think she enjoyed the change of scenery and all the activity." Melissa tried to carry the heavy iron pot to the stove, but obviously her overused muscles wouldn't cooperate, and it clanked back into the steel sink.

Watching her struggle while he did nothing made him feel a bit like a heel. He knew she'd worked even harder today than he had. He crossed the floor. "Here," he said, and reached in front of her to grab the wooden grip, "let me."

"No! I can do it." Melissa recoiled, but kept her hands clamped on the handle. He saw naked fear in her dove gray eyes. He supposed he couldn't expect her to instantly overcome what might have been years of intimidation, although whenever he'd looked outside this afternoon, she seemed to be getting along just fine with her customers.

He dropped his hand. "Why are you so damned jumpy? And why do you think you have to do everything yourself?" He couldn't keep the impatience out of his voice.

"I don't think that," she said. "It's just that . . ."

"Just what?"

She glanced up at him through a veil of dark lashes. "I'm afraid you'll think I'm not doing my best for you and make me give up my laundry business."

"Why? I told you I didn't care how you spent your free time."

"You also said that I'd better keep up my end of our agreement. That's what I'm doing." She looked him full in the face then, and her low voice held both anguish and determination. "I need to make money for Jenny and me, money that no one can take away. I don't want her to have the kind of life that I've had. I don't want to see her sold by a drunken husband to a stranger in a barroom. She's a brand-new life—she has a chance for something better, and I have a chance to give it to her. I mean to do it." Her breathing was labored, and her eyes glittered with unshed tears. It was the longest speech he'd ever heard her make in one breath, and Dylan felt his face flush all the way to the roots of his hair.

He shifted his weight from one foot to the other. All this time he'd supposed that Melissa was just glad to get away from Logan. He'd never thought about how humiliating that day must have been for her.

"Look, if you want to work, go ahead. There isn't that much to do up here anyway."

She looked relieved, then cautioned, "I'll try hard to have dinner ready on time, but sometimes it might be late."

He shrugged. "Well, I guess that's the way it'll have to be. I'll tell you what," he said, "you make the biscuits and I'll finish this." He looked around at what she'd assembled on the table, a piece of boiled canned beef and a few fresh vegetables. "Stew, right?"

"You want to help?" She gaped at him as if he'd suggested putting on one of Jenny's diapers and dancing down Front Street. Apparently she'd never had such an offer before. "But I can do it, really—"

"You look as stiff as an old gunnysack left out in the rain. I'll give you a hand. But just until you're limbered up."

"All right," she conceded, and he reached for the pot handle again.

This time his hand brushed hers, and their eyes met. She gazed up at him, not so frightened now, he thought, but more curious. Standing this close, he caught a whiff of the soap and starch she'd used all day. The scent wasn't perfume, but in a way it suited her, clean and unadorned, and it went to his head like the most expensive of fragrances.

Stunned, Dylan stared down at her, recalling the first time he'd seen her. She had seemed plain then, a pale ghost of a female with a downcast gaze and a carefully blank expression on her face. He'd felt resentment, and maybe even a bit of revulsion, when she'd been foisted upon him. When had his feelings begun to change? At what point had she ceased to be unattractive? Dylan didn't know. He only knew she no longer seemed homely to him. Just the opposite.

Although her hair was the color of frost-covered daffodils, her eyelashes were dark, he noticed, framing her eyes with thick, silken spikes. And her bronze brows were as fine and delicate as butterfly feelers. His gaze dropped to her mouth, pink and tender-looking. Would that mouth be soft under his if he were to kiss her? Would it?

Just then, the baby let out a loud squawk, the kind of noise that babies make when they exercise their lungs and voices, and the spell was broken.

"Oh," Melissa said, as if she too had been entranced, then pulled away.

Dylan followed her lead, widening the floor space between them. Jesus, what had he been thinking of? He took the pot and put it on the stove. "Okay, let's get this going," he mumbled.

"Yes, of course," she said, and ran her hands over her sleeves. She went to the table to roll out biscuit dough.

He felt as awkward as a schoolboy. Why, he couldn't guess. He'd known his share of women and bedded more than a few. Kissing one wouldn't be the end of the world.

This was not an ordinary woman, though—people in Dawson believed that she was his wife. These circumstances weren't ordinary either, and by God, he didn't want to make them any more complicated than they already were.

She had a goal? Well, so did he, and he had to keep his mind on it.

He resolved that he would stop noticing how nice Melissa was beginning to look, and how good she smelled. He swore he wouldn't wonder again what it would feel like to kiss her, or imagine his fingers twined in her long pale hair.

But as he watched her working at the table, slender and utterly feminine, he knew that ignoring her would be as difficult a feat as getting rich by digging in the gold fields with a teaspoon.

Late that night Dylan lay on his side of the bed, caught between sleep and wakefulness, when the baby started to fuss.

He saw Melissa get up to tend her. Her thin nightgown looked like a pale moonbeam as she crossed the room in the semidark of the Yukon summer night. She carried the child back to bed, murmuring the softest of endearments to her.

"What's the matter, button?" she whispered in a voice mothers saved for their children. "Are you hungry? Is that what's wrong with my button? Well, we can fix that, can't we."

He felt the mattress sag as she lay down again. Her voice, soft and lulling, had nearly made him feel drowsy when he made the mistake of glancing at her.

The bodice of her gown was open, and Jenny lay at her full white breast, suckling contentedly.

Stifling a groan, Dylan swallowed hard and turned his back to her. Watching her with the baby, he'd never expected to see anything so intimate, or worse, so arousing. Hot blood suffused his groin, and his heart began pumping hard in his chest. He'd never known such exquisite torture.

As he lay there, trying to ignore the woman on the

other side of the rice sack and wishing for the oblivion of sleep, he almost wished he were digging for gold with a teaspoon.

That would be a hell of a lot easier.

Chapter Seven

"Have you heard that singin' washerwoman? I swear she's got a voice like one of God's own choir," a bearded man remarked to his companion.

"That she does, but she's right here on earth and she don't seem to be married. I was thinkin' I might call on the young gal personal-like and ask to her to some festivities," his companion replied, and washed down a doughnut with a mug of beer.

"You? Why, she's too much of a lady to be seen with the likes of you. Besides, she's got that baby there with her. I bet her man is workin' in the gold fields and she's makin' ends meet with her laundry."

"Well, I won't know till I ask, will I?"

Eavesdropping on this conversation between two rough miners standing behind him at the bar, Dylan scowled. After what he'd seen lying next to Melissa the night before, he had no little difficulty in checking his impulse to deck them both. After all, he told himself, in some circles it was considered a dueling offense to even mention a lady's name in a saloon.

He turned and gave them a sour look, but they didn't notice.

Rafe, who stood next to him, obviously did notice, and he laughed so hard he started coughing.

"Come on, Dylan," he said, recovering his wind, "let's find a table to sit at." Lately it had seemed that the lawyer grew tired as quickly as an old man, and he'd taken to carrying a walking stick. It was an impressive thing, with a big gold filigree head and black lacquered ferrule, and it certainly looked correct on a spiffy dresser like Rafe. But Dylan noticed that he leaned on the stick more than carried it.

Grabbing the whiskey bottle, Dylan led them through the crowded saloon to a table, and Rafe eased himself into a chair, chuckling at Dylan again.

"I'm surprised you think this is funny," Dylan commented, flopping into the opposite chair. He downed his own shot. "Wasn't that what you were worried about when Melissa decided to start that laundry business? That she'd be exposed to 'unsavory opportunities'?"

"I'm not laughing about that. I'm laughing at you. You might not admit it, but you're the one who doesn't like their interest." Rafe had a wicked gleam in his deep-set eyes. He flicked a speck of lint from his crisply tailored coat.

"I just don't want her to be pestered by people like Ned Tanner." Dylan inclined his head toward the two miners. "Or men like that."

"Maybe she wouldn't see it as pestering," Rafe suggested, keeping a keen eye on him.

"If you think she's looking for another man's attentions, I can guarantee you that you're wrong. It's the last thing she wants." Dylan put his feet on the chair next to him.

"And how would you know?"

Dylan thought back to Melissa's impassioned speech about giving Jenny a chance in life. "I don't need to be a genius to figure that out. Besides, your mumbo jumbo at McGinty's back table didn't do away with Coy Logan. She's still legally married to him, if you'll recall."

Rafe shrugged and took another deep swallow from his whiskey glass. "He deserted her. I'm sure any judge would grant a divorce decree given the circumstances."

Dylan didn't want to think about that. As long as she was technically some other's man's wife, he felt a measure of safety from the thoughts that kept creeping up on him. "It makes no difference to me—that's her business. All she wants is to make money, and from what I can tell, that's just what she's doing."

The day was overcast, although the sun peeked through the clouds from time to time. A cool, stiff breeze threatened to carry away the wash drying on Melissa's clotheslines. She had erected a little tent over Jenny's cubbyhole to keep the wind from blowing in the baby's face.

Melissa stood over her iron kettle, stirring a batch

of starch with a broken oar. She paused for a moment to roll up her sleeves and then leaned on the oar.

Despite the breeze, this was hot, hard work. In fact, everything about the laundry business was grueling. She had given up on perfection; most of the clothes that were brought to her were so grimy with embedded earth and sweat, they would never be truly clean again no matter how hard she scrubbed. She had to settle for mostly clean, but her customers were very satisfied.

Now and then they would linger to make small talk, lonely miners with their mostly clean wash wrapped in brown paper and tucked under their arms. Her experience with men was limited, but she sensed their interest by the questions they asked. How had she gotten started with this laundry business? Wasn't this a hot summer? Did she like to dance? Melissa was polite, but she reminded them that she was *Mrs.* Harper, and suggested that they might want to do business with her husband at his trading store. Some of them actually did.

She'd also had a couple of unpleasant experiences. The gold rush had drawn men from all walks of life, most of whom, she was surprised to learn, had come seeking escape more than gold. They sought refuge from nagging wives or mothers-in-law, bill collectors, punishing jobs, and the law. A few of them reminded her of Coy; they eyed her speculatively, as if assessing her ability to be dominated, and possibly because she was making more money than they were.

One man offered her money to sing to him—in

private. Another erupted into a rage when she couldn't remove a wine stain from his shirt front. But the Mounties also made their presence known, and they patrolled her side street just often enough to keep any situation from getting out of hand.

Yes, the work was hard, but oh, it paid so well. She hoarded every single grain of gold dust she received, and she weighed it every night. For good measure she'd sewn a button closure on her apron pocket where she kept her poke, and once in a while, especially when her back ached the most, she'd heft that pocket to feel the weight of it. While she'd had every intention of paying Dylan for Coy's debt, in her heart of hearts, the plan had been more like a child's solemn promise than a certainty. How on earth would she do it? Now, though, she was beginning to believe that she would achieve that goal.

She had seen and heard nothing of Coy since the afternoon at the Yukon Girl Saloon, and for that she was grateful. He had taken her fragile hopes for a better life and crushed them before he deserted her. At first she had been as wary and watchful for his return as she'd been with Dylan. People like Coy rarely went away, but turned up again like the famous bad penny. And she knew Coy well enough to have trouble believing she'd seen the last of him. But as the days passed with no sign of him, she began to relax her guard. She wished that she weren't still his wife, but eventually perhaps that could be remedied.

Occasionally, she would glance up from the bubbling cauldron of starch to look at the side window of Harper's Trading. Dylan wasn't standing there. She wasn't sure if she hoped to see him or not. He was still a mystery to her. She sensed that something drove him, and that an old grievance—a disappointment, maybe—that lurked in his past had colored his viewpoint.

However her original fear of him was turning into curiosity, and lately she'd caught herself watching him in the morning while he shaved. It was always the same—he stood at the mirror barefoot with no shirt, his jeans hanging low, his sun-blond hair brushing his wide shoulders—

"Ma'am, are you Miz Harper?"

Melissa lurched back to the present and saw two men approach in a wagon that had pulled into the side street. In the wagon bed they carried a large, tarp-covered object.

"Yes, I'm Mrs. Harper," she answered, stopping her oar. Strange how easy it had become for her use Dylan's last name. She hoped that a wagonload of dirty clothes wasn't hidden under the tarp.

The driver nodded, then set the brake and wrapped the lines around the brake handle. "Ma'am, we have your order back here," he said, and both men jumped down.

"Order? I haven't ordered anything."

"Says here you did." He waved a piece of paper at her so quickly she saw nothing but the largest print before he jammed it into his back pocket. She had been able to read *Bill of Sale* and *Paid.* "Leastways, we was hired to make a delivery here."

The other man, ignoring the conversation, had already begun to untie the ropes holding the tarp in place.

"But what is it?"

The man unpacking the delivery flipped the canvas back with a flourish. "Here you go, ma'am."

There Melissa saw a large sign that read, MRS. M. HARPER'S LAUNDRY. It was beautifully painted, with scrolls and fancy black lettering outlined in gold leaf.

"Who bought this?" she asked, astounded.

"Well, lessee." The man pulled out the bill of sale again and handed it to her. She read Dylan's bold signature, and the price—seventy-five dollars! It seemed no matter how hard she worked, her obligation to him kept growing. And she hadn't even asked for this.

"Oh, please, no, I can't accept this. You'll have to take it back."

"You don't like it?"

"Oh, no, it's a wonderful sign, a beautiful sign. But I can't keep it. Please, can't you take it back?"

The man rubbed his stubbled chin, obviously unprepared for this possibility. "No, we can't do that, ma'am. See, the thing has been bought and paid for proper, and we was paid to put it up for you. Anyways, what would the sign painter do with it if we took it back to him? He can't sell it to somebody else, 'less you know another Miz Harper doing wash in Dawson."

"But I—"

"It's a gift, Melissa."

She turned and saw Dylan approaching. His stride was graceful and long. The wind whipped his hair away from his handsome face and flattened his shirt against his torso, outlining the frame and muscle of him. Intermittent sun highlighted the gold hair on his arms, making it sparkle. She wished she could learn to ignore his striking looks.

"You said you wanted a sign. I had one painted."

"But I meant when *I* could afford it. I didn't expect you to pay for it."

He shrugged and gestured at the back of the wagon. "Well, it's here today, and I *wanted* to pay for it. So—what are you going to do, Melissa?"

The delivery man watched her expectantly. Dylan smiled and looked vaguely triumphant, as if he knew he would have his own way. Melissa didn't know what else to do but accept. It bothered her that once again, she'd had no say in a decision that affected her. But mingling with her annoyance was a sense of pleasure that Dylan had actually thought of her, and done something nice to surprise her.

"All right," she said to the men, "put it up."

The next day was Sunday, and by strict order of the North West Mounted Police, the lively, sleepless Dawson that everyone knew six days a week came to a dead stop. Every business in town, including the saloons and dance halls, closed up tight. The only sound to be heard was the faint strains of hymns coming from the Catholic and Anglican missionaries who had traveled to Dawson to save those who lusted after wealth and its associated evils. An air of grudging repentance hung over everything.

Dylan chafed at the enforced weekly inactivity. It was one thing if a man decided to take a day off—it was another when it was demanded of him. He couldn't even keep the store closed and work within its walls. Businesses were required to keep their lights burning so that the Mountie on the patrol could see inside and be certain that no one broke the law.

On most Sundays, Dylan used the time to walk through the hills. He missed owning a horse, but so far there weren't that many to be had up here, or much livestock of any kind. Two weeks ago Dawson had seen its first cow arrive, floated in by a man named Miller, who immediately sold the milk for thirty dollars a gallon.

Today, though, Dylan remained in the room over the store, looking out at the deserted streets. The sky was low and gray again. God, he really hated what this town had become. Six days and nights a week it was loud and crowded. And although it was surrounded by wilderness, in just a few weeks it had grown to almost the size of Portland and Seattle.

The town hadn't been so bad when he arrived. It hadn't been where he wanted to be, but there was a beauty to the place, a grandeur in its harsh vastness that had appealed to him. Now it had two banks, two newspapers, five churches, and telephone poles lined the streets. It was like a damned carnival. The scars of men's futile dreams crisscrossed the surrounding land, which was further disfigured by the machinations of those dreams—sluice boxes, ugly cabins, tailings, and mining shafts.

It seemed like a lifetime since he'd seen the green, forested hills and sheer rock cliffs that he'd left behind in The Dalles. The Columbia River, fierce and wide, cut a relentless course from its headwaters in Canada through the Cascade Mountains on its way to the Pacific Ocean. In its path it carved the most beautiful river gorge Dylan had ever seen. He sighed and jammed his hands into his back pockets.

The desire to see it again, to live upon that land once more, was what made Dawson bearable. He'd have the money he needed, he hoped within the next few months. Then he'd go back to The Dalles and live the way he wanted to. His father would see that a man didn't have to cheat or lie his way through life to succeed.

Behind him at the washstand, Melissa was just finishing giving Jenny her bath in the flowered porcelain bowl. The sound of water splashing, and the cooing between mother and baby were not so bad, he conceded. In fact, they were kind of homey. He glanced over his shoulder in time to see Melissa button Jenny into one of the dresses she'd made for her.

"How's she doing today?" he asked.

Melissa cradled Jenny in the crook of her arm, with the baby's dress trailing over, and brought her to the window. "Oh, she's doing just fine, aren't you, button?" she replied with a smile, more to Jenny than to him. "She's fed and washed, and has clean clothes."

In this muted light both mother and child looked as pretty as the dawn. Although Melissa was busy every day from morning till evening, Dylan realized that she looked much better than she had when he first met her. She was still too thin, but her shape was beginning to round out. Her gray eyes were clearer, and her skin had acquired a luminous, peach-colored bloom. Either hard work agreed with her, or liberating her from that bastard Logan had helped. Hell, maybe it was both, he thought.

One way or the other, she was becoming a distraction that Dylan hadn't anticipated the day her husband traded her to him. Back then, clutching the baby to her thinness she'd looked not much older than a child herself.

That had definitely changed.

He put out a finger for Jenny to grab, and her little hand closed around it with a strong grip. She stared at him, seemingly even more fascinated with him than he was with her. Something about the child stirred his heart. She smelled of fresh soap and water, not unlike her mother.

Standing this close to Melissa, he felt blood begin to pound through his veins. The crescents of her lashes made him think of dark, smooth sable. Her cheek, softly curved, wore a pale rose stain like a sunset sky. And her mouth, full and coral-pink, parted slightly when the tip of her tongue peeked out to touch her upper lip.

She was a married woman, and Dylan had never dallied with another man's wife, no matter how tempting. Or, as in this case, no matter how low the man or thin the couple's bonds had stretched. His mind might know better, but his body didn't give a tinker's damn about morals or ethics. It wasn't to have been a problem when he agreed to this arrangement. But as he gazed at the slightly damp spot on her lip where her tongue had touched, he asked himself again what harm could be found in just a kiss—

"Would you like to hold her?" Melissa asked.

He looked up and found her gray gaze resting on him. Feeling suddenly self-conscious, he pulled his hand from Jenny's fist and backed up a step. "Oh, well, no . . . I . . ." He brushed his hands against his pants legs and shrugged.

The baby, clearly unhappy with losing Dylan's finger, scrunched up her face and started crying.

Melissa barely stifled a giggle. Here was this big man-savage, who kept a nasty-looking knife tied to his thigh and a meat cleaver under his store counter, a man who could be so completely intimidating that he'd steal her breath. But he backed away from Jenny as if she were a twenty-foot-tall ogre.

"She won't bite you—she doesn't have any teeth," she teased, enjoying her advantage. She knew that Dylan was curious about Jenny. She'd seen him stop to look at the baby while she slept, or dangle his watch in front of her, but he'd never picked her up.

"But she's so little," he said over Jenny's squalling. "I'd probably hurt her."

She couldn't help but smile. "You won't hurt her, although it looks like she's pretty upset with you for taking your finger away from her."

Uncertainty was written on his handsome face. "Well, I don't know how to—"

Melissa closed the distance he'd opened between them and thrust Jenny into his arms. He held her awkwardly, his inexperience glaring.

"You just need to support her head and back," she said, and pantomimed the proper technique. "Hold her a little closer."

As soon as he got the hang of it, Jenny's bawling stopped, and she stared up at Dylan and smiled, waving a slobbery fist at him. He smiled back, then looked up at Melissa. "She's soft." He sounded surprised.

This time Melissa couldn't check her laughter. "Yes, she is. Babies *are* soft. Haven't you ever held one before? Maybe a little brother or sister? Or a niece or nephew?"

He shook his head. "No. My brother is only a couple of years younger than me. Anyway, we were never what could be called close."

This tidbit of information threw another log onto Melissa's fire of curiosity. It might be her chance to learn something about Dylan. "Did he come North, too?" Picking up the washbasin, she walked to the door.

His laugh was short and biting. "Scott? Hell, no.

As far as I know, he's still in The Dalles, following my father's example and learning his ways."

"Is that bad?" Balancing the bowl on one hip, she opened the door and stepped out to the landing to toss Jenny's bathwater over the railing.

"Yeah, it is for the people the old man forecloses with his banking business." He shook his head and chuckled again, keeping his gaze fixed on the baby. "He never seemed to think he did anything wrong. I suppose his motto could be, do unto others to serve yourself." Holding Jenny as if he carried a priceless art object, he sat down in a chair at the table. "Besides, Scott has a wife." This last he said with special bitterness.

She closed the door again and considered him. "You don't look like a banker's son. At least not the way I'd imagine one to look."

"Yeah? And what does a banker's son look like?"

"Well, you know, more starched, I guess." She gestured in his direction. "Shorter hair, and probably no knife or buckskin pants."

"That's what my brother and father thought, too."

"Does your family know you came up here?"

He frowned then, his brows lowering to rest on his eyelids, and making him look as fierce as he had the day she saw him wield the meat cleaver. He stood and carried Jenny to her crate.

"No, they don't know where I am, and they aren't my *family*." The word was as sharp as a broken bottle. "I was the sand in their picnic lunch—the conscience that kept asking them what they were doing—and they were embarrassed by me. My father and my brother put widows, children, and old men out of their homes if they couldn't pay their mortgages. Piled their belongings up in front of their houses and told them, it was nothing personal . . . just business. It was just *greed.* I was ashamed of them, and I don't care if I never see them again. Not exactly what you'd call a loyal group, huh?" He walked back to the window, beyond which drifted the tolling of a distant church bell.

When he was mad, he seemed to fill whatever space he occupied. He looked taller, broader at the shoulder, bigger than ever. Strange, Melissa was less afraid of him this time, perhaps because she realized that his anger was not really directed at her. But it was a palpable thing, growling at the past.

"You've cut yourself off from everyone? Even your mother?" She thought of her own mother and that she'd never see her again, and felt a catch in her heart.

"She died during an influenza epidemic. I was about eleven, I guess. Anything else you want to know?" He turned and faced her then.

The question sounded more like an accusation, and she realized that he was more vexed than she'd thought.

"Yes, what do you want for dinner?" It was a silly question, but it just popped out of her mouth.

He stared at her, then burst out laughing. His smile revealed straight, white teeth, and dimples. The tension in the small room evaporated. He shook his head ruefully and rubbed the back of his neck. "Melissa, you're a different kind of woman," he admitted.

She didn't know why—after all, it wasn't really a compliment, exactly—but it sounded like the nicest thing anyone had said to her in years.

Two days later, Melissa was up to her elbows in hot sudsy water, scrambling to finish an order of boiled shirts for Big Alex McDonald. Called the King of the Klondike, his wealth and business interests were so vast that when asked by the Bank of Commerce to list them, it had taken several hours and the entire bank staff to sort them out. He'd promised Melissa an extra two hundred dollars if she had the shirts ready by morning, and she intended to do it.

While Jenny reached for the rawhide string of beads that a customer had hung above her little niche, Melissa sang "Sweet Marie," and scrubbed.

"You sing mighty nice, Lissy. I didn't know you could sing so nice."

Melissa froze, her hands wound in the fabric of Big Alex's shirt. Even without hearing that familiar, hated diminutive, she knew the voice of the speaker behind her. Her heart took off at a gallop, like a runaway horse inside her chest.

Coy Logan sidled up to the washtub and stood across from her. She stared at him, speechless. She had foolishly lulled herself into believing that she had seen the last of him.

If possible, he looked even more dissipated and threadbare than he had the day he'd sold her. He had a gurgling, wet cough that sounded like he'd spent too much time in a damp place. His clothes hung on his skinny frame and looked as if he'd slept in the gutter with them. One grubby shirttail hung out, and his fly was partially unbuttoned. "I been hearing all about the pretty laundry lady who sings to pass her time." He glared up at her sign with narrowed eyes. " 'Cept I heard her name was Mrs. Harper, so I didn't figure right off that it was you they meant."

Desperately, Melissa glanced around, hoping someone, *anyone* would come by. Dylan had gone to meet a steamship at the river, and she had no idea when he'd be back. The Mounties had already dropped by here earlier, and she didn't expect to see them again until much later. Men and animals and wagons traveled up and down busy Front Street, but none turned down here. Never had this side street seemed so deserted and isolated.

"What do you want, Coy?" she asked, trying to keep her voice steady. Over the past few weeks she had been shedding her fear, a layer at a time, the way a person would peel an onion. But seeing Coy brought it all back, and she was wrapped tightly within it again. Habits and attitudes were even harder to let go of than they were to learn, she realized.

He eyed her up and down with assessing, bloodshot eyes, taking full measure of her. "You're looking damn fine, Lissy. I like that braid in your hair and those new clothes." His tone was ingratiating and jovial. "Just like I figured, you clean up pretty good." He smiled, revealing scummy-looking teeth, and licked his lips in a way that made Melissa's stomach turn over. There was nothing left of the man she remembered sitting at the kitchen table with her father and brother. He hadn't been a prize catch then—now, though, he seemed to have slid to the bottom of life.

"You still haven't told me what you want," she said, and gripped the edge of the washtub with her nerveless fingers.

"You been making money too, by the looks of it," he went on, fingering a shirt on her clothesline. "Seems like I did you a big favor by letting Harper take care of you for a while."

Automatically, Melissa started to reach for the apron pocket where she kept her gold pouch, but stopped herself in time. If Coy knew she had that gold dust, he'd take it from her without a moment's hesitation.

"You're not supposed to come around here, Coy. That paper you signed in the saloon said so."

"Shee-it, I don't give that"—he snapped his grimy fingers—"for any paper. Anyways, I got me a hankering to have my wife back. So pack up your stuff and let's go on."

She stared at him, horrified. "I'm not going with you. You deserted me, *sold* me, and I don't belong to you anymore!"

"Got a little gumption, too, dontcha," he said, pushing his greasy hair back with one hand. He appraised her again with a vaguely leering look that made her heart thump even harder. "I kinda like that—so long as you don't overdo it." She saw the meanness flash through his eyes. He coughed again, wet and phlegmy, then dragged the back of his hand across his mouth.

Once more Melissa looked toward Front Street, searching for someone to interrupt, even if it was just one of her laundry customers. But there was no one. She felt like a drowning swimmer who could see the shore, but was too far away to reach it.

She took a deep breath and tried to sound brave. "I don't want anything to do with you anymore, Coy. I want you to go away."

"You're starting to try my patience, girl," he warned, sounding more like the man she remembered. "I'm giving you five minutes to get your gear, or I'll take you with me now, as you are. I don't think you'll like that since I don't have your old clothes anymore."

He gripped her forearm, and Melissa tried to wrench free, but he was stronger than he looked. "Why should I go with you?" she demanded, trying to hear over the pulse pounding in her ears. "You left me here, and that's the way I want it. We're divorced."

His anger was in full sway now, but he was cunning enough to keep his voice down to avoid drawing attention from some passerby on Front. "I ain't stupid, Lissy, and I got my rights. I don't care what that lawyer friend of Harper's said. We ain't in the

United States, we're in Canada, and that Louisiana dandy ain't got no say here. I know there wasn't nothing about that divorce that was legal. You're still my wife, and that girl is still my baby." He pointed at Jenny, and Melissa felt the wild horse in her chest climb to her throat. Jenny— "And I don't give a damn what Dylan Harper says. You been practicing adultery with that son of a bitch. Unlawful carnal knowledge, they call it. I call it whoring. The law is on my side. Your daddy gave you to me, and you belong to me. Even if you are a whore."

"No, Coy, please—you don't know what you're talking about," she cried, aghast at his filthy accusations.

He tightened his grip on her arm, making her fingers tingle, and yanked her around to his side of the washtub. He slapped her once, sharply, making her ears buzz and tears spring to her eyes. "You come along, or I'll teach you a good lesson for talking back to me."

Then, with a truly evil glint in his beady eyes, he snatched up the baby in one arm. Jenny started crying. "Now, let's have a little of what you been giving away to Harper," he said, and with his free arm pulled her up against his sour-smelling body. She struggled to turn away as she saw his mouth coming toward hers, but he held her head fast. Oh, God, please, send someone—

Suddenly, as if God had taken pity upon her, she was free. Dylan was there. He grabbed Coy by the hair and yanked him away from Melissa. Taking advantage of the instant, she plucked Jenny out of Coy's arm and clutched her as tightly as she dared, trying to quiet the baby's shrieking.

Standing behind him, Dylan gripped Coy's forelock and dragged his head backward to his shoulder in a chilling embrace. His knife, its long blade gleaming in the sun like a mirror, he touched to Coy's throat. "Didn't I tell you not to come around here, you sniveling dog's pizzle?" he growled.

Melissa watched the struggle, and thought Dylan looked a hundred times more frightening than Coy did. His face flushed blotchy red, and a vein throbbed in his temple.

Dylan tightened his grip on Coy's hair, his green eyes blazing like burning emeralds. "Didn't I tell you to stay away from her?" he repeated. *"Answer me!"*

Coy made a strangled noise in his throat that sounded like an affirmative.

"That's right, Logan," he said next to Coy's ear. "But I didn't tell you what I'd do to you if I caught you here." Dylan put a little pressure on the blade against his neck, cutting a nick that dripped blood.

Melissa let out a little squeal. "Dylan, no!" She had suspected that in his darkest moments, Dylan Harper was very capable of killing a man. If he killed Coy, the Mounties would hang him for certain.

"Dylan!"

Looking up, Melissa saw Rafe making his way toward them, walking as fast as he could. He looked weaker every time she saw him, but his voice carried thunder, as it had that day in the saloon. Dressed as impeccably as ever, he held his gold-headed cane like a scepter, and the frown on his thin face gave him the look of a scowling skull.

Dylan kept his grip on Coy, the fury still pouring out of him, his jaw locked. He didn't lift his gaze or acknowledge his friend's approach. Melissa believed he was aware of nothing around him except the debate in his own mind either to kill Coy or to spare him.

Coy's eyes were as wide as stove lids, and the color had drained from his sallow face. Acrid, fear-scented sweat leaked from him in sheets, adding to the already foul odor that he exuded.

"Let him go," Rafe ordered. His commanding tone almost disguised his winded panting. He stood a scant two feet from Dylan with Coy sandwiched between them. "Dylan, goddman it . . . let him go! If you kill him . . . you'll lose every . . . thing . . . think, man . . . he's not worth it!"

Rafe backed off then as a coughing fit overtook him, the worst Melissa had heard yet. Gray-faced, he stumbled to an overturned lard barrel next to the clotheslines and sat down, pressing a fist to his heart. Melissa hurried over and put a hand on his bony shoulder. His lips were tinged a faint blue, and his eyes bulged alarmingly with each round of coughing, but he kept his gaze fixed on his friend.

After what seemed like an eternity, Dylan released Coy's hair and gave him a hard shove that pushed him into the dirt. Dylan's own breath was coming fast, and the muscles along both of his jaws rippled with tension. Coy skittered sideways along the ground, his legs working as if he pedaled an imaginary bicycle.

"This is the last time, Logan," Dylan said between gritted teeth. "If you *ever* show your face around here again, no one will be able to save you. No one."

Incredibly, Coy made one last protest after he gained his feet. "Lissy's my woman, and that's my kid. They belong to me, and I know my rights," he harped with watery bravado, waving a shaking finger at them as he backed away. "I got rights, by God!"

Still gripping his knife, Dylan took two menacing steps toward him and spit at his feet. Coy danced backward. "You've got shit. You gave away everything—your wife, your child, and the right to call yourself a man—the day you sold them to me for twelve hundred dollars. Melissa belongs to herself now. The next time I see you around here, you won't be walking away. I'll have to call Father William to take you off to his hospital."

Gawping like a landed fish, apparently Coy could think of no reply. His small eyes full of fear and impotent hate, he turned and hurried back toward Front Street as fast as his skinny legs could carry him. To return, Melissa hoped, to the rock from beneath which he'd crawled.

No one spoke for a moment, and the ensuing silence was broken only by Rafe's ratchety breathing and Jenny's diminished wails.

Dylan put his knife back in its sheath, then strode to Melissa. "Are you all right?"

Putting her finger under her chin, he tipped her face up to his, and she saw the fury rush back into his green eyes. Flinching, she tried to pull back.

"Jesus—*Jesus Christ!* Did he hit you?"

She supposed that Coy must have left a red imprint of his open hand on her cheek. She nodded, trying to find her voice, but her throat was too tight. Her insides quivered like Fannie Farmer's aspic, and her outsides didn't feel much better.

Dropping his hand, he paced in front of her, his rage back in full force. "I should have killed the son of a bitch! Damn it, I should have! I'll find him—"

Melissa found her voice and pulled on his arm. "No, Dylan, no!" she begged. "Rafe is right. The police would banish you from Dawson. He won't come back now. Just let him go." Beneath the fabric of his sleeve she felt tightly drawn muscle.

After pacing a moment longer, he nodded grudgingly, then slipped an arm around her shoulders. She yearned to lean against him, to give into the infinite comfort of his strength. Was it possible that such comfort and safety might be found in a man's embrace? Melissa had thought so once and had been fooled by the very man who had just left. She wouldn't take the chance again. She straightened and pulled away from Dylan's arm.

"What about the baby?" he asked, and reached down to draw Jenny's blanket away from her face. The baby's whimpers ceased.

"Oh, she's fine now." She pressed a kiss to Jenny's forehead. "Thank you," she whispered from her tight throat.

"And you?" Dylan asked Rafe.

"By God," the other man wheezed, "no one can call this a dull town. I was on my way to the saloon when I glanced down here and saw you in an altercation with Logan. It's a good thing I happened along before the Mounties did."

Melissa thought it was a good thing that Dylan had happened along before Coy could do anything worse.

Chapter Eight

Dylan led Melissa up the stairs. "I have to finish Big Alex's shirts," she fretted. "He promised me two hundred dollars extra if I have them ready by morning."

"Don't worry about that now," he said, and opened the door for her. He didn't begrudge her the money, but privately, he thought that Alex McDonald was a fool, wealthy or not.

"But I have to worry about it. I promised Big Alex, and two hundred dollars is a lot of money. It would feed a family for a year back home." She stood on the landing, her face paper white except for the fading red imprint of Logan's hand. Pale blond strands had worked themselves loose from her braid and hung on either side of her slender face. Looking closer, he saw a bit of swelling just below her eye.

He sighed. The sight of it, added to everything else that had happened in the last few minutes, shook him to the core. He had just come back from meeting the steamboat *Athenian* down at the waterfront when he'd seen Melissa struggling with Logan. Not only had the bastard pushed Melissa around, but he'd held a blanketed bundle that Dylan knew could only be Jenny. And for an instant when his anger had made time seem to stop, he'd gripped Logan's hair and felt a driving desire to dispatch him to hell. Rafe's thundering voice, warning him about loss and deportation, had finally penetrated the red mist of Dylan's rage.

"Melissa, I want you to give up this laundry business," he said after he waved her inside.

She was putting Jenny down in her crate, but sprang back up again, the baby still in her arms. "Give it up! No, no, I can't do that."

He sank into a chair at the table and crossed his ankle over his knee. He could smell Logan's stink on him, and it made him want to pull off his clothes and burn them. "I think I gave Coy Logan a good scare, but I can't guarantee that he won't be back. He's mean and stupid, and that's a bad combination. He could hurt you—he could even steal Jenny to get even with you, or to punish you. He could—" He threw his hat on the table in weary disgust and plowed both hands through his hair. "Oh, hell, who knows how the pea brain works in a man like that?"

"But I'll be safe. The Mounties come by every day," she offered hastily, and put the baby down.

"They didn't today, did they?"

"Yes, earlier—"

He shook his head. "Nope. I think you ought to quit. I don't want to have to worry about you every time I leave you alone."

She stood there for a moment, silent, and still quivering from the horror of her experience with Logan. Or so he thought.

"No. I won't quit. I refuse to quit, and I told you why." She kept her eyes down, and her voice was almost a murmur, but there was no mistaking her resolve.

Dylan's eyebrows rose. He was so astounded that she'd spoken up, he stared at her, his mouth partially open. "Melissa, there's more to life than just money."

"That's true if you've never been without it. I have, and don't intend to be again. Do you know why I married Coy?" she asked, gripping her apron pocket, the one with the button on it. "Can you guess?"

He shifted in his chair. The question had certainly crossed his mind. "I thought maybe Jenny had something to do with it," he mumbled.

She frowned, then blushed back to her ears. "You mean I was desperate and in trouble and had to marry him?"

He shifted again, beginning to feel damned awkward. "Well, yeah, something like that. It happens all the time." He wanted to add, why else would a woman like her, smart and pretty, have shackled herself to a man like Logan?

"Well, it didn't happen to me. I *was* desperate and in trouble, but not the kind you think. In the house where I grew up, I lived my whole life tiptoeing around my drunken father, hoping not to be noticed. If I was noticed, I got hit, or yelled at. There were nights when he came home drunk, with a mean drunk's temper. It happened a lot, but on the days when he set out supposedly to find work, it was guaranteed. He never failed to run into a pal, some old friend he wanted to catch up with, and he'd spend his days—and what little money we had—finding the bottom of a whiskey bottle instead of a job. We wouldn't have had anything to eat if my mother hadn't worked for the Pettigreaves. She kept the roof over our heads and food on the table." She twisted the hem of her apron into a wad in her hands as she paced in front of the stove. Her braid, looking like a frayed rope, swung back and forth behind her. "I remember one night when I was five or six years old—my father was arguing with my mother. He was horrible—drunk and calling her names, filthy names. I crept into the parlor, scared for her. I was carrying a little sailboat that she'd just given me for my birthday. My father saw me, and, oh, he was so mad. He slapped me, and then he jerked the boat out of my hands and smashed it under his heel. He said that would teach me not to spy on people.

"My brothers weren't much better, but I think that's because my father beat them with his belt until they couldn't sit down. He thought it would make them behave. All he did was turn them into men just like himself."

Her voice began to quiver, and Dylan saw that her eyes were filled with tears that didn't quite spill over. He stood up and caught her upper arms, fighting the urge to take her into his embrace. "Melissa, you don't have to do this."

She pulled away from him. "Yes, I do! I want you to know why I married Coy Logan. I was a fool, but not the kind you think. I wasn't . . ." Impatiently, she scrubbed at her wet eyes with the hem of her apron, and her brow furrowed as she searched for the right word. "I wasn't *dazzled* by Coy, or swept off my feet like a heroine in some romantic story. He was a friend of my brothers, and he dawdled in our kitchen and made jokes with me sometimes. He made me laugh. He was kinder to me than my own father or brothers." She laughed now, a funny little chuckle that sounded as if her heart were breaking. "It's hard to believe, isn't it?"

Dylan wanted to kick himself for starting this. Though Melissa hadn't discussed it in much detail until now, he'd guessed that her life hadn't been an easy one. Listening to her talk about it was painfully hard—her words twisted his heart. But he thought he owed it to her to let her finish the story. He leaned against the wall, his arms crossed over his chest.

She stood by the sink and gazed at the floor, as if watching the events of her life roll by on the planking. "When he said he wanted to marry me, I knew I didn't love him and that I never would. But I liked him. Sort of. My mother urged me to accept him—I guess she thought the same thing I did. That marrying Coy would get me away from the arguing and yelling . . . the hopelessness." She raised her eyes and looked up at Dylan. "But he was just like my father, after all."

"Does your mother know that?" Dylan asked.

Melissa swallowed hard, and her voice quivered again. "No. She died right after Coy and I got married. It—it was as if she wanted to see me on my way, and then was too tired to go on. She went to sleep one night and didn't wake up. The doctor said her heart just gave up. I think it was broken, from hard work and all those years of disappointment."

Dylan pushed himself away from the wall and sat down opposite her. He wanted to keep his distance from her, to hold her at arm's length from his soul and his body, but the armor around his own heart wasn't as impenetrable as he'd believed. How could he envision the lurid scenes her words painted and remain completely detached? An instinct to protect her made him wish he could sweep her out of her chair and onto his lap. Instead, he reached tentatively across the table and covered her trembling hand with his own. Despite the punishment it took every day in wash water, her skin was remarkably soft.

"Melissa, I'm sorry."

Melissa felt as if a low jolt of electricity had shot through her arm. Dylan's hand on hers was warm and vital and comforting. Though she kept her gaze fixed on the oilcloth covering the table, she sensed him watching her. Without wanting to, once more she thought about the inevitable time when they would go their separate ways. Despite her desire for independence, in her heart she had begun to anticipate that day with dread.

"Feeling a little better?" he asked.

She nodded and took a deep breath. "Thank you.

Now maybe you understand why I want to make as much money as I can. I want to take care of myself and Jenny, and not have to depend on anyone. I'm learning that cash is the best friend a person can have."

Dylan's brows drew together slightly, and he let go of her hand. "I wonder why I've known women who were only interested in money," he muttered, more to himself.

Melissa remembered the day he'd found her with his trunk open, and the dark-haired woman whose picture he kept buried inside. Whoever she was, Melissa guessed he shared a history with her that now gave him no happiness. "That woman in the photograph—Dylan, who is she?" she blurted.

His expression turned as dark as thunderheads, and he said nothing. In the gulf of awkward silence that opened between them, the sound of a jangling saloon piano from the street below floated through the open window. Melissa wished she had the question to take back again.

"I'm sorry, it's none of my bus—"

"Her name is Elizabeth Petitt Harper," he answered, surprising her. "She's my brother's wife."

Melissa digested this for a moment. At least the woman wasn't his own wife. But it seemed a bit odd that he would carry a photograph of his sister-in-law, especially since there seemed to be no affection among the Harpers. Unless of course, the real reason that Dylan had left the family had something to do with her and him—

"Your brother's wife?"

He drummed his fingers once on the tabletop, then pushed his chair back and stood up. "If you and Jenny are going to be all right, I have to get back to the store."

She looked up at him, feeling foolish, as if she'd asked him something far more personal. "Oh—well, of course—we're fine."

He plucked his hat from the table and turned it in his hands. "You go ahead with whatever work you feel you need to do, Melissa. If you want to keep doing wash for people, I won't say anything more about it." He put on the hat and walked toward the door, then turned to consider her for a moment. "You're right—it doesn't matter how a person plans, there's never any telling what the future will bring."

After Dylan left, Melissa took Jenny downstairs and finished Big Alex McDonald's shirts. She would collect that bonus, despite what had happened today. Coy's surprise visit had rattled her more than she wanted to admit, even to herself. But with shaky resolve, she gathered the shreds of her thin courage and determined to go on.

As she stoked the fire in the little stove behind the building, she knew she couldn't live her life cowering in the shadows. She had done that for too many years. In trading Coy's debt for her, Dylan had done more than just rescue her from a life of abuse. Though laconic and enigmatic, he had unwittingly given her the chance to escape, to discover who she really was.

Anyway, she decided, even if Coy meant to return and harass her again, she didn't believe he'd come back that same day, especially after the furious warning that Dylan had given him. Nevertheless, as she rung out the shirts, she cast so many wary, searching looks at the entrance of the street she began to get dizzy. Each time she found no one there.

But if there had been, she knew that Dylan was in the store, close at hand.

Dylan.

She had tried to ignore the picture he presented every morning as he stood at his shaving, his bare back sculpted with light and shadow, and the sun glinting on his streaked hair. She tried, but her pulse told her that she failed. She had done her best to stop wondering how Dylan's full mouth would feel if he kissed her—would it be better than Coy's brutal, sloppy attentions? Her imagination had her believing so. She had struggled to convince herself that Dylan was only a man, better than most she'd known, but nothing remarkable. That, she had begun to suspect, wasn't true either.

The significance of Elizabeth Petitt Harper remained a mystery to her, and Dylan seemed unlikely to reveal it. But to her chagrin, Melissa realized she felt a niggling bit of envy. Obviously, he cared enough about the woman to carry her picture with him all the way to Dawson. And whatever she had been to him, she'd burned a lasting memory into his heart.

She flung a dripping shirt on the clothesline and jammed the wooden pins over the tails. Melissa might share Dylan Harper's food and sit at his table; she could wash his clothes and even sleep in his bed, with the sack of rice still in place, of course. But despite all of that, he'd made it plain that he didn't welcome personal questions.

Envisioning his bare back again, she thought that perhaps it was just as well.

That night Dylan didn't go upstairs for dinner. Instead, he sat at his counter in the store, eating stew and cornbread from a tray he'd ordered at one of the chophouses on Front Street. He'd eaten a lot of his meals this way before Melissa had come to stay with him, and he'd never given it much thought. Now it seemed lonely. The coffee was cold and not as good as hers. The biscuits weren't as flaky, and even the stew seemed greasy. And he knew that she would be waiting for him—he felt a little guilty about that. But he wanted some time to himself to think, without her simple beauty to distract him.

He let his gaze drift to the tarp-covered object sitting in the corner. He'd asked the captain of the *Athenian* to buy it for him in Seattle, and it was the reason he hadn't been in the store when Logan had appeared.

When he thought of that dark slime of a man, Coy Logan, touching Melissa, every jealous instinct inside him came alive. At first he hadn't recognized any feelings beyond outrage, but now he knew what they were, and he didn't like it.

He took a sip of the lukewarm coffee and looked around the walls of the store. His simple life in Dawson sure had become complicated. He'd drifted North, hoping to leave behind all of his memories of Elizabeth and his falling out with the old man. He'd been able to escape them for a while. In fact, he'd pushed everything and everyone far, far away from him. A loner by nature, he hadn't missed the company at first. But the Yukon winters were longer and harder than any he'd ever known, and one dark afternoon he'd waded through the snow to the saloon next door. There he'd traded drinks and conversation with a laughably out-of-place, dandified newcomer from Louisiana named Raford Dubois. Rafe's frail appearance had proved to be deceiving, however. What he lacked in physical strength his wit made up for. He could skewer a man with words as neatly as a fencing master wielded a rapier. He and Dylan had had nothing in common, but Rafe had turned out to be a loyal friend. Dylan had enjoyed watching Rafe lampoon the occasional sourdough with his razor-sharp intelligence. And tipping a few with Rafe had not distracted Dylan from his single-minded goal.

Melissa was a different story.

When he came upstairs in the evenings for dinner and saw her standing at the stove, sometimes he wanted to turn around and run back down the steps. He found it so easy to take Rafe's matchmaking to heart. Carrying the scene a little further, he could envision a future with Melissa standing at the stove in another kitchen, the one he would build for her in Oregon with the money he'd earned. She would look beautiful—rested and happy, so different from the haggard, worn-out drab he'd met at the end of June. When she looked up at him, her gray eyes would hold a look of welcome, and the promise of something more intimate to follow. And there would be Jenny, a giggling toddler by then, and as blond as her mother, dragging around the wooden pull toy that he had whittled for her. He would never remember that he had not fathered her; in his mind she would be his and Melissa's. During the long winter nights in Oregon, he and Melissa would burrow deep into the warm bedding and explore each other's bodies with wonder, reverence, and passion. She and Jenny would be his family, one that he had made, one that loved him as his other had not.

"Damn it," he swore aloud, and pushed away the tray, disgusted with himself. He was doing it again, painting that rosy, unrealistic picture in his head of an ideal life. Hadn't Melissa made it plain enough that the last thing she wanted now was a man? Who could blame her after what she'd been through? And what did he want with another woman? Elizabeth's greedy fickleness had cured him of the notion of settling down.

All Dylan wanted was the chance to live a simple life, governed by his own rules and his own code, which were so different from Griffin Harper's. During their last confrontation, Dylan's enraged father had divulged something so staggering that upon hearing it, Dylan had felt as if he'd been punched in the stomach. Those words had been the last the old man spoke to him. Dylan had turned on his heel, packed up, and left behind a house furnished with stolen keepsakes and treasures, plunder taken from others less fortunate in loan foreclosures. Robber barons—that's what men like his father were called.

He shook his head and wondered why he hadn't realized the truth before that moment. His brother, Scott, was a willing student of their father's cutthroat business practices, but Dylan had always felt like a stranger, the outsider in the family. The only thing he had in common with them was his last name.

Dylan remained sitting at the counter with the plate of cold stew and his gloomy thoughts until the late July sky began to grow dusky. He knew he couldn't put off going upstairs any longer—it was almost ten o'clock. Sighing, he stood and grabbed his hat. Then he went to the corner of the store and picked up the bulky, tarp-draped shipment from the *Athenian*.

With Jenny asleep in her arms, Melissa pulled the rocker closer to the window and sat for a moment to look out on the rooftops of Dawson. The sun skimmed the far edge of the earth and touched the taller buildings with gold. Now that summer had ripened, for a few hours the sun would actually dip below the horizon and let the town sleep in full darkness.

Watching the street, she decided that the milling throng of people on Front had diminished a bit over the last few weeks. Certainly, the circus atmosphere was still there—pianos jangled until morning, and men who'd worked hard in the gold fields all day came into town at night, eager to spend what they'd earned on a saloon girl or the turn of a card. The Novelty Theater featured a hootchie-kootchie girl named Freda Maloof, whose daring act consisted of a scarf dance, and the Oatley Sisters' Concern Hall packed customers in six nights a week. But every steamship that left Dawson carried away stampeders who had managed to scrape together the fare to return home.

As Melissa sat and rocked, the gray and lavender shadows of the Arctic evening grew longer, and still Dylan didn't return. Behind her on the table, the place she had set for him waited, although she was certain the chicken she'd roasted had turned cold and dry over the past three hours. Too tired and anxious to eat anything herself, the meal would simply go to waste if he didn't return soon.

Miserable, Melissa gripped the arm of the rocker. She knew it was her fault that Dylan hadn't come home. If she hadn't asked about Elizabeth Harper, he wouldn't have gotten angry enough to stay away. That *had* to be the reason he wasn't here now.

What a stupid, nosy question she'd asked him, she thought. It was so unlike her to meddle in other people's business, but her curiosity had gotten the better of her. Well, she supposed it had been more than curiosity—a tiny demon of jealousy had prodded her. And a dreadful realization it was, that she would be jealous of a woman about whom she knew nothing. But Melissa had heard the ghost of an unmistakable yearning in his voice when he spoke of his brother's wife, and for an instant she'd wished that she was the one who held that place in his heart. That he was the father of the sleeping child she held against her breast.

Finally, after the evening stars had begun to emerge, Melissa heard Dylan's boots on the stairs. She sat up straight in the rocker and listened intently. His footfalls were slower than usual, as if he were too tired or—please, no—too drunk to take the steps two at a time, as he often did. Outside on the landing, she heard a couple of loud thumps, like he'd sat down heavily, or staggered around and bumped into the wall. On the other side of the door he fumbled with the latch as though he couldn't remember how it worked—she knew that sound, she'd heard it often enough in her life. Oh, God, he *must* be drunk.

With a shaking hand, she lit a match and held it to the wick in the oil lamp on the table next to her. Although Dawson had been wired for electricity, neither this room nor the store downstairs was equipped for the new technology. The lamplight filled the room with harsh brightness; if trouble was approaching, she wanted to see it coming.

Despite the progress she'd made, her old fears and

foreboding came rushing back over her like floodwaters after a storm. The last few weeks that she'd lived in relative peace hadn't been enough to make her forget a lifetime of hiding from an angry, drunken father, or her marriage to Coy, or completely convince her that Dylan would never hurt her, drunk or sober. Her palms damp with foreboding, she rose from the rocker and put Jenny down in her bed.

No matter how drunk he might be, Dylan wouldn't hurt Jenny, she told herself; he liked Jenny. Her feverish thoughts fluttered around in her mind like trapped birds. Watching the door swing open, she took a deep breath, prepared for the worst.

Then she saw the reason for Dylan's dragging footsteps and the thumping noises she'd heard on the landing. On his shoulder he carried a big canvas-draped object. She stood rooted to the floor, staring as he lowered his burden to the planking.

Finally, he straightened and glanced at the waiting place setting on the table. "Um, sorry I missed dinner. I just . . . well, I can't explain—" He broke off and gestured at the canvas. "Anyway, I thought you might like this."

Melissa took one step closer. He didn't seem angry any longer, and he certainly wasn't drunk. In fact, he appeared almost bashful. "What is it?"

Jenny, awake now and watching the proceedings with great interest, followed Dylan's movements. It seemed to Melissa that the little girl fixed her blue eyes on Dylan's tall form whenever he was near. She wasn't the only one who did.

"I didn't think it was right that the baby should have to sleep in that damned box." He pulled off the tarp to reveal an expensive-looking cradle.

"Oh!" Melissa exclaimed and clasped her hands over her chest. She'd been prepared for the worst, but nothing in her experience had taught her to prepare for the best. "It's beautiful!" She crossed the floor in two steps and crouched beside the bed, extending a hand to caress the pale oak rails. She'd never seen a baby bed quite like it. Instead of having a base that rocked like her chair, this cradle hung suspended between two sturdy, fixed bases, allowing it to swing between them. Inside lay a snow-white feather tick and a lovely pale pink muslin quilt.

Melissa's throat closed, and sudden tears stung her eyes. Her poor little Jenny, her baby, now had a proper bed to sleep in. She'd been born in a tent in the dead of a howling Canadian winter to a frightened, exhausted mother and a lazy, bullying father. There had been no gifts for Melissa's child to welcome her to the world, no loving family of grandparents and aunts and uncles who vied to hold her, nurture her, guide her. Rather than the safe, downy nest a mother wanted for her child, Jenny's existence had been a precarious one.

Until Dylan Harper had come along.

"Do you think she'll like it?" He sounded uncertain—it was the first time she'd heard a note of hesitancy in his voice, and it surprised her. Everything about him bespoke a man who always knew exactly what to do.

"Oh, yes, I know she will! She . . . I haven't been able to buy much for her." In truth, Melissa had longed to part with some gold to buy her baby a few things, but given Coy's outstanding debt to Dylan, she hadn't felt free to spend anything she earned, not even for necessities.

Melissa looked up at Dylan now, and try though she would, she couldn't ignore his rugged appeal. He seemed as tall as a totem pole, and his sun-streaked hair gleamed in the lamplight. "Where in Dawson did you find something so nice?"

Resting a hand on one end of the cradle, he said, "I didn't buy it here. I asked the captain of the *Athenian* to get it for me when he made his last run to Seattle. That's why I went down to the riverfront this afternoon—to pick this up."

Melissa stood and gazed into his eyes. "Dylan, thank you," she whispered, clearing her tight throat. Unable to express the jumble of emotions she felt—relief, a mother's gratitude, guilt over her assumption that he was drunk, and one or two more she was afraid to examine too closely—she could say nothing more.

"I hope maybe this will help make up for the lousy day you had," he murmured.

"I've had days that were much worse," she answered, hearing the subtle change in the tone of his voice. It was warm, personal . . . intimate.

Slowly, he took her hands in his own. Lifting them to his chest, he forced her to move closer and stand with her hands trapped between their bodies.

With his touch the atmosphere around them became charged. In that instant the world seemed to contain only the two of them. Even Jenny, for a single moment, faded to the background, and Melissa's vision was filled with this green-eyed, sun-blond man. Suddenly, she felt hypnotized. She knew she ought to pull her hand away, but she had no desire to do so. Dylan's gaze skittered lightly over her face, connecting with her eyes, glancing over her mouth, her brow, her throat, searching, searching. She watched, unmoving, as he angled his head and lowered his face to hers, his lips parted and slightly moist.

She did nothing but breathe in the scent of him and accept his kiss. It wasn't a kiss exactly—his lips just brushed over hers, lightly, teasingly. The sensation was like none she'd ever known—sweet, tender, exciting. Goose bumps raced over her scalp and down her back. She took a deep breath and a tiny moan formed in her throat.

The sound jarred Dylan, and abruptly he broke off the kiss with a suddenness that was almost violent. He felt Melissa flinch. What the hell was wrong with him? This was exactly what he'd promised her would not happen that afternoon outside the Yukon Girl Saloon.

But his body had made no such agreement. He felt his blood coursing through him, pounding to his groin where fierce arousal was in the making. His hair-trigger response was like that of a green kid instead of a grown man. What would he have done next? Given into his urge to wrap his arms around her and bury his face against her neck? And after that? He looked down into Melissa's startled face and released her hands.

"I'm sorry, I didn't mean to—"

"Oh, but I didn't mi—that is, well, it's all right."

"No, damn it, it isn't all right. And it won't happen again. I promised I wouldn't take advantage of"—he gestured around the room impatiently—"of this. Of you being here."

Looking stricken, her face flamed with color. Obviously, he'd embarrassed her, and she was doing her best to cover it. Hadn't she suffered enough humiliation today? In her whole life? Whatever she might think of him, he wasn't about to have her think he was trying to seduce her by buying presents for her child.

Yanking off his hat, he tossed it on the bed. It landed on the rice sack still firmly situated in the middle of the mattress. *Shit.* If that wasn't enough to remind him of their situation, maybe a horse kicking him in the head would do the trick. Not for the first time since Melissa had come to stay, he felt the confinement of this small room. He tried to tell himself it was because he didn't like sharing his privacy, but more often he realized the small quarters were making it harder to keep his word to her.

"Shall we see how Jenny likes her new bed?" Melissa proposed as she fiddled with her cuffs.

Grateful for the change of subject and activity, he jumped to agree. "Good idea." Dylan moved the cradle to the end of his bed, and Melissa retrieved Jenny from that damned crate that he so disliked.

But after she laid the baby down on the new tick, the tension between them melted as they stood over the cradle and watched Jenny together, their arms brushing. He gave the bed a little push to start it rocking. The little girl smiled up at them, and Dylan felt a rush of tenderness greater than he'd ever known.

Jenny was not his child, and Melissa was not his wife. They would never be his family.

But right now he wished for all the world that he knew how to change that.

That night Melissa fell into bed, exhausted from the long, stressful day. But as she lay curled up against the sack of rice, waiting for sleep, she felt both contented and restless at the same time.

From the beginning Dylan had made it plain that he had his own plans, and that he'd taken in Jenny and her as a simple act of temporary charity. And she had feared him as much as she had feared any man she ever knew; he could be violent and frightening and harsh.

But not toward her. Time and again, he'd gone out of his way to do good things for her. When she thought of them—the clothes he'd bought, the rocking chair, the sign for her laundry, and now the cradle—why, no one had ever given her so much. Or been as thoughtful.

Then tonight when he'd kissed her, she'd felt a

wild quickening, an urge to respond. Rather than just enduring his caress, she'd wanted to take her hands out of his so that she could stroke his long hair and feel the muscles under his shirt. But he'd pulled back before she wanted him to. Even now she felt tempted to peek over the sack between them just for the pleasure of looking at him in the low light. In the relative quiet of this room, she listened to his breathing—he was so close, and she just knew he lay there in only his drawers with the sheet pulled up to his hips. She'd seen him thus many other times.

Instead, she rolled over and punched her pillow with a long sigh.

Fire, oh, she was playing with fire. For one thing, she didn't know for certain that Dylan was not somehow entangled with a woman back home. Indeed, she didn't know much about him at all, except that he was in exile from his family, just as she was. And like it or not, she was still Coy's wife. But even if she were not, and while Dylan might be as free as a bird, she knew that he valued his independence as much as his integrity.

With this jumble of thoughts whirling in her head and plaguing her heart, she finally drifted off.

Sometime later in the night, Jenny's cries pierced the layers of Melissa's exhausted sleep. She moved leaden limbs to tend her daughter, but when she hoisted herself to her elbows, she saw Dylan bending over the baby's cradle and carefully lifting her to his shoulder.

"Hold on there, little Jenny," he whispered. "We'll

let your mama sleep, okay? She had one hell of a day." The baby quieted immediately, and Melissa watched as he carried her to the rocking chair, where it sat in a shaft of moonlight. He wore only his drawers, and his hair brushed his bare shoulders. The noise in the street faded away, and Dylan rocked her child in his arms. They sat limned in silver. His hair looked almost white, and sharp shadows fell across his face as he smiled down at the baby and pressed a kiss to her forehead. When he spoke again, his whisper was as soft and light as a dandelion puff, as if he told a secret that only Jenny was meant to hear. "I love you, sweetheart."

Melissa kept her silence and lay back against her pillow, her throat tight with emotion. She thanked God that Dylan Harper had found such tenderness and affection for her baby.

Then she prayed that he might learn to feel it for her, too.

Chapter Nine

Two days later, Melissa sat down on a soap crate next to her washtubs and stared at the wet street, her elbows on her knees and her chin in her hands. A soaking drizzle had fallen from the dull gray sky since morning, and it showed no signs of clearing. Pungent smoke from cook fires all over town hung in the air, held in place by the heavy clouds overhead.

Fortunately, they'd had few rainy days; damp weather made her hard job even more difficult. Although she and her clotheslines were under the cover of a canvas awning Dylan had thoughtfully erected, the moisture-laden air kept the wet clothes from drying. Even her skirt was clammy nearly to her knees. Thank heavens Dylan had offered to let Jenny sleep in the store.

As she sat, she did some mental calculations and realized that with the bonus Big Alex had given her, she now had almost one thousand dollars in gold.

One thousand dollars! she marveled, looking out on the rainy day. In Portland she and Jenny could live for two years or more with that much money.

But her first obligation was to pay back Dylan. Earning this gold hasn't been easy, but it had been quick, and she would be able to make more as long as there were dirty clothes in Dawson.

She had some competition now, but she still had more work than she had time for. She had one advantage, however, that the competition did not—a clientele who loved to hear her sing. Melissa had no business experience, but she was smart enough to realize that her singing was an asset that cost her nothing. She didn't go so far as to give performances, but her habit of entertaining Jenny had brought her customers from all over the region. Lottie Oatley, who sang for the miners with her sister, Polly, had even visited her one day and offered her a job in their concert hall.

But Melissa was satisfied to continue with her laundry business. Now if only her heart could find the same contentment. She resisted the urge to look back over her shoulder toward Dylan's side window, as she'd done so many times in the last few days. She never found him there—that was good. Wasn't it?

Since he'd bought her the cradle for Jenny, Dylan had been in her thoughts during almost every waking moment that didn't require her undivided attention. Her thoughts about him concerned more than just how nice he'd been to her, too. She'd actually found herself beginning to regret the rice sack that served as a barrier between them in his bed. Were all men careless and rough during intimacy? she wondered. Or would it be different with Dylan? Just considering the idea made her cheeks flame hotly.

Melissa's thoughts were interrupted when she heard the splash of approaching boots. She looked up to see the familiar red wool coat of Sergeant Foster Hagen of the North West Mounted Police. He was tall and ramrod straight, with riveting silver eyes and a carefully waxed handlebar mustache. He wore his Mountie hat squarely over his brow, completing his no-nonsense appearance. Though the rain had picked up its pace and soaked his uniform, he gave no indication of discomfort, accustomed as he was to all kinds of weather, fair or foul.

And while his bearing made him noticeable, she wasn't likely to forget him in any case. He had been the arresting officer who sent Coy to the government woodpile.

He glanced up at her sign on the side of the building, and then at her again. "You are Mrs. Coy Logan, are you not?"

She rose from her seat. God, what had Coy done now? she wondered anxiously. "Yes, I am, but I don't know where my husband is, Sergeant. Except for a short . . . visit two days ago, I haven't seen him in weeks."

"Oh, I know where he is, ma'am. Please"—he gestured at her soap crate—"won't you be seated again?"

Melissa's hands turned ice cold, and she closed them into fists at her sides. He must have done something really bad this time—dear God, maybe he'd been given a blue ticket, banishment from the Territory. She didn't care if that was the case, but as his wife, perhaps the authorities could force her and Jenny to leave as well. "I would rather stand, Sergeant, if you don't mind."

He nodded stiffly, and for a moment his proper military demeanor shifted uncertainly. He looked up at the sign again, and then at her. "Well, Mrs. Lo . . . ma'am, it is my regrettable duty to inform you—"

Melissa tightened her fists.

"—that your husband, Coy Logan, died early this morning at St. Mary's Hospital. Pneumonia, I believe Father William said it was."

The air whooshed out of her lungs, and she stared at the sergeant. "He—he's dead? Coy is *dead*?"

He inclined his head, and a trickle of rain ran from the wide brim of his hat. "Yes, ma'am, I'm afraid so. You say you haven't seen your husband lately?"

Melissa looked down at the wooden pallet under her feet. She swallowed and swallowed, but her throat was suddenly as dry as cotton. "Except for a minute two days ago, I-I hadn't seen him in weeks. Coy thought that he could do better in Dawson without the burden of a wife and child. So he left me here." She didn't lie, but despite her shock, she was careful not to mention the details of her illegal divorce.

The unflappable Mountie looked distinctly uncomfortable. He slapped his gloves against the palm of his hand and twiddled with his impeccable mustache. "Yes, well, we found him passed out behind one of the saloons last night. Apparently he regained consciousness long enough to tell one of the sisters where you could be found."

She raised her eyes again. "Did he . . . do you know if he left any message for me? Or for his daughter?"

Now Sergeant Hagen shifted from one foot to the other, while a puddle formed around his boots. "Nothing I would repe— No, I don't believe he did, Mrs. Logan. I'm truly sorry. The sisters said he had no money or personal effects."

"Do you know, that is, should I arrange for a funeral?"

"No, that won't be necessary. There was some confusion and, well, he was already buried in our potter's field before I had a chance to find you."

"Potter's field—does that mean his grave isn't marked?"

"Yes, it does." He tipped his wet hat deferentially and added, "My sincere condolences, ma'am." Then he walked back through the mud to Front Street.

Coy was dead.

She was a widow.

Just like that. Melissa sat down hard on the soap crate. The man who had married her and taken her from her unhappy home in Portland, who had fathered her baby and brought her to this wilderness outpost was gone.

He'd looked dissipated a couple of days ago, but her horror upon seeing him again had been so great that she hadn't realized he was ill. She folded her hands tightly in her lap. Maybe that had been why he'd come around that day. *He* must have known he was sick, and he'd expected her to take care of him.

Of all the things she had thought might happen to him, she'd never imagined that he'd pass from this earth as a charity patient to be buried in a pauper's unmarked grave. Try though she might, Melissa couldn't rouse any grief, or any other emotion but one. And she struggled to push it to the back of her mind because it was heartless and unworthy.

Feeling suddenly very cold, she stood again and went to fetch the child she had conceived with the late Coy Logan.

When Melissa walked into the store, one look at her chalky face told Dylan that something was wrong. Rafe, who sat pitching cards at a chamber pot again, obviously noticed it too—the ten of clubs took a wild turn and fell far short of its intended target.

"Melissa," Dylan said, "are you all right?"

She moved like a sleepwalker across the floor to Jenny's crate, which they'd brought downstairs to use in the store. Picking up the baby, she touched her cheek to the little girl's silky head.

Dylan stepped out from behind the counter. "Melissa," he repeated, worried. He reached out and grasped her arm. Standing this close to her, he could smell the rain in her hair. "Did Logan come back?"

She shook her head. "No. He won't bother us anymore." Her gray eyes were as blank as a wall. "Coy is dead."

For one wild moment, while he looked at her paper-white face and fragments of thought tumbled around in his head, he wondered if she had killed Logan. He tightened his grip on her slim arm. "Dead?"

"Sergeant Hagen said it was pneumonia." She went on to explain the Mountie's news in a dull monotone.

Rafe used his cane to push himself from the chair. With decorous gravity he led Melissa back to the now vacant seat. "Please sit down, dear madam. This is quite a shock, I'm sure." He offered to bring her a glass of water and a headache powder, which she declined. Then he collected his deck of cards from the enamel pot, stepped away from her, and withdrew his gold pocket watch. "I am due at a card game at the Pioneer Saloon," he said to Dylan in a low, winded voice. "I hope I have the kind of luck that has just been left on your doorstep."

"What are you talking about?" Dylan murmured back.

Rafe gave him his jack-o'-lantern grin. "I imagine it will dawn on you later." Patting Melissa's arm on the way out, he left the store.

Dylan returned his attention to her. "Coffee? It's been sitting on the stove since the morning."

"That's all right. I don't mind."

He poured a cup of the bitter black liquid and gave it to her. She held it without drinking it, as if she were a mannequin in a shop window. Pulling up a stool, he sat down, wishing he could think of something eloquent to say. Under the circumstances it didn't seem right to tell her he was glad that Logan would never pester her again.

"I'm sorry, Melissa."

At that, she looked up at him with eyes glittering with tears. God, did she *still* care about that no good—?

"But I'm not sorry," she said. He heard anger and fear creeping into her voice. "I'm not sorry at all. I'm glad he's dead, and I shouldn't be. I feel so guilty about it. Remorse is one of the only feelings that elevates us above animals, and I feel no remorse for Coy." She leaped from the chair so suddenly, Dylan worried that she might drop Jenny. But she put the coffee on the counter and with a kiss, laid the baby in her crate.

"You don't have to be sorry, Melissa," he said. "He chose his own path and made his own decisions. He was a grown man, even if he didn't act like one."

Color returned to her face, and fury, perhaps a lifetime's worth, erupted in her. "But he's dead now. I should be able to forgive him. Forgive the times he hit me and belittled me and ordered me around like I was a—a *dog*. I should overlook the names he called me—*stupid, dummy, wh-whore.* Just like my father!" She paced the plank flooring, and her damp skirts slapped against her ankles. She held her hands interlaced in front of her as if she appealed for understanding, while tears streaked her face. "I can't forgive any of it. I never loved Coy, but if he'd treated me decently, I could have been a good wife to him. Maybe I could have even learned to like him. Instead, I hated him and I wished him dead so many times that now it's come true!"

The mousey, timid female Dylan had first met was completely gone. In her place stood a person outraged by the wrongs she had endured. She scrubbed her tear-wet face.

At that moment Ned Tanner walked into the store, raindrops beading on his oiled hair. His curious, eager gaze swept over Melissa, who looked as wild-eyed as a harpy. Dylan jumped from his stool and literally pushed Ned back out to the duckboards.

"But Dylan, I need a new ham—"

"I'm closed, Ned," he barked and slammed the door.

The interruption took some of the fire out of her tirade. Dylan gripped her shoulders on her next pass over the flooring. She wasn't a small woman, but she felt as delicate as a bird beneath his touch.

"Honey, you know you can't wish someone dead. It doesn't work that way. And it doesn't matter if you don't forgive him. That he died didn't change what he did to you. Logan was a drunk and a bully, and he was headed for a bad end." Dylan thought back to the raging fury that had coursed through his own veins when he'd held his knife to Logan's scrawny neck. "If he hadn't died of pneumonia, somebody probably would have killed him eventually."

She turned her face up to his, and the anguish he

saw in her expression twisted his heart. He hoped that Coy Logan was in hell, getting his worthless ass fried for what he'd done to Melissa.

"But in a way, if I can't at least be sorry that he's dead, it makes me no better than he was."

He shook his head. "It makes you human. It's human to be angry at someone who hurts you."

"Do you think so, Dylan?"

Oh, she had a way of looking at a man as if he knew more than God himself. "Sure. Otherwise you'd be a martyr. And martyrs are so tiresome."

She gave him a wobbly little smile that went straight to his soul. "Maybe."

He dropped an arm over her shoulders. "You'll never forget how he treated you, but I'm betting that after enough time goes by the memory of it will fade. It will be a part of your life that's in the past." He nodded at Jenny. "And she won't remember it at all."

"That matters more than anything," Melissa agreed. "It was so horrible to hear my father call my mother those awful names and treat her like she was his servant. He—he must have been kind to me some times in my life, but I can't remember them. I only remember the bad times."

He sighed. "Maybe someday, they'll fade too." Though their pasts were vastly different—hers one of poverty and his, privilege—neither of them had good memories to hold to their hearts. And as he looked down into her face, for just this moment it seemed as if they had only each other.

Giving in to the greedy urge to hold her, Dylan enfolded her in his arms. To his surprise, she relaxed in his embrace, and his body responded with a pounding ache that made him think about flinging the rice sack upstairs out the window. Her lips, soft and pink, were just inches from his own. Her hair, fragrant with rain and soap, lay against his jaw. The other night he'd called himself a fool for nearly kissing her, and he'd promised it would never happen again. Right now, with her so close to him, sweet-smelling and soft beneath his touch, he couldn't remember why . . .

Melissa felt Dylan's finger under her chin, tipping her face up to his, and it seemed like the most natural thing in the world. She stood mesmerized by his green eyes, entranced by the long, sun-streaked hair that brushed his wide shoulders. Just above the hollow in his throat she saw his pulse beating, strong, steady. His wild maleness called out to her, asking her femininity to answer.

When his mouth covered hers, thoughts of Coy and her father and Dawson retreated like fog under a blazing sun. His lips were hot and full and soft, and the feel of them was like nothing she'd ever known. The peculiar quickening that she had felt around him before doubled its tempo now, suffusing her body with heat and restlessness. He traced her lips with his tongue, silky and warm, so that they were as moist as his own. Melissa's pulse jumped and her breath deepened. He tasted ever so faintly of coffee, and smelled of buckskin and freshly cut wood. Returning his kiss, she reached up timidly to put her arms around his neck, bringing her torso in contact with his. At her touch, he drew in a swift, deep breath.

Nothing existed for Melissa but Dylan and his kiss.

Jenny began fussing for her dinner then, and the moment ended.

Melissa pulled back, feeling a little awkward. "I guess she's getting—"

"You'll want to be feeding—" They both spoke at the same time.

He smiled. "Will you be all right now?"

"Yes." She smiled shyly.

Leaning over, he put a light kiss on her cheek. "You go on, then. I'll be up a little later for dinner."

She plucked Jenny from the crate and cast a lingering look at him. "Then I won't rush to get it started."

He opened the door for her, and as Melissa walked out to the duckboard, she realized that she felt a lot better.

That was due mostly, she knew, to Dylan Harper.

It took a while, but mingled with the turmoil in her heart over her feelings for Dylan, and the stunning news of Coy's death, Melissa finally realized one important thing.

She was free.

Not just because Rafe Dubois had said so in the

Yukon Girl Saloon. And not simply because she had stopped using her husband's name.

She was truly free—an independent woman. Coy Logan would never appear at her washtubs again, demanding that she come with him. He would never hit her again or call her names or make any other demands of her.

She had the right and the freedom to live her life as she saw fit, to raise Jenny and give her every advantage she could afford. Just how she would do it, and what it would entail, she didn't know yet. That evening after dinner, while the baby slept in her new cradle, a conversation with Dylan made her stop and think about it.

"What do you want from life?" he asked. He sat at the table with his chair tipped back against the wall. From the window a shaft of evening sunlight fell across the chiseled planes of his face, touching his lashes with gold.

Melissa sat across from him, taking small, careful finishing stitches on a new dress she'd made for Jenny. What did she want? She had never really stopped to think about it, although she supposed the truth had been there all along.

"To be safe and comfortable." She paused to wet the end of her thread before putting it through the needle's eye. "I never wanted to be rich, really. Well, I guess I used to daydream about the grand house where my mother worked, and I'd pretend that I lived there and had servants to wait on me and a driver to take me around in an automobile. But that was like putting myself in a fairy tale."

"Safe and comfortable. That sounds reasonable. I just want to raise horses."

"Horses?" This was a revelation, she thought. As far as she knew, he didn't even own a horse in Dawson.

"It's all I ever wanted."

"You must have wanted a wife, a family?" Melissa blessed the opportunity to pose the question.

He frowned. "At one time I thought I did. I know better now."

Disappointed by his ambiguous reply, she asked, "How did you get interested in horses?"

"My father and brother were all caught up in their banking and mortgages and damnable loan foreclosures. Even if they had been less ruthless, that wasn't the kind of business I wanted to be in. I told the old man that I could make a success of horse breeding if he'd let me give it a try. I invested everything I had to get started, and his bank loaned me the rest. When he realized that I could make money at it, he agreed to let me use his stables."

"Who did you sell the horses to?"

"A couple of the ranchers in the area took a few. But most of them went to the army at Fort Vancouver. These weren't nags rescued from the glue pot—I sold them fine, blooded horseflesh that were to be ridden by officers."

She adjusted her thimble. "You must have come North with a lot of money."

He shook his head. "I was down to about four mares and a stallion when I left The Dalles. I'd sold the rest to pay off most of that bank loan—I hated having that thing hanging over my head. Then I planned to rebuild my stock. But those plans fell through."

She wanted to ask why he'd left, what had led to his split with his family. But the last time she'd asked about it, he'd gotten angry.

Once he'd started, though, he continued as if in answer to the question she didn't dare ask. His green eyes had taken on a distant look, his expression conveying that he was no longer in this small room above the store, but far away and trapped in the past. Melissa had an almost overpowering urge to lean across the table to touch his hand, to let him know that his feelings mattered to her, to tell him she understood how it felt to be plagued by memories.

"I knew I didn't fit in with the rest of the family," he said huskily. "I was always different. I grew up in a big house with a cook and a maid, but I didn't care about that stuff."

Melissa lowered the dress to her lap and stared at him. This man with his long hair, with the knife on his thigh, and an Indian amulet around his neck—he'd grown up in a house with someone like her own mother to wait on him?

A huff of laughter rumbled out of him, as if he'd read her mind. "Yeah, you wouldn't know it to look at me, huh?" He toyed with a tiny pearl dress button on the table. His hands were nicely shaped, she thought, long-fingered and strong-looking.

"Well, I didn't think you looked like a banker's son." To her, he more closely resembled a mountain man.

"Nope, I never did. I moved out of the house when I was fifteen and went to live in a room over the stables. I hunted game in the hills and dressed like this and made friends with a few Deschutes Indians. The old man hated it. Money didn't mean anything to me, especially when I saw how the rest of them lived." He let his chair drop back to the floor. "Back in the house, he and Scott dressed for dinner every night like they were going to the damned opera or something. They invited the mayor for dinner, or other politicians they wanted to influence. They sat in the *drawing room,* smoking cigars and drinking brandy. I tried to stay out of the old man's way because if I didn't, we were sure to tangle."

The dress in her lap forgotten, Melissa leaned forward slightly, waiting for him to volunteer the reason that he'd finally left. And what his brother's wife had to do with it all.

"It sounds like such a lonely life," she said.

"Yeah, I guess it was sometimes, especially when I was young. Other kids talked about their families and the things they did together. I always wondered what that would be like."

"I guess you didn't have much reason to stay there," she put in.

He shrugged. "I did, and I didn't. I'd planned to

make enough money to move the operation to my own land, but things starting falling apart before I could do that. And there was Eliz—" Then he stopped himself and glanced up at her before returning his attention to the dress button in his fingers. "My father meddled in my business. He didn't know a goddamned thing about horses, but that didn't stop him from telling me how to run things. His way wasn't my way. If you aren't honest in business dealings, people figure it out soon enough. I never lied or cheated anyone. I didn't need to. The last argument I got into with him was because he wanted me to sell one of the mares to a business acquaintance he wanted to impress. I refused."

"Why?"

"Because I'd seen the man's other horses. He rode them hard, put them away wet, let them develop saddle galls. God, it gave me nightmares to think about it. I stood in the dining room and told him to keep looking—my horses weren't for sale to him. And that night, hell rained down on The Dalles."

"What happened?" she asked quietly.

He considered her for a moment, as if trying to decide whether he wanted to open an old wound, one that might be only half healed as it was. Then he inhaled a deep breath and propped his elbows on the table.

"It was an ugly scene. I went back out to the stables, and my father followed me, ranting on and on. He covered a lot of familiar ground about expecting me to fail in life, and what an embarrassment I was to him. Then he threw in something new—that he'd been a fool to pretend that my mother's bastard was his own son."

Melissa stared at him. "Was it true?"

Dylan leaned back in his chair again and tossed the button on the table. "It seems my mother was two months gone with a cowboy's baby when Griff Harper married her. My grandfather asked him to make an honest woman of her. He said he agreed because he felt sorry for her. But it didn't hurt that she was sole heir to very valuable ranch land over in Pendleton. He got that after my mother died." He looked up at her. "I guess I should have realized it sooner. I didn't look like anyone else in the house. I never felt like I fit in."

"But you didn't know any of this before? Not for sure?"

He shook his head. "Naw. I'll tell you, though, when I was a kid, sometimes I thought I might be a foundling. Scott was the one who got all the attention. In the end, he got everything. Even my horses. Scott wouldn't even know which end of the animal to put a bridle on. But that's okay—at least I can sleep nights. I don't have to think about the people I cheated or put out of their homes or threw off their land." A moment of silence fell between them. Finally, he pushed himself away from the table. "I guess I'll go check on the store." He did that every night to give Melissa a little privacy to wash and get ready for bed.

Melissa had always supposed that the reason her

life had been hard was because she'd grown up in poverty. But Dylan's life, in a way, had been no better, and he'd grown up with wealth.

"I guess there's misery everywhere," she said, more to herself.

He stopped with his hand on the doorknob and gazed at her over his shoulder. "That there is, Melissa. That there is."

Chapter Ten

After kissing Melissa in the store and telling her about his past—most of it, anyway—Dylan sensed a subtle change in their relationship.

As much as he didn't want to, he found himself following her softly rounded shape with his eyes, and his trips to the side store window became even more frequent. When he saw her customers hanging around her, chatting, he wanted to go out there and tell them to stop bothering her, that she had work to do. But deep down, he knew the miners didn't bother her nearly as much as they did him.

Her beauty was not glamorous or queenly, as Elizabeth's was. Melissa had an uncluttered, quiet grace that made him think of clear, cold streams and wildflowers. He could not begin to imagine Elizabeth changing a baby's diapers or tending to the other messy aspects of motherhood. Melissa did it all and yet retained her prettiness and much-improved spirits.

Whether or not she could admit it to herself, her mood had brightened considerably since Logan's death. Dylan noticed that she had finally begun to stop flinching at loud voices and no longer looked over her shoulder whenever she went outside.

He told himself again and again that a woman and a child played no part in his foreseeable future. It was all very well to imagine his fairy tale scene with Melissa and Jenny in the kitchen when he came home at night, but it was just that—a pretty daydream. He figured the first five years of his horse-ranching operation would be nothing but hard work, and he'd have to live in a cabin while the house and all the outbuildings were constructed. He would have no trouble doing that—fancy trappings didn't matter to him. But it would be too hard for a woman. Even if it wasn't, Dylan was not willing to risk his heart again.

And that was the crux of the matter.

A wife deserved a whole husband, and he knew he wouldn't be able to give completely of himself. He would always hold something back, the part of his soul that would let him love her fully.

But still he watched Melissa with a yearning that continued to grow every day. Just being around her was a sweet kind of torture—he felt better than when he'd lived alone, but to have to only look and not be able to touch—it was hell.

The afternoon after Logan died, Rafe dropped by the store. To avoid climbing stairs, which stole his already feeble wind, he'd made arrangements to move from his rooming house to a first-floor room at the now completed Fairview Hotel. Although there were no guest rooms on the first floor, Belinda Mulrooney had fixed up one for him—for a price, of course. A nice place, he observed drolly, but all the walls were nothing more than canvas with wallpaper pasted on them. "Anytime a guest so much as farts, it can be heard by the entire establishment."

Rafe looked far worse than Dylan had ever seen. His face was more ashen, and his deep-set eyes had taken on a slightly sunken look. The skin of his face stretched tightly over the bones. Dylan felt a chill of foreboding rush down his spine. But Rafe's clothes were as dapper as ever, and his biting wit suffered no debility.

From the street outside Dylan heard strains of "Nearer My God to Thee," honked out of a Salvation Army band that had staked out a spot on Front.

"I see you now have the luxury of musical accompaniment," Rafe remarked, gesturing with his cane at the brass and tambourine ensemble.

Like an old man, he lowered himself into the chair where he'd spent so many hours pitching cards and observing Dylan's corner of what he called man's last folly of the century. "Except for the war with Spain," he would add with his rich drawl. "That truly is supreme idiocy."

"Are you doing all right, Rafe?" Given his gray-faced appearance and shuffling gait, it seemed like a foolish question, but Dylan had to ask.

Rafe sent him an arch expression. "Why? Don't I look all right?"

Dylan chuckled. Even as ill as he was, Rafe could

still make him laugh. He realized that he would miss his friend very much when he was gone.

"Have you yet realized what good fortune befell you with Logan's death, Dylan?" he asked, his breath shorter than ever.

Dylan was wary—he suspected this had something more to do with Rafe's transparent effort to secure a protector for Melissa and Jenny. Pretending indifference, he poured a bag of coffee beans into a canister. "And what might that be?"

"She is a widow now."

Dylan's head came up. *A widow.* Of all the realities that had occurred to him since Logan's death, the most obvious of them all had not: Melissa was now a marriageable woman. He'd only considered that Logan wouldn't bother her again, and that Jenny wouldn't suffer the same abuse her mother had. But the imaginary wall that had stood between them, and which he'd used as a flimsy shield against the hunger that she aroused in him, suddenly had crumbled. She was no longer another man's wife.

Dylan shrugged. "Yeah, she's a widow. I'm not going to be the one who changes that."

Rafe sighed, and it sounded like a cross between a wheeze and a rattle. "Don't let an incident with one woman turn you into a bitter, cantankerous man."

"Hmm, from the voice of experience," Dylan said with a laugh, refusing to be pulled into the conversation.

"Good. If you learned nothing else from me, at least I set an example of what not to do with your life. You know, I was like you once, certain that I'd never let any woman get close—I told you about that. But I never told you about Priscilla Beaumont." His voice dropped and his tone became introspective. He stared at a coffee can on the shelf as if a memory unfolded before his eyes. "She was a beautiful young lady, graceful, charming, kind, and from an old, well-respected New Orleans family. Suitors lined up with their calling cards every day of the week to pay their respects and to propose. Gently, but firmly, she turned all of them down. There was another gentleman who had already captured her affection, she told them, although she would not reveal his name to them. That was because the gentleman in question—a cad, really—did not want to be bothered with such foolishness as love." He smiled faintly. "She was lovely, as fair as a spring flower. He did everything he could to push her away, even though in his heart he truly cared about her." He looked up at Dylan. "Obviously, I was the cad."

Dylan had already guessed as much. "What happened?"

Rafe took another deep breath, and the rattling wheeze sounded again in his chest. "Eventually, her father forced her into a marriage that he arranged with a shipowner's son. A year after the wedding, she died from an overdose of laudanum."

"Well, Jesus, Rafe, I'm sorry."

Returning from his reverie, he sat up a bit straighter, and his voice took on a brisker tone. "Don't be. I'm sorry enough for both of us. Just don't make the same mistake. True love, an *affaire de coeur*, comes along only once or twice in a lifetime, my friend. Some people never find it at all. Forget about what happened with Elizabeth and put it behind you. I have seen the way you look at Melissa and the way she looks at you." He hoisted himself to his feet again. "A body would have to be blind to miss the sparks that fly between you two."

Dylan felt his face grow hot all the way to his scalp.

Just then, a delivery driver walked in. A big hulking giant, he looked like the epitome of a teamster. "Mr. Harper, I got your goods outside that came up on the *St. Paul*."

Grateful for the chance to escape, Dylan pulled his shirt off over his head. "Okay, let's get them unloaded."

Rafe caught his arm as he passed him. He looked especially haggard suddenly, as if talking had used up his small reserve of strength. "Don't throw away this chance, Dylan," he said in his low voice. It seemed to have grown huskier over the past few weeks. "Trouble comes by the barrelful in life; good things are doled out to us on a teaspoon."

Rafe walked out then, his progress slow and measured, and Dylan watched his retreating back.

On the other side of the street, the Salvation Army band took up "In the Sweet By and By."

Melissa automatically clutched her apron pocket, feeling for her gold pouch. Then she picked up Jenny and left her pot of boiling water, intending to buy a box of starch from Dylan's stock. He might resist taking money for Coy's debt, but she would tolerate no argument about paying him for her laundry supplies. If she was making money from her venture, so should he. But when she rounded the corner of the building, she stopped in her tracks, captivated by what she saw.

Standing in the back of wagon and silhouetted by a blue summer sky, Dylan hoisted a keg to his shoulder. Obviously, the work was hot, and his torso gleamed with sweat that also dampened his belt. His muscles, thrown into bright relief by shadow and sun, contracted as he shifted the keg and handed it down to a burly man on the duckboard. His jeans hung low and snug, and Melissa's eyes were drawn to the hollow of his spine, to his arms where tendon and sinew flexed and lengthened.

"Is that the last of it?" the burly man asked. They'd stacked merchandise on either side of the front door.

"Yeah, that's it." Not seeing her, Dylan dragged the back of one gloved hand over his forehead, then jumped down off the tailgate of the wagon right into her path.

"Oh—hi," he said. He looked down at his bare chest and then gestured at the wagon. "Um, I just had some stuff delivered from the waterfront."

Melissa tried not to gape, but this was a different Dylan from the man who stood at his shaving mirror in the mornings. He was more vital and earthy and powerful. And he called to someting just as vital and deep within her. She watched, fascinated as a rivulet of perspiration ran down the center of his flat belly to be absorbed by the low waistband on his jeans. Seeing him this way only fanned the low, hot flame he had lighted when he kissed her. "I—well, I just wanted to get a box of starch."

He nodded, and scribbled his signature on a manifest that the wagon driver handed him. "Go ahead and help yourself. I'm going to wash off in the back." He kept an enamal washbasin and a bar of soap behind the building near her stove.

Watching him round the corner, she felt like a silly young schoolgirl gaping at the object of her crush. But the truth was that her feelings went deeper than a crush, and her daydreams about him didn't end with a simple kiss. She was tempted to follow him back to the washbasin . . . she could imagine sheets of water flowing through his hair and down his back, sparkling in the sun, catching on his long lashes and the tip of his nose. Picturing it made her insides jumpy and tight.

Stop it right now, she told herself sternly. Turning to walk into the store, she gave herself a sharp talking-to. She would have to stop thinking about Dylan the way she'd . . well, *that* way, and as if he were really her husband. Even if she wanted to marry again, he'd made it plain that he had no interest in acquiring a wife.

She shifted Jenny to her other arm to reach for a box of starch from the shelf, and as she did, she caught sight of his blond head passing the window.

Just looking at him made her catch her breath. Melissa knew that a treacherous emotion had begun to creep into her heart.

She was falling in love with Dylan Harper.

. . . your experience with one woman . . .

. . . put it behind you . . .

. . . don't throw away this chance . . .

Rafe's story, and his warning, kept repeating themselves in Dylan's mind as he walked toward the stairs that evening. Was his friend right? He knew that Rafe was dying, and for a moment he stopped to consider his own mortality. Rafe was just five years older than he was, and it sounded as if he'd collected regrets for the whole of his short life. If he himself were hit in the street by a runaway wagon tomorrow, or contracted some fatal disease, would he take regrets with him to his grave? he wondered. And even if he lived to be an old man, did he plan to do it alone, with no one to share his triumphs and setbacks?

The prospect was depressing as hell.

On Melissa's clotheslines, shirts and underwear flapped in the breeze along with diapers and dresses. No one could say she was lazy or purely ornamental. She did two jobs, really, the laundry and the housekeeping. He'd never thought her weak—after all, a woman who'd crossed the Chilkoot Pass while pregnant and survived Coy Logan wasn't weak. But she'd revealed herself to be even stronger than he would have guessed. Her strength didn't lie only in her physical resilience. She possessed a vitality of spirit that amazed him.

He knew she worked hard, though. Maybe, he thought—just maybe she would like to get away from the stove and have someone wait on her for a change.

Glancing down the street, he saw Belinda Mulrooney's Fairview Hotel. It was said to be a magnificent establishment, just as she'd promised. During her first twenty-four hours of operation, the bar alone took in six thousand dollars. Even if the place did have canvas walls, the dining room was reported to be lavish.

He took the stairs two at a time and opened the door to find Melissa at her usual spot at the stove. She glanced up at him and smiled, then ducked her head, blushing shyly. She had rebraided her hair, and she wore a clean, starched apron. She was a sweet sight to come home to, he couldn't deny that.

"I was thinking we might have dinner out tomorrow," he said, stopping at Jenny's cradle to let her grab his finger. The baby grinned at him and gurgled; even she looked better than she had when he first saw her.

"Out? Do you mean on a picnic?"

He glanced up. "No, I mean at the Fairview Hotel."

"Oh, Dylan, really?" Melissa's eyes were wide with excitement, and her smile was as bright as ten candle flames. "I've heard it's a grand place. But what about Jenny?"

He shrugged. "We'll bring her along. She should be all right. Belinda owes me a couple of favors—she might even have a maid whom she can spare to watch her for an hour or so."

"We'll have to dress up, won't we?" she asked, casting a sidelong glance at his buckskins.

He laughed. "Oh, I might surprise you. I guess you haven't seen *all* of my clothes." Then he added, "I believe I heard Belinda even has an orchestra playing."

Melissa's brow furrowed slightly as she stirred the stew. "Do you think they have dancing there?"

"No, the orchestra is out in the lobby. Why? Is dancing against your religion, or something?"

Idly, she stirred the pot on the stove. "Well, no, of course not. I just—I don't know how, that's all."

He went to the table and sat down, afraid that if he didn't he'd be tempted to stand behind her and nuzzle her slender white neck. "Really? I thought all girls knew how to dance."

"There wasn't a lot of call for ballroom dancing where I grew up," she said.

"It was forced on me when I was a kid. 'No *gentleman* can conduct himself in society if he cannot properly escort a lady around a ballroom,' " he mimicked in a pinched-up voice that made her giggle. It was good to see her smile, he thought.

"I think we were only told not to use our sleeves for handkerchiefs."

"Oh, I heard that one too." This scene wasn't far from the one he'd envisioned. Sitting around the kitchen at night after dinner. Talking, laughing, being close. "Would you like to learn? To dance, I mean?"

"Maybe someday, I guess. I'll get someone to teach me."

"I'll teach you," he said, and knew he offered only for the chance to hold her.

"What, you mean now?"

"Yeah, sure, why not?"

She looked at him with those clear gray eyes as if he'd lost his senses. "But dinner—"

"We can take a couple of turns. We'll just be a minute or two."

"There's no room in here. Don't you need a dance floor to dance?"

"No, not to learn a few steps."

"But there's no music."

"Sure there is. Can't you hear McGinty's piano player next door?"

Yes, Melissa heard it. The sound was always there, in the background. And Dylan had managed to deflect all of her excuses. But she didn't want to stumble all over his feet and make a fool of herself. Dancing—that had been the last thing on anyone's mind in her old neighborhood.

He held out his hand to her. "Come on, Melissa. If you won't dance with me, I'll just have to ask Jenny."

She laughed. "Oh no, you won't. I just fed her and she'll spit up all over you if you jiggle her."

"Then I guess I'll have to jiggle *you*. Come on now, don't say no."

Oh, that teasing grin was so hard to resist. She

couldn't imagine what had put him in such a playful mood, but it sure beat an angry, cleaver-wielding man.

"Well, I suppose . . ." She put down her cooking spoon, and he immediately whisked her into his arms. He cocked his head and listened for a moment.

"They're playing 'On Top of Old Smokey' down there. Let's see, that's a waltz. Put your left hand here"—he positioned it high on his right arm—"and I'll take your right one here." He closed his fingers around hers and put his other hand on the small of her back. "Now just relax and follow me."

Relax! As if she could, with the clean, male scent of him drifting to her and his warm arms holding her. He stepped back and pulled her along, but her feet didn't move, and she tumbled against his chest. Had she noticed before how broad it was?

"Oh, I'm sorry," she gasped, recovering her balance, but not her dignity. Her face turned flame hot.

He chuckled. "That's okay, but this time when I step back, you step forward. When I move to my left, you move to your right. You know, just follow along."

Melissa had grave doubts, but she nodded, unwilling to be released from his grasp just yet.

He led them through a series of less-than-graceful maneuvers on the small floor space, her skirts snagging on the chair legs, until the music changed to a much faster tempo and beat. Their movements narrowed to just standing in place and turning in a circle. It all seemed so silly, Melissa got the giggles and couldn't stop. Dylan laughed with her, and finally they collapsed into the chairs at the table.

"You get the idea," he said, and pushed his hair away from his forehead with both hands. "Kind of."

"Yes, kind of." It felt so good to actually laugh with someone for a change—to have something to laugh about—and not have to worry about being told to pipe down, damn it. "We'll just have to wait until we have a bigger kitchen to dance in," she added, and then realized how it sounded. "I mean a bigger floor, anyway."

Dylan's laugher died, but the smile stayed in his eyes as he gave her a contemplative look. It passed so quickly she wasn't sure what she had seen, except she felt as if he been examining her soul with his riveting green gaze. "Maybe we'll have a chance to try again someday," he said.

Pushing herself away from the table, she replied hastily, "I'll finish putting dinner together."

For the rest of the evening after they ate, Melissa bustled around the small room in a flurry of busyness. Dinner out, in a hotel dining room! And with Dylan. She had eaten in a restaurant only one other time in her life, and that had been in Seattle when Coy relented and let her buy hot tea and a doughnut in a cafe. Surely, this would be more exciting.

While Dylan sat at the table and held the baby, she brought out her nicest new dress and pressed it carefully. She even ironed a clean dress for Jenny, although she worried that it might be a little small for her—she was growing so fast. Jenny sitting on

Dylan's lap looked so natural, she thought. He had endless patience for her, and he genuinely seemed to enjoy entertaining her. Melissa got that little pull at her heart again. If only he were really her father.

As for her clothes, Melissa had a nice dress to wear, but her heart sank when she realized how functional and bulky her work shoes were. They weren't intended to be worn for a dressy occasion. And she had only two pairs of stockings, both black cotton.

Thinking back to the day she and Dylan had gone to the marketplace, she remembered seeing all kinds of pretty lingerie for sale—petticoats, corsets, silk stockings. Of course it was disgraceful that it was all out on public display, but just the same it had been lovely. Standing at her ironing board, she could feel the weight of her apron pocket, heavy with gold, against her thigh. She had feared spending even one cent of that dust she'd worked so hard for. It represented her future, which was uncertain at best.

But tomorrow night would be very special. Maybe she could afford to part with just a little money to buy nice stockings and a pair of dress shoes. And possibly some cologne to go in the atomizer Dylan had bought for her.

At about ten-thirty, after Jenny was asleep, Dylan stood and stretched. Melissa tried not to stare, but she was fascinated by the way his shirt buttons strained against the lean muscle beneath them.

"Well, I guess I'll go down and have a last look at the store."

"All right," she responded. This was her time to get ready for bed. When he returned, she would be in her nightgown and lying under the covers with the lamp out.

But tonight when he closed the door behind him and went downstairs, Jenny woke up squalling. It took Melissa the better part of a half hour of rocking her and walking her and swinging her in her cradle before she settled down again.

After the baby finally went back to sleep, Melissa stripped down to her chemise and drawers and stood at the porcelain basin to wash. She glanced out the window next to her. Outside, the early August sky was growing dark; the midnight sun was finally waning and the nights were getting longer. Down in the street the parade continued, and she heard music coming from several of the dance halls and saloons on Front Street.

Her arms and neck were covered with suds when she heard Dylan coming up the stairs. Oh, God, she thought, as she looked in the mirror at her state of undress. She began splashing water haphazardly, trying to rinse off the soap and dry herself before he came in, but she succeeded only in soaking her chemise in the process.

The door opened and Melissa jumped, letting out a gasp. There Dylan stood, looking at her as if he'd never seen a woman before, taking in every inch from her bare feet to the top of her head. Looking down she saw that her wet chemise was as transparent as organdie, showing off her nursing breasts and nipples to their fullest. The expression in his eyes was possessive, powerful.

But it wasn't fear she felt.

"P-please turn around," she demanded with a shaking voice.

With a last sweeping glance at her form, he took a deep breath and complied. "I thought you'd be done by now," he said, sounding a little short.

"I would have been, but the baby woke up, and—"

"Look, I'll just wait outside on the steps until you're finished. You can call me." He walked out again and slammed the door behind him.

Melissa scurried to finish her ablutions and shimmied into her nightgown, worried about keeping him outside too long, but almost afraid to let him back in.

Outside, Dylan flopped down on the top step, resting his elbows on his knees, and tried to ignore the nagging ache in his groin. That image of Melissa—full, ripe breasts, nipples like sweet cherries, a tiny waist, and gently curved hips—burned a picture in his brain that knifed through his heart, bounced down to his crotch, and back again. How the hell was he supposed to go back in there and sleep in the same bed with her and pretend that he hadn't been affected by her? Sullenly, he propped his chin on his hands. He wasn't a monk, but by God he was living like one, and he didn't like it for one damned minute.

For the briefest moment he thought about visiting one of the prostitutes that had settled over on Second

Avenue in the heart of the business district. But he abandoned the idea. It wasn't just physical satisfaction he wanted. He could buy that any hour of the week, except Sundays, of course. He wanted more, and with a sinking feeling he realized that the only woman who could give it to him was Melissa.

In the soft warmth of her he might find solace and peace, possibly even the sense of belonging he'd craved since he was a kid.

But making love to Melissa was out of the question. Men needed only the urge to make love. Women needed a reason. And he cared too much about her not to give her a good reason. Where would that leave them? Nothing could come of their pairing. He would be going back to The Dalles, and she would continue with her life, someplace.

Behind him the door opened a crack. "I'm finished now."

"Okay," he grumped.

He heard her bare feet scamper across the plank flooring, and then the ropes under the mattress creaked as she flew into bed.

He stood up and stretched his back, wishing he had somewhere else to sleep tonight, without the torture of temptation lying next to him. He'd once thought of sending Melissa off to a hotel. Now he wondered if he should be the one to get a room. Tipping back his head to look at the emerging stars, he knew he couldn't do that either.

He would just have to suffer through it.

* * *

Had the clock that sat on Dylan's trunk ever sounded so loud? Melissa wondered. She lay in the darkness, listening to the timepiece noisily tick off the minutes that dragged by. The room had a chill tonight, and she burrowed down beneath the light blanket.

She suspected that Dylan was awake as well and envisioned them lying in his bed like two tailor's dummies, stiff and tense.

How could she sleep after he'd walked in on her while she was practically in the altogether? It was bound to happen sooner or later, she supposed, considering their tight living quarters. The embarrassment of being seen in her underwear, though, was only a pinprick compared to the other feelings roiling inside her.

With each passing day, she felt a womanliness ripening within her, a sensation she'd never fully experienced before. Coy had not summoned such feelings, not before she married him and certainly not after. This restlessness, this itchy yearning, seemed to be caused by just one man: Dylan Harper.

She rolled over, turning her back to the rice sack. But nothing could come of how she felt about him.

He'd made that plain. And maybe it was for the best.

Chapter Eleven

The next day Dylan stood downstairs in the store, feeling as if his eyelids weighed five pounds each and were made of sandpaper. Irritable from lack of sleep, he wished business were a little slower today, but he'd been busy from the moment he unlocked the front door. At least it kept him from going to the side window to look for Melissa.

"Mister, have you got any tenpenny nails? I'm building me more sluice boxes."

"Harper, you'd better give me another bottle of that Electricatin' Liniment. My back's killin' me from all that digging, and I used up the last of that stuff on my horse. Oh, and throw in a canned ham while you're at it, and some Eagle's condensed. I ain't payin' no thirty dollars a gallon for fresh milk."

"You ready to sell me that new hammer I need, Dylan?"

The goods and gold changed hands at a brisk pace, but Dylan's mind was not on business.

He thought he must have dozed off sometime during the night, but only after he lay on his side of the rice sack for what seemed like hours. He alternately cursed and blessed the barrier between himself and Melissa. If it hadn't been there, he wasn't sure he would have remained the disinterested gentleman that he'd promised to be that afternoon on the duckboards outside of the saloon.

He hadn't talked to Melissa yet today. When he'd left this morning to come down here, she still slept, with the blanket pulled up to the collar of her nightgown. But her pale hair, loose from its braid, had flowed across her pillow and over the edge of the mattress, making him think of a lovely sleeping princess in an old legend.

He shook his head. Brother, if that wasn't a lot of moony drivel. Tonight he had to sit across the table from her at the Fairview Hotel and pretend that she had no affect on him.

Just get through this, he told himself again. Just get through this. In a couple of months or so it would all be over. He'd sell this place, buy himself a steamboat ticket back to Portland, and get passage to The Dalles. Melissa Logan would be just a memory of a good deed he'd been talked into.

At least he hoped so.

As the afternoon wore on, traffic finally slowed, and he decided he'd close early to go buy himself a bath and a shave. It might not feel altogether bad to dress for dinner again. At least he didn't have to do it every damned day, as he had back home.

Just as he was about to move the lard bucket he used for a doorstop, Melissa walked in with the baby in her arms. Jenny gave him a big smile that went straight to his heart.

"Oh, are you leaving?" Melissa asked, her delicate brows rising with the question.

If she was here, he really didn't want to. God, but she was pretty, he thought. She looked better every day, like a neglected flower that had finally found its way to sunlight. A rosy glow tinted her cheeks and lips, and her gray eyes were bright and clear. Even her hair seemed to shine. And her clothes only hinted at the lush shape that lay beneath them. Her slender waist would fit perfectly between his hands. Her hips were sweetly curved like the swell of a wave. And those full breasts, ripe with milk . . . Jesus, he was driving himself crazy thinking about her.

"I was just going to run an errand, but help yourself to anything you want."

"I didn't come down to shop, Dylan. I'm going upstairs now to get ready for dinner." She glanced at his plain work shirt and at his knife. "I wondered if you wanted me to iron something for you to wear."

Obviously she still didn't believe he owned anything else but boots and buckskins. "Don't worry, I'll leave the knife at home."

She flushed a becoming shade of pink. "I didn't mean to sound critical—"

He pushed the lard bucket away and waved her out the door. "Just think about what you'd like to order for din—"

"Mr. Harper? Are you Dylan Harper?" A flush-faced young man came running toward them from the street, dodging wagons and pedestrians. He was breathless and looked as though he were coming to report a fire.

"Yes, I'm Dylan Harper."

The young man pressed his hand to his side. "I have an urgent message for you." He pulled a folded note from his pocket.

Dylan felt his heartbeat double in his chest. He grabbed the paper and opened it.

I would like to see you, my good friend. RD.

He looked up at the other man. "Did Rafe Dubois give you this?"

"No, sir. Miss Mulrooney herself put it in my hand. She only said to deliver this note with all possible speed and to tell you that it's urgent. I'm to bring you back to the hotel with me."

"Dylan?" Melissa questioned worriedly.

"You and Jenny wait for me here," he told her, not looking up from the spidery handwriting on the note. "I need to find out what this is about."

But Dylan figured he already knew.

At the Fairview Hotel, Dylan followed Belinda's clerk to Rafe's room. This end of the hallway was quiet, although through the front part he could hear the buzz of voices behind what were really nothing more than curtained cubicles with paper glued on.

The clerk gestured at the door and hurried away, as if he didn't want to know what was on the other side of it. Taking a deep breath, Dylan lifted his hand and knocked lightly.

Belinda herself, dressed in purple taffeta but looking drawn and pale, opened the door. The canvas walls surrounding the door frame shivered slightly, like the painted backdrop of a stage play.

"How is he?" Dylan murmured.

She shook her head and stepped out into the hallway. "I don't think it will be long, Dylan. I have to get back to the front. You'll stay with him for a while?"

He nodded. A cold knot of dread formed in his stomach at the finality of her words. Walking into the room with leaden feet, he heard Belinda close the door behind him.

Inside, the two window shades were pulled against a bright afternoon sun, creating a gloomy sanctum. There was a closed-up, musty odor in here, even though the building was less than two months old. Dylan had smelled that odor once or twice before—it had preceded death.

Though his eyes were closed and he wore a striped nightshirt, Rafe lay propped on pillows in a polished brass bed. In fact, there were so many pillows behind him, he was practically sitting up. Seeing that, at first Dylan thought that the situation wasn't as critical as he'd feared. Maybe this was just a passing malady, and Rafe would recover.

But when he pulled a chair close to the bed and sat down, he realized his hopes were groundless, and the icy knot inside him grew colder still. The lawyer's breathing was as labored as he'd ever heard, and his lips had a faint blue cast. His crepey skin looked like putty-colored wax with a day's growth of beard, and his face was oddly puffy, especially around the eyes. Seeing him now, it was hard to believe that he was only thirty-four years old.

"Rafe, it's me, Dylan."

His eyes opened a slit, then, as if satisfied that Dylan was there, he closed them again.

"Glad you came." His words were slurred and slow in coming. "I guess my luck . . . has finally run out. I always knew . . . it would."

"God, Rafe, shouldn't I get a doctor?" Dylan asked, straining against his helplessness. He wasn't accustomed to just sitting by and doing nothing. "If there's a chance one could help—"

"Been and gone . . . been and gone. 'Sorry, friend . . . your heart has failed.' Not a startling revelation. It was never . . . a secret that I would die."

No, it hadn't been. But Dylan hadn't known that he would be around to see his friend off on his final journey. In his mind he'd believed Rafe would always be there, sitting at a card table in the Yukon Girl, or leaning against the bar with a bottle and a glass. It seemed to him that one way or another, over the years he had lost everyone and everything that mattered to him. A fever had taken his mother. Elizabeth had been lost to greed. His horses were forfeited. And now Rafe. Sometimes he wondered if that was all life was about—loss.

He put a hand on the thin forearm lying on top of

the blankets. "Is there anything you'd like me to do for you? Any debts paid or scores settled? Anything?"

Rafe grew a deep, ragged breath and glanced at Dylan again. The sunken, drowsy look in his eyes was more pronounced than it had been just the day before. "The Lemieux case—the parish magistrate will hear it tomorrow . . . *Mon coeur est sans espoir . . .*"

He rambled like a man talking in his sleep. Dylan leaned forward a bit, waiting for Rafe's mind to clear. "Do you want me to get Father William?" The priest was eternally busy, but if Rafe wanted to see him, Dylan would offer the man whatever donation he asked for his hospital.

"No, that's not it," he replied, sounding lucid again, but weaker. "That poke there on the bureau . . . there's some gold dust in it. Give it to . . . give it to Melissa."

Dylan was surprised. "Melissa?"

The conversation was interrupted by a strangling coughing fit from Rafe. When he finally recovered his wind, he was soaked with sweat and his energy was just about gone. "Yes, damn it . . . give it to her. She might need it."

"Okay, Rafe, okay. I'll take care of it."

Apparently satisfied, he drew in another noisy, labored breath. He made a feeble effort to smile, but even that seemed to be beyond the exhausted man. "We had a hell of a good . . . time, didn't we?"

Dylan smiled and nodded, feeling his throat tighten. "That we did."

"And you've been a good friend. I doubt that was . . . always easy. I tend to drink a bit."

Dylan wished he could laugh at the understatement. "You're a true friend, too, Rafe."

"It's over now. I'm not afraid, but . . . God, I wish I'd done everything . . . differently, and this isn't a good time to discover that. I want you to . . . think about your own life . . . don't waste it on old grievances. Don't waste it at all."

Dylan gave his arm a light squeeze, then released it. He was horrified to find that his fingers had left impressions in Rafe's flesh, but he didn't seem to notice.

A few moments of silence fell between them, and Dylan watched Rafe's chest labor in his effort to breathe.

"Priscilla . . ." He spoke so faintly, Dylan couldn't have called it a whisper. "Tell Priscilla . . . that I'm sorry . . . tell her I love . . ."

Those were the last words that Rafe Dubois spoke. A rattle began to sound in his throat. Then he exhaled a final time.

An unearthly stillness settled over the room.

Suddenly, Dylan found himself alone.

He stood and put his hand on Rafe's chest and felt no movement, no heartbeat. Then he sank back into the chair, feeling far older than his own twenty-nine years.

* * *

When he left Rafe's room, Dylan found Belinda in the busy hotel bar and told her that he'd arrange for the undertaker.

She signaled for a bottle and one glass and led him to a relatively quiet corner table. The sound of the lobby orchestra carried easily through the fabric walls. Overhead, her cut-glass chandeliers sparkled with electric light.

"Dylan, I'm sorry. I know you two were friends." She pointed out one of the bartenders. "I had Andrew, there, look in on him, but he said it was hopeless."

About to pour a drink, he set the bottle down on the table, hard. His emotions were raw and his temper short. "Christ, Belinda, in this whole town couldn't you have found a real doctor? Since when is a goddamned bartender an expert about whether a man will live or die?" he snapped.

A woman not known for her patience, she demonstrated exceptional restraint in the face of his rudeness. The only change in her expression was a slight lowering of her brows. "All of my bartenders are American doctors and dentists. They can't get British licenses to practice here so I gave them jobs mixing drinks instead of medicines."

Feeling foolish, he rubbed the back of his neck and sighed. "Sorry—I didn't know."

She picked up the whiskey bottle and poured his shot for him. "That's all right," she said, then looked up at him and winked. "Just pay your tab when you leave." She pushed herself away from the table and went back to work.

Dylan drank his shot and paid six dollars for it. Apparently no one drank for free in Belinda's place, regardless of the circumstances or the occasion. After he left the hotel, he made arrangements with an undertaker on Second Avenue to collect Rafe's remains and organize the funeral. Then he stepped back out into the sunny glare and jostling crowds on Front Street and began walking, with no particular destination.

For the first time in two years, he felt lost, disconnected. The isolated little tent town he'd once known was growing so quickly, it changed its face on an almost daily basis.

Change wasn't necessarily bad, he reflected as he passed the skeleton of a new building. And it was unavoidable—plans and people changed, friends sometimes drifted away. Or died. But there was comfort in *some* things staying the same, and that was what he missed. Rafe had been a dependable constant, his best friend in Dawson and one of the few truly good friends he'd ever had, for all that some had viewed him as an acerbic though stylish drunk. No one could comment on this carnival with the wit and perception that Rafe had conveyed.

After wandering along Front Street, Dylan finally found himself in front of his own store. He looked up at the second-floor window. Melissa was up there. He felt drawn to her, as a traveler adrift on a moonless night would gravitate to a light in a window.

She and Jenny had added something to his life here, and he'd gotten used to having them with him. For just a moment he wished he could go up there and bury his head in Melissa's lap and tell her about his worries. She would hum to him and stroke his hair and make everything seem right again.

He could tell himself that Rafe's incident with Priscilla had no relevance to himself and Melissa—and he would probably be right. But in the corner of his heart, he knew the difference wasn't that great.

God, he didn't want to die the way Rafe had, alone and calling for a woman he'd yearned for but never held close. A man ought to make his life count for something more than a lot of regrets about things left undone and unsaid.

Hell, he just wanted to go home—to leave this place and go back to Oregon. But leaving here would mean saying good-bye to Melissa, too, and he was beginning to think he might not be able to do that.

He went into the store for a bottle of whiskey—someone should lift a glass to Rafe's memory. His gaze fell on the empty chair in the corner where his friend had spent so many hours, pitching cards at a chamber pot and commenting on the human condition. A dull ache crept up from his chest to his throat, and he felt his eyes start to burn.

Damn it, he thought and grabbed the whiskey bottle by the neck. If he stayed here by himself, he'd end up bawling like a little kid—for his friend and for himself—and he didn't want to do that. Striding to the door, he yanked it open and headed upstairs.

That small room was home, and right now the only one he had.

Melissa had looked at the clock at least a dozen times in the last forty-five minutes. Hours had passed since Dylan left. She'd gone downstairs to see if he was in the store. She'd even peeked over the swinging doors at the Yukon Girl. There was no sign of him, or Rafe either.

Now she paced the small floor, wearing the clothes she had put on to go to dinner. She had avoided sitting much for fear of wrinkling her nice dress, and her feet were getting tired in her new shoes.

Jenny had started fussing as well, as if she, too, were waiting for his return. But it looked as if he wouldn't be back in time for the Fairview dinner.

Melissa had no idea why Dylan had left so abruptly. She assumed it had something to do with Rafe—something very serious—but what, she couldn't guess.

Unless . . . Oh, God, what if Rafe had grown worse?

He had stopped to talk to her yesterday when he dropped by the store. He'd shuffled and wheezed like an old man and hadn't looked much better than one.

Maybe he needed someone to take care of him. Maybe he'd even been become bedridden. Nothing was as bad as not knowing.

Jenny's displeasure rose in volume, and Melissa picked up the baby to walk her. "Oh, button, please don't start in now," she urged, jogging the baby as she paced. Her tension mounted with each circuit.

Finally, after what seemed like an eternity, she heard Dylan's footsteps on the stairs. Putting Jenny in her cradle, she turned just as he walked in, and with one glimpse of his face, knew something terrible had happened. Beyond his handsomeness and his presence that filled any room he entered, he looked haggard, as if he hadn't slept in days. Even his wide shoulders seemed to droop. Her heart jumped in her chest, and she was engulfed by a feeling of dread.

"Dylan, what's wrong?"

He put a bottle on the floor next to him and sank into a chair, weary and boneless. When he looked up at her, she saw loss in his green eyes. "Rafe is dead."

She gaped at him. "What?"

He nodded and leaned forward to put his head in his hands. His long, sun-streaked hair fell forward, obscuring part of his face. "Not more than an hour ago."

Her hands and stomach were suddenly icy. "How? What happened? Did someone kill him? Was there an accident?"

"You know he's been fading for the past few weeks. He had that weak heart. It finally gave out."

Rafe had told her about it once. He said he'd gotten it from rheumatism fever when he was a boy.

"Oh, Dylan, no," she murmured, feeling her eyes sting with tears. Rafe had been the one who rescued her from Coy, even if the proceedings at the saloon had been only for show, so that Dylan could give her a place to go from there. "I'm so sorry."

She wished she could offer the solace of her arms. Sometimes an embrace was more comforting than words. But though she had felt him watching her when he thought she wasn't looking, after that one kiss he had kept his distance. So instead she sat across the table from him, her heart aching with love for him and grief for Rafe's passing.

"Did you get to say good-bye?" she asked. How she wished she'd known yesterday that she would never see him again.

"Yeah. Belinda Mulrooney sat with him until I got there. He didn't last long after that."

She gazed at the checkered oilcloth on the table, trying to conquer her quivering voice. "At least he didn't die alone. That would have been terrible." She plucked at a loose thread in the cloth. "I hope he was at peace."

He lifted his head then and looked at her. "I don't think he . . ." His words had a croaky sound. "He had a few regrets. His life wasn't long enough to let him do all the things he wanted." He sat back in his chair and pulled a leather pouch from his pocket. "He asked me to give this to you." He pushed it across the table to her.

"Me?" She sat back and blinked. "I-I can't accept this, Dylan. He was your friend. You should have it."

His gaze skittered away from hers, and he shrugged like a guilty-looking child who claimed to not know who took the last cookie. "He thought you might need it."

Might need it. For the day when Dylan told her he was going home. She reached out and lifted the pouch—it was heavy. She drew a shaky sigh. "Will there be a funeral?"

He massaged his forehead with his fingertips. "The undertaker is arranging something for ten o'clock tomorrow morning," he replied woodenly. He leaned over and picked up the bottle he'd brought in with him, then went to the shelf for a glass.

Melissa's eyes riveted on the dark brown bottle as if it were rattlesnake. The memory of a hundred nights, maybe a thousand, came crowding in on her mind, blotting out everything—Rafe's death, Dylan's grief, her own love for him. All she saw was a whiskey bottle in her father's hands, in Coy's hands, and imagining everything that had gone with it—the arguing, the hitting, the voices raised in anger—

"What are you doing?" she asked.

Dylan looked at her with a puzzled expression. "What does it look like I'm doing? I'm going to have a drink."

Melissa knew that he went down to the saloon now and then—sometimes she could even smell the alcohol on his breath. She didn't like it, although she didn't have to be around it, either. But he'd never brought a bottle upstairs before.

"No, you can't," she said and pushed her chair away from the table. "I mean, not here you can't. Not here."

"What do you mean, I can't?" he demanded.

"You have to take that bottle out of here. I don't care where." She heard the harpy tone in her voice, the creeping hysteria, but she couldn't stop it.

His brows dropped even lower. "The hell I will. What's got into you? I just watched my best friend die, and I want a drink." With angry defiance he uncorked the bottle and sloshed the amber liquid up to the rim of the short glass, but made no move to take a sip.

Jenny began to complain again, but Melissa stood fast, trembling with years of suppressed anger and hurt. "I lived with that"—she pointed at the liquor—"all my life and I don't want to anymore. I'm not asking for much—please, take that outside or downstairs or wherever you want to pour it down your throat. I don't want to be around it."

Rafe's gray, sunken face stayed in Dylan's mind as clearly as if he were looking at its photograph. He was in no mood to analyze what bothered Melissa. She stood on the other side of the table, reminding him of a pinched-up temperance worker, and sounding like Elizabeth at her worst and most demanding. Her gray eyes flashed, and the color was high in her cheeks.

"Please, Dylan—this isn't a joke," she stressed.

Disillusionment and grief combined to give him a temper one inch long. He slammed the bottle down near the edge of the table. A dollop of whiskey shot out of the top and splashed his hand. "Now you listen to me," he said, pointing at her. "I'm not your father, and I'm not your husband. That means you're not my wife. This is *my* room. I built it with my own two hands, and I'll do whatever I please here, when I please."

Her face became flushed, and her chin quivered ever so slightly. "Shall we leave, then, Jenny and I?"

"No, damn it!" No. He plowed his hand through his hair, knowing he'd said the wrong thing.

He stared at her, dressed for a dinner they wouldn't be going to. She'd pulled her hair back with a wide blue ribbon that matched the stripe in her dress. The gown showed off to perfection the fullness of her breasts, her small waist, the curve of her hip. Didn't she understand? Didn't she know how beautiful she was to him? Or how scared he was? He was afraid of losing her, but afraid of losing himself by loving her.

But, then, how could he make her understand what he barely understood himself? He'd come upstairs, hoping to somehow escape his grief, hoping for comfort, and he couldn't ask her for it. He took a step toward her, his hands extended like a supplicant's, trying to keep his churning emotions out of his voice.

"When a man dies, having lived just half of his years, with nothing to show for his life—no children, no legacy—" He choked to a stop, unable to find the words he needed.

Melissa's expression softened, and he saw her tense shoulders relax a bit. "You don't see yourself in Rafe, do you? He always knew his time would be short."

He stepped closer and took her hand in his. She looked so irresistible, so vital and warm. "Knowing doesn't make someone ready," he said, trying to grasp the depth of his own bewilderment. He rested his forehead against her shoulder and sighed.

"No, I guess not," she agreed. "I don't know if there's an answer." He felt her stroke his hair with a light, tentative touch that sent delicious soothing shivers down his back. Inexplicably, in this aftermath of death he felt a need to reaffirm his own existence and everything that made him a man. He took her chin between his thumb and forefinger to tip her face up to his. Her soft, pink mouth lay just within reach of his own, trembling slightly, moist.

"Melissa," he murmured. "I . . ." But he had no more words. He had only the urge to feel her lips under his, and he pulled her to him to take her in a kiss. The instant they touched, warmth spread through Dylan that soon turned to fire, sweeping along his veins and melting the frost that lay on his heart from watching a man die.

He put his arm around her waist and held her closer, while he probed the slick warm depths of her mouth with his tongue. A quiet little moan rose from her throat, stoking his arousal to a hard, insistent throb. She felt so good in his arms. He let his hand drift from her chin, down the side of her slender neck to her full breast, where he longed to lay his head.

Drawing a deep breath, she threaded her arms around his neck and let her weight rest against him.

Breaking the kiss, he trailed his lips down her

throat where her pulse beat as swift as a bird's. Dylan didn't think he'd ever wanted a woman as much as he wanted Melissa right now. Shifting his weight, he took a step back and pulled her with him to rest against the length of his torso.

The sharp sound of breaking glass interrupted them as effectively as a dousing of cold water. Melissa broke from his embrace and stared at something on the floor behind him. Turning, Dylan saw that he'd bumped into the whiskey bottle he'd left sitting on the edge of the table. Its shattered remains lay in a star-burst puddle of whiskey. The biting odor drifted up to them.

"I wish you had taken that out of here," she cried, her hand at her mouth. She lifted angry gray eyes to his. "I *hate* that smell. Oh, God, I just hate it." The remnants of Dylan's passion fizzled away in the face of her outburst.

She hurried to the sink and grabbed a towel. Then, in her best dress, she sank to her knees and blotted at the whiskey and broken glass.

He touched her shoulder. "Melissa, I'll do that."

She shook her head, but wouldn't look up at him. She had shut him out again, apparently for indulging a vice that reminded her of her father and her late husband.

Reality intruded and shook Dylan. Elizabeth hadn't accepted him for what he was and had worked hard to change him. He wouldn't change for anyone, and he sure as hell wouldn't be forced to suffer for the sins of another man.

"Then I'll go."

Feeling as lost and alone as he had when he'd come up earlier, he stormed to the door, slamming it so hard the windowpanes rattled.

Chapter Twelve

Swiping angrily at tears that would not stop, Melissa took off the silk stockings and new chemise she'd bought, then changed into her everyday clothes. She moved woodenly, feeling as if the world and all its trials had settled on her shoulders. She wished she could go to bed and wake up in the morning to discover that the today's events—Rafe's death and the scene with Dylan—had been nothing more than a horrible nightmare.

But too edgy and overwrought to sleep, she put her irons on the stove to heat, hoping that work would distract her. Dylan's hurtful words had reminded her of the importance of her original goal, to gain independence.

He'd been right, of course. She'd had no right to tell him what to do—her own bad memories had gotten in the way of her judgment. And regardless of what they had told the world, and despite the fact that she sometimes caught herself thinking otherwise, Dylan was not her husband. His commitment to her and Jenny was a temporary one, and no amount of wishful thinking on her part would change that.

How, then, had she let him kiss her, *fondle* her, as if she were a—a strumpet? Deep in her heart, though, Melissa didn't feel cheapened by his touch. Rather, she only longed for more. She had no explanation for the heat and wild yearning he'd evoked from her. The feel of his fingertips on her neck, his palm hot against her breast, his lips on her throat, gentle yet predatory and demanding, beckoning her in a way that she felt compelled to answer—she'd never known anything like it.

Dipping her hand in a pan of water, she sprinkled a shirt and smoothed it flat on the board. The twill sizzled beneath the hot, heavy iron, raising a cloud of steam. Maybe she wouldn't really make Dylan a good wife anyway, she thought, her tears running faster. She'd driven him out of his own home to deal with his loss by himself.

In the cradle Jenny's cranky wailing grew worse. Sighing, Melissa set the iron back on the stove and went to give the cradle a nudge to make it rock. It was so unlike the baby to be this cross, but everyone else here had had a hard day. Melissa supposed Jenny was entitled to one as well.

But when Melissa picked up Jenny, the baby felt hot with fever, and instead of quieting, her squalls grew louder. Melissa touched frantic hands to the little girl's head and face.

"Oh, God—oh, Jenny, honey. You're burning up!" No wonder she had been so irritable all afternoon.

Melissa clutched the baby to her, uncertain of what to do. She had no experience in caring for a sick child—for all of her short life Jenny had been healthy. How she wished for a mother or grandmother or sister to consult, someone who could tell her what should be done. The baby in her arms was so hot—

With only maternal instinct to guide her, she laid the baby in the center of the small table and snatched a washcloth and an enamel pan from the shelf. Hardly taking her eyes from Jenny, she hurried to the tin sink and pumped water into the basin.

She charged back to the table, sloshing water on the floor. What was Jenny sick with? Melissa wondered as she wrung out the cloth to put on the baby's forehead. The town was full of illness and disease, and nowhere was it worse than in Lousetown across the river.

Over there, the lights did not shine brightly. The wealth and excess of Dawson's Klondike Kings were absent. Sewage oozed through the narrow, muddy streets, spreading sickness. People without money, or the hope of escape, crowded together in tents and in squalid, makeshift dwellings. These luckless stampeders lived in filth and poverty, and died from typhoid and cholera. Maybe some contagion had found its way to Jenny. It might have even been one of Melissa's customers who had carried some miasma to her as she lay sleeping in her little nook.

The cold compresses seemed to have no effect, and the baby's wails continued. Maybe she was hungry,

Melissa thought. With shaking fingers she ripped at her bodice and sent buttons flying across the table. But again and again, Jenny turned her face from Melissa's breast, refusing to eat. She kept screaming, the likes of which Melissa had never heard from her before. She tried to soothe Jenny every way she could think of, but after nearly a half hour of more cold cloths and rocking, the little girl showed no improvement. If anything, she seemed worse.

With Jenny in her arms, Melissa went to the open window and looked out on the twilit street below. There crowds still elbowed each other on their way to the saloons, dance halls, and the opera house. Her child needed a doctor, but Melissa didn't want to take her out, possibly exposing her to the chill night air or something else that might aggravate her condition.

Perhaps she could hail someone on the street to send a doctor here. Scanning the passing faces for a likely rescuer, she saw a man with kind eyes. "Excuse me! Please, I need help!" she called down.

But he didn't hear her and soon passed from view.

"My little girl is sick—can someone bring a doctor?" No one looked up at her window. Two more tries with a louder voice yielded nothing. Apparently her words couldn't carry over the clash of voices and music and tramping feet.

Whirling away from the window, she cursed herself for making Dylan leave. She'd never seen him drunk—so what if he'd stayed here and had a drink or two? It seemed so trivial now in the face of this calamity. Jenny's life was in danger.

Her only remaining choice was to go down to the street and stop someone. Melissa carried Jenny back to her cradle, then ran to the door and flew down the steps, nearly tripping on her cumbersome skirts.

Emerging from the side street, she nearly collided with a young man pulling a tired-looking mule behind him. His face was familiar, and she recalled that she had done laundry for him once.

"Whoa, careful there, ma'am." He shot out a hand to steady her, then his eyes dropped to her open bodice.

Too frantic for much modesty, with a trembling hand Melissa dragged the edges of her dress together to cover her camisole. "Oh please," she babbled. "Please, I need help for my little girl. She's burning up with fever. Can you get a doctor?"

Apparently galvanized by her urgency, he tugged at the brim of his hat and nodded shortly. "Yes, ma'am! I'll find Doc Garvin. He fixed me up when I caught my hand chopping wood." He held up a hand that was missing its index finger. "Come on, Susannah," he said and tugged on the mule's lead to get it started.

Melissa turned and ran back up the stairs to Jenny. When she flung open the door, the baby was still yelling, but Melissa thought she sounded weaker. She picked her up and pressed her hot, silky head to her own cheek.

"Help is coming, button. The doctor is coming."

Jenny was so small, so new—her life hadn't even begun yet. Melissa struggled to hold a demon of fear at bay, the one that whispered to her that babies died every day. Fevers, measles, influenza and more—they snatched away young lives to leave behind heartbroken mothers and gray-faced fathers.

No, not her child, God, she prayed fiercely. Not her Jenny. If she were taken, Melissa thought she might as well be dead too.

If she lost her baby, she would have no one.

Dylan sat with Seamus McGinty at the back table in the Yukon Girl Saloon. The place was as busy as any other night, and a dense layer of tobacco smoke hung over the crowd of gambling, drinking, dancing miners. Dylan couldn't decide if Rafe would have appreciated this atmosphere for his wake, but for his own part, he wished he had somewhere else to go.

After trying to remember the number of times Rafe Dubois had sat at this very table, Seamus had declared that no one would be allowed to sit at this shrine henceforth. Then the husky, blue-eyed Irishman had required Dylan to witness that oath with a shot from his cherished bottle of poteen. Angel's tears, Seamus called it, and had drunk nearly half of it lamenting the news of Rafe's passing.

Dylan thought he'd never seen a man who so enjoyed mourning.

"Angel's tears, Dylan," he repeated, and lifted his glass, "to send him off proper, and may God speed him on his way. Jaysus, they're crying in heaven tonight, they are."

"I think you're right, Seamus." Dylan raised his

glass too, but he still nursed his first drink. The Irish moonshine was powerful stuff that tasted as if it could blister a man's insides.

He really wished he could get foolishly, insensibly drunk, to forget about Rafe's death and Melissa's shrewish rejection that had driven him to sit here with McGinty when he'd have rather been with her. What the hell did she want from him, anyway? He'd done everything he could for her, given the circumstances, and still she had made him leave.

But mingled with the dull anger over being banished from his own home was the memory of Melissa in his arms—soft, warm, and so damned womanly he'd wanted to carry her to his bed right then and there. To show her how a man—a real man—made love to a woman, wild but tender, conquering her not with brute force, but with her own desire. Just the thought sent the blood coursing to his groin again.

"Dylan, man," Seamus said, interrupting his thoughts, "will ye be drinking that poteen or sipping at it like a kid with a sarsaparilla?"

Dylan looked at his glass and picked it up. "What the hell," he muttered, "she's already mad at me." He held the glass to his mouth, ready to pour the fiery liquor down his throat, when a miner elbowed his way through the crowd to the table.

"Hey, McGinty, have you seen Doc Garvin?" he panted.

The Irishman looked him up and down, amusement mingling with his tragic expression of mourning. "What's your hurry, son? You lose another finger?"

The miner shook his head, then pointed over his shoulder. "I need to find him for that singing laundry lady. Her baby is ailing."

Dylan froze, his fingers locked around his glass. "The singing laundry lady? The one next door?"

The miner nodded. "Yeah, that's her. She flew down her stairs and stopped me on the street, looking as pale and wild-haired as a ghost. She said her little girl is sick with a fever."

Gripped by the greatest terror he'd ever known, Dylan jumped from his chair and knocked it over. His heart pounded in his chest, and adrenaline sent a prickly feeling shooting down his arms and legs. He whirled to face Seamus. "Is Garvin in here?"

"Yeah, I think he's at a table by the window, eating his dinner," McGinty replied, looking stunned as well.

Dylan plowed back through the crowd with the miner on his heels. Several tables were lined up along the front windows, and all of them were occupied.

"Which one is he?" Dylan demanded, clutching the miner's sleeve.

The other man peered at the faces of the diners. "I-I'm not sure now. I haven't seen him for a while, and I was pretty shook up at the time, getting my finger chopped off and all."

Impatient, Dylan turned away. "Doc Garvin," he thundered. His voice carried over the blur of all the other conversations, rising above the din of the piano and shuffling feet and clinking glasses. The noisy saloon fell silent. "Is Dr. Garvin here?"

At the farthest table, a customer with a weary youngster's face held up his hand. "I'm Dr. Garvin."

Dylan didn't want to insult the man by voicing his first impression, but despite his formal suit Garvin appeared to be no older than sixteen. Dylan looked at the miner for confirmation.

"Yessir, that's him."

Dylan strode forward. "There's a sick baby who needs your help."

Dr. Garvin nodded, then gestured at his barely touched chicken dinner. "I'll be right with you as soon as I finish eating."

Dylan clamped his hand on the man's wrist. "I'm sorry to interrupt your dinner, Doc, but I need you to come with me *now*. That little girl won't wait."

Dr. Garvin glanced at Dylan, then at the long knife tied to his thigh. Tossing his fork onto his plate, he wiped his hands on his napkin and picked up his bag from the opposite chair.

"Very well, then. Let's go."

When Dylan led Dr. Garvin up the dusk-shrouded stairs, the first thing he heard was a peculiar squalling sound coming from the other side of the door. It was a baby's cry, sort of, but so unlike anything he'd heard from Jenny, he wondered if there was a mountain lion cub inside.

Dylan opened the door, and he saw Melissa, pacing in a circle with the baby clutched to her. She looked ashen, and her hair hung in fine, pale strands around her face, just as the miner had said. The front of her dress gaped open, revealing her plain camisole beneath.

As soon as she saw him, she stopped. Her earlier anger was gone, and the terror he felt in his own heart was written on her face. "Oh, Dylan, Jenny is sick with something—she has a fever and—"

He gripped her shoulders lightly. "I know, honey, I heard about it. I brought Dr. Garvin."

She pulled away from his hands and lurched toward the young man following behind, apparently just now seeing him. The agony of fear and heartbreak was in her voice. "Doctor, please—you must save my child. She won't eat and she's burning with fever. It just started today."

Putting down his bag, Dr. Garvin took off his coat and draped it over the back of one of the chairs. "Bring her to the table, madam, and also a lamp if you have one."

Dylan grabbed the oil lamp from the small table near the window. Melissa hovered at the edge of its light, her trembling hands tightly interlaced at her mouth.

Dr. Garvin appeared calm, and he made comforting noises as he poked and prodded the screaming Jenny, who thrashed and kicked, but his grave expression gave Dylan another icy knot in his stomach. It was the same feeling he'd had this afternoon when he'd seen Rafe. Then the doctor unbuttoned the baby's dress to reveal an angry red rash on her chest.

"Oh, dear God," Melissa gasped. Dylan felt as if his heart had plummeted to his feet.

"Her temperature is one hundred and five," the doctor said. Melissa moaned and Dylan winced. "But children her age routinely get and survive high fevers that would be much harder on an adult. Her pulse is very rapid, though."

"But what's wrong with her? Is it measles?" Melissa asked.

The young doctor shook his head. "No, I believe she has scarlet fever. Everything points to it—the sudden onset, her high fever and pulse. Her throat is inflamed, and now this rash— Some people call the fever scarlatina."

"Scarlatina," Melissa repeated parrotlike. "Scarlatina." For a moment she looked so dazed Dylan thought she might faint. He put his hand under her elbow, meaning to catch her if she did.

"How would she get this fever, Doc?" Dylan asked. "I haven't heard of anyone being sick with it around here."

Dr. Garvin wrapped up Jenny again and put her in Melissa's arms. "It's hard to say. Obviously she came in contact with it somehow. The contagion can cling to rooms and clothing with great tenacity. It's more common in children than adults, and I can't say I've seen much of it in Dawson. But there are people from all over the world in this town, and there are a lot of other fevers here, too. I'm really not surprised by this."

"You say it's carried on clothes?" Melissa asked, her voice high and tight.

"It can be."

Dylan saw her stricken look, and his heart clenched in his chest. She would blame herself for the baby's fever.

"B-but she'll get well?" Melissa asked. "You have medicine you can give her?"

The doctor sighed. "Ma'am, I believe you'd rather I tell you the truth than a lie."

She nodded her head almost imperceptibly.

"Scarlatina often has a bad outcome. And the medications I'd give to a grown man would kill a baby."

What little color that remained in Melissa's face drained away.

Dr. Garvin looked apologetic. "It's highly contagious, so both of you might get sick too if you haven't already had it. Some people though, especially adults, seem to be resistant to the disease. And I think your baby has a relatively mild case of the fever—with good nursing some children pull through just fine. The rash will spread, so sponge her with soda water once in the morning and once at night. In a day or two you'll also notice that her tongue has turned the color and texture of a strawberry. Try to get her to eat though—your milk will be just fine for her. Other than that—" He sighed. "I'm afraid this is a wait and hope situation."

After promising to check in the next day, Dr. Garvin put on his coat and picked up his bag. On his way to the door, he patted Melissa's arm. "I won't tell you not to worry. But worrying won't get the job done. Put more energy into taking care of Jenny and yourselves. If you two should fall ill"—he looked from Melissa to Dylan—"there will be no one to tend your baby."

Melissa stared at the closed door, feeling as if the crack of doom had just sounded. Her baby, the dearest little soul she'd ever known, was close to death, and she was the cause. She turned to face Dylan. He stood with his arms crossed tightly over his chest, and his handsome face was wiped clean of all expression. She knew she'd been angry with him earlier, but for the life of her, she couldn't recall why now. Whatever the cause, it must have been trivial. She could think of nothing but the overwarm bundle in her arms, her own flesh and blood.

She looked down at Jenny's flushed face, at the rash that crept up to her tiny neck. "I'm so sorry, button," she whispered, her breath coming in hitches. "It's all my fault. I only mean to earn a better life for us. I never thought you'd get sick from someone's clothes."

"Melissa," Dylan murmured, "it's not your fault. Blaming yourself won't make Jenny well. Besides, you don't know if that's how she caught this fever."

"Of course she did!" Melissa snapped back, unable to keep the emotion out of her voice. Didn't he understand how guilty she was? She began pacing again. "Either she got it from the clothes or from the miners." She let an angry, rueful tone slide into her words. "Oh, I was going to prove to everyone how strong I was, that I could make it in the world on my own, and it didn't matter if Coy left me with just the dress on my back. Well, he's dead now and so is Rafe. And Jenny—"

"Don't say it!" Dylan barked. Frowning, his eyes like hard green stones, he strode forward and took her shoulders again in a hard grip. "Melissa, you've got to be strong to take care of her. You can't afford the luxury of self-pity right now."

Scared and swamped with contrition, Melissa stared up at him, at the planes of his face where his own worry and grief had etched lines, and his eyes that seemed haunted by events long past. Drawing courage from his warm touch and firm words, she struggled to bridle her runaway panic. "Yes, of course, you're right," she admitted and took a deep, steadying breath. Then she added in a small voice, "It's just that she's so little, and I'm so scared for her."

He gave her shoulders a light squeeze, then released her. "I know. But all you can do is your best. And I'll be right here if you need help."

Melissa took heart in that, and she felt like kissing him for it. In her whole life, she'd never had anyone to depend on. She'd heard a lot of empty promises, but Dylan—she knew his word was good. He'd stand by Jenny and her. "Thank you, Dylan."

She shifted into action then, and followed the doctor's instructions about the soda bath and feeding Jenny. At first the baby wouldn't eat anything. After several tries, though, she finally took a little milk.

With full darkness upon the town, Dylan and Melissa sat in edgy silence, keeping watch over Jenny, who slept fitfully. Her fever did not abate, but the little girl hung on through the hours. Melissa was grateful for Dylan's company—she couldn't think of even one other man of her acquaintance who wouldn't have been asleep or gone by now. There was so much goodness in him, as intimidating as he could be, yet it seemed he was determined to spend his life alone.

Just after midnight and while Jenny was quiet, Melissa, who'd been sitting next to the cradle for hours, walked to the window, flexing her tense, aching shoulders as she went. Resting her forehead against the cool glass pane, she gazed dully at the laughing, free-spending carnival rolling along under the street-lights on Front. Above, a sliver of moon riding low on the horizon hid behind a mask of gauzy clouds, and a few stars twinkled around it. Now that August was waning, the chilly nights fell earlier and lasted longer.

With her focus so fixed on this room, she marveled at how precarious life was, and how heartless the world could be. It continued on, unaware and unconcerned about the fate of one child who lay in the cradle next to Dylan's bed.

She heard Dylan's chair legs scrape across the plank flooring, and then felt his warmth behind her as he laid his hand on her shoulder. His touch was firm but gentle, the contrast reminding her of the kind man who lurked beneath a threatening persona.

He worked at the tightness in her muscles, coaxing them to relax, but her thoughts were bitter.

"I'm beginning to see what you hate about this place," Melissa said without turning. "It's all a gaudy spectacle on the surface, but I think there's a lot of suffering that we don't see. What good is making money if it costs you everything else that matters?" She shook her head as she gazed down at the street. "If I'd had the chance to refuse, I never would have come up here. Why did you? What made you choose this place?" She heard him sigh behind her, not in exasperation, she thought, but as if pondering her question. His hand fell away.

"When I left The Dalles, I'd already lost all I had that mattered to me. I didn't know where to go. I just wanted to put some distance between me and them—the old man, my brother . . . Elizabeth."

Melissa turned to face him then. She wouldn't question him about her—he was the one to bring up the woman's name. Maybe this time he would tell her what he'd run away from so that she could understand why his eyes had their haunted look.

He went back to the table and sat down again, slouching low and crossing his ankle over his knee. "Remember when I told you about the night I left home, that it was because of an argument I had with my father about the horses?"

She nodded, leaning against the windowsill behind her.

"Well, there was a little more to it than that." He shifted his gaze to an empty coffee cup on the table before him, turning it idly as if looking for the grit to give voice to his story. "I met Elizabeth Petitt four years ago at her homecoming party. She'd just gotten back from some fancy eastern school. Her father, William Petitt, was one of the bank's biggest customers. I agreed to go to keep peace with my own family—the old man told me to put on decent clothes and stop looking like a hired hand for one night." He sent her a wry smile that stopped short of his eyes. "How could I resist such a bighearted invitation? I'd planned to stay for just a half hour or so, make small talk, and then leave. I don't know why, but I'd supposed that the daughter was probably a homely bluestocking her family wanted to marry off. But when I was introduced to Elizabeth, it was like I lost everything, my sense of time, my heart, my mind—everything. From that moment I was doomed." He shook his head, and his expression turned bittersweet. "She was beautiful, with long black curls and dark eyes, and so different from the other women I'd known. On the surface she was ladylike and cultivated, almost girlish, I guess. But beneath all that I discovered a wanton, uninhibited, free-thinking woman. She had me tripping all over myself like a fifteen-year-old boy. I turned into the worst kind of blind, love-sick fool anyone ever saw. I couldn't eat, or sleep, or think of anything or anyone but her."

Melissa lowered her eyes. It was almost impossible to imagine Dylan as he described himself then. He was so serious and controlled, even in anger. The day she'd seen him pin that miner's sleeve with his meat cleaver crossed her memory. That was the Dylan Harper she knew—dangerous, swift-moving, and certainly unpredictable. As difficult as it was to picture him so besotted, she found it harder still to think of another woman bringing that out in him.

He plowed his hand through his hair. "Elizabeth listened to everything I had to say, and there was a lot—I'd kept most of my thoughts and ideas to myself. Finally, I thought I had someone to talk to, someone who understood my love for the land and the horses. At least I thought she understood. I don't know why—there were never two people with less in common. But I didn't realize that at the time, and it wasn't until a lot later when I figured out that while I'd told her all about myself, I knew almost nothing about her. Before I knew what I was doing, I'd asked her to marry me."

"I suppose it isn't that we don't know people," Melissa put in softly. "I think sometimes we make up our minds to ignore the things about a person that give us doubt, or make us worry. I know that's what I did with Coy."

He considered her for a moment, as if seeing a new side to her. "You're smarter than you give yourself credit for. I think you knew from the beginning that you were taking a gamble on Logan. It was a bold risk, but the odds were so high you were bound to lose."

She walked to the cradle and looked at Jenny. "Maybe you're right," she admitted, letting her eyes meet his. "I wanted to leave home so badly, I was willing to take a chance on Coy. It was too much to hope that everything would work out, that somehow he would turn into the kind of man you—" She looked away then, and felt her cheeks flushed as if she too suffered from fever. Reaching down, she swabbed Jenny's head with a cool cloth.

Her unfinished remark hung between them awkwardly. "I'm probably not the man you think I am, either, Melissa."

She looked up again, the cloth wadded in her fist. "But you've been kind to Jenny and me. You took us in when we had no one to turn to."

He shrugged and straightened in his chair. "I didn't have much choice, considering the circumstances. But I'm no teetotaler, and I hate wearing a suit. I like being outdoors, I don't have much interest in front parlor politics, and I expect to get my hands dirty when I work. Elizabeth didn't care if I took a drink, but she didn't like anything else I did except—" He glanced away. "Well, she didn't like much else."

Adjusting the baby's dress, Melissa stroked Jenny's hot, downy hair with the back of her fingers. She thought again of Elizabeth's patrician features and wondered if the woman had been out of her mind. There was nothing about Dylan that she didn't like, except her helpless attraction to him. "It sounds as if she could have had any man that suited her fancy. Why would she choose one she felt she had to change?"

"Why," he repeated. Then he looked up at Melissa

and grinned. In this light she thought the smile looked almost malevolent. "Over time, the reason made itself clear enough. It was money."

"Money? Didn't you say she came from a wealthy family?"

"Some people never get enough. I began to suspect that her father and mine had plotted the whole thing from the beginning, but . . ."

Pushing himself from his chair, Dylan went to the stove and shook the coffeepot. His movements were restless, like those of an animal pacing in a cage. She knew the coffee in the pot must be only lukewarm, but apparently he didn't care—he filled his cup. But he left it on the stove and paced to the window, where he stared at the blue-black night sky.

"But?" she prompted quietly.

Keeping his back to her, Dylan shoved his hands in his back pockets and sighed. "Hell, I thought I was in love with her, and I figured it didn't much matter how we'd come together." Shaking his head, he added, "I was truly bewitched by her."

With the benefit of hindsight, Dylan wondered why he hadn't seen Elizabeth for what she was. Being in love with her, that shouldn't have mattered. But, then, she had been very clever in her duplicity, cloaking it with a sizzling, teasing passion that had made him view her exactly as she must have wanted him to: helpless but so charming, so beautiful, so ornamental. He felt like a fool now.

He wasn't about to tell Melissa that the only time Elizabeth had not found fault with him was when she writhed beneath him in his bed over the stables. It had been a puzzle to him then, and even now he wasn't sure he grasped how a woman with such dainty, impeccable manners and dress could turn into a demanding, insatiable hellcat who'd left him sweating and exhausted, with his back on fire from the long red welts she'd raised with her nails.

Dylan glanced over his shoulder at Melissa's downturned head. Guileless, gentle, and modest, she was so unlike Elizabeth. Faint smudges beneath her lower lashes told of her fatigue, but she still looked beautiful to him.

"The harder I tried to please her, the more demanding she became until she had me by the b— Well, let's say she wanted her own way about everything. I knew something wasn't right between us, but I couldn't put my finger on it. Finally, the night I had that blow-up with the old man, I went to her place and asked her to come away with me, right then, that moment. I was practically on my knees, begging her to go, when her father came into the parlor and told me that our engagement was off." He turned to face Melissa. It hurt to talk about it, but somehow, it hurt more to keep it to himself. "She had decided to marry my brother, Scott, instead. Elizabeth confirmed it and said she'd been waiting for the right moment to tell me."

"Oh, Dylan," Melissa moaned.

He walked back to the table and flopped into the chair again. "What a perfect ending it was—to everything. I guess they deserve each other. I hope I never care that much about anyone again."

He could tell her that, but he knew it was already too late.

Dylan cared about Melissa.

Chapter Thirteen

The day and night that followed were a blur to Melissa. The passage of time was marked only by sunrise and sunset, and by the soda baths she gave Jenny, who, though still feverish, doggedly clung to life. Melissa refused to do more than catnap while Jenny slept, and occasionally she woke up stiff, feeling like an old woman from dozing in the chair.

Once someone came upstairs looking for the singing washerwoman, but she called through the door that they had a sick child in the house and she couldn't work. She had certainly lost her desire to sing. There was nothing to sing about.

Keeping the trading store closed, Dylan maintained the vigil with her, leaving only to attend Rafe's funeral. She wished she could pay her respects as well, but it was impossible. At any rate, there was nothing she could do for Rafe now, but Jenny needed constant care.

Dylan returned from the ceremony hollow-eyed and looking exhausted.

"Did Dawson do well by Rafe?" she asked, looking up from Jenny's cradle.

He nodded and went to the coffeepot on the stove. "The funeral drew quite a crowd, and a lot of eulogies were spoken for him. I think more people knew and liked him than he realized. Nearly everyone there pitched in some money to get him a good headstone. McGinty, Big Alex, Bill Ladue, they all gave. Even Belinda."

Thinking of what Dawson winters would be like, her mind conjured a tiny casket covered with roses and a string of mourners trailing behind it in a bitter wind, their black figures set against a cold, gray sky. She gazed down at Jenny and said, "What a desolate place to have to bury a person. It would be so hard to leave someone alone in a grave with ice and snow and darkness. I don't think I could . . ." She looked up at Dylan. "I just don't know what I'd do if . . . I couldn't stand it."

He walked over to her and handed her his cup of coffee. "We're not going to worry about that now, okay? Jenny's going to get well, and everything will be fine. As for Rafe—" He sighed. "If it's possible, I think his spirit has gone to be with someone who died before him, someone who meant a lot to him."

Late in the afternoon, Dr. Garvin came by as he'd promised, and Melissa thought the young physician looked surprised to see that Jenny had survived thus far.

"This is promising, very promising!" he declared upon examining her. "Her fever isn't gone, but it's down."

Dylan stayed out of the way, but Melissa saw the hope and relief in his eyes.

Dr. Garvin instructed her to maintain the regimen of Jenny's treatment and told her to take care of herself as well.

For the rest of the day and that night, Dylan stayed close by. Melissa silently blessed his company, although she insisted that he get more sleep than she did. He brought their meals in from restaurants and chophouses to save Melissa the chore of cooking, and took his turn walking Jenny. She drew strength from his quiet presence, and sometimes while both he and the baby slept, Melissa would watch over them and feel such a rush of love she thought her heart would break.

The long hours in the small room gave her a lot of time to think, and she came to two decisions. First, she knew she would take in no more laundry here in Dawson. Jenny might have caught her fever in a number of ways, but Melissa refused to expose her to any more danger. She'd made good money washing for the miners, but no amount of gold was worth risking her child's health.

As to her heart, she knew that to speak her feelings now was out of the question. She and Dylan were both distracted and worried. But when this was over, she thought, when Jenny was well again—the baby *would* get well, she was positive—Melissa determined that she would tell Dylan how she felt. She had come to realize that life was too perilous and uncertain to let the chance for love slip away.

She looked at him as he lay across the end of the bed, his chest rising and falling, the worry in his face smoothed out in sleep, and let her eyes trace the line of his full mouth. The stubble of his day-old beard shadowed his face, emphasizing his strong male features. She wished she could trail her fingertips along his jaw and over his lips, just for the pleasure of touching him. The kisses that they had shared seemed like a dream now, beautiful but not real. The rice sack still occupied the space in the middle—Melissa had come to hate the thing.

Dylan was bitter about Elizabeth, and he had every reason to be. She had as much, if not more, reason to be bitter about Coy. But what good could it bring? It would be a mistake to let those experiences color their lives. After all, who knew when fate could steal away a life? Their recent brushes with death—Rafe's, Coy's, and Jenny's fever—had given her a new perspective. They needed to put the past where it belonged, behind them, and leave it there.

Yes, both she and Dylan had been disheartened by life. And the events they'd experienced were lamentable.

But to have nothing to show for one's years but regret and a longing heart seemed the greater tragedy to her.

Melissa stood on the bottom rail of a corral, watching her husband lead a horse in a circle around the enclosure. He was tall and straight and lean, with long hair that flew behind his shoulders in the wind. Perched on the horse's bare back was a young child with curls as fair as the man's. Her childish voice urged the horse on, although Melissa couldn't catch the words. They were beautiful together, the man and his daughter, outlined by the bronze and pale blue of sunset, and Melissa felt so proud of them. The little girl's giggle floated to her on the soft breeze, and as they drew near, she saw the dark green glint of her husband's eyes, reflecting a mingling of joy and frank desire that made her breath come faster.

"I think she's getting better, Melissa," he said, and the child giggled again . . .

Melissa woke with a start and sat up. She realized she'd fallen asleep with her backside still in the chair and her torso hunched over on the bed.

"She's really better. Look." Dylan was standing next to her with Jenny in his arms. She saw one little fist wave and heard the baby's contented gurgle.

She shot from her chair and looked at Jenny. Swiftly, she moved her hands over the baby, feeling for fever. There was none. She still had the horrible-looking rash, but it was improving, and she smiled when she saw her mother.

"Oh!" Melissa said, laughing with relief. Dylan put Jenny in her arms, and she gazed down at her face, laughing again. "Oh, thank God! Jenny, my dear little button, are you feeling better?"

Jenny gurgled and smiled broadly.

"Hah!" Melissa laughed again triumphantly and did a little dance around the room, being careful not to bounce Jenny too much.

Dylan watched her and laughed as well. "I was

sitting by the window, watching the sunset, and I heard her. When I came over here to look, she was awake and sort of giggling."

Suddenly, everything in the room and beyond the window looked beautiful. The sun, dipping down behind the clouds, turned the room a burnished, mellow gold. Melissa drew a deep, bracing breath and exhaled it. She felt as if a great weight had been lifted from her shoulders and she could stand straight again.

Certainly, Jenny was not well yet, but Melissa was positive that she'd turned the corner toward recovery. From the dark night of Rafe's death and Jenny's terrible illness the sun had shone again. Impulsively, she crossed the room to Dylan and surprised them both by kissing him soundly on the mouth.

Dylan actually felt himself flush all the way to his ears, and he saw color rise in Melissa's cheeks too.

She ducked her head and said, "I'm sorry if I seem forward. But I want to thank you, Dylan, for being a good friend to me. For bringing the doctor and staying with us, for helping me take care of Jenny." Melissa's words bore a heartfelt sincerity that touched him. They were straightforward and honest, not coy or sly. "You didn't have to do any of it. I'm very grateful." She gazed at him with those clear, gray eyes that sparkled despite her fatigue.

He felt tongue-tied for the first time in years. He wanted to tell her how he felt, that any danger posed to her or Jenny roused every protective instinct he had, as if they were really his family. But the words wouldn't come, despite Rafe's last advice to him. He was wary, not of Melissa as much as of love itself. The wound Elizabeth had inflicted with her treachery was still too new, and the scar on his emotions was still too tender for him to even consider giving his heart again.

Remaining silent, he put his arm around her and held her and Jenny to his heart. Strands of Melissa's hair had come unraveled from her braid, but it still smelled of soap and clean water. A tangle of emotions were sluicing through him so quickly he didn't know what to say. Relief for Jenny, his feelings for Melissa, regret for Rafe's passing—they jumbled together and nearly made him blurt out three words that he would not be able to take back.

"I just did the right thing, the decent thing," he said, resting his chin against her head. Truth be told, a few weeks ago he'd wished that none of the Logan clan had ever set foot in his store. But now he envisioned with dread the day that he would leave this woman and her child. Maybe Rafe was right; maybe he'd be a fool to let them slip away from him.

"I guess I haven't known many decent people in my life, then," she said. She lifted her face to look into his eyes, and something intimate and elemental passed between them. He felt it shoot through him, and he knew she did too. For a moment the isolation of the dusk-dim room made it seem as if they were the only people left in Dawson. All the troubles they'd endured faded, the memory and weight of them falling away like autumn leaves.

With Melissa's soft coral lips just inches from his own, the need to kiss her was overwhelming. Her eyes drifted closed. He knew he should stop himself, but she was here and he hungered for her.

Dylan dipped his head and touched her mouth lightly with the tip of his tongue . . . first her upper lip . . . then her lower. Her swift, light intake of breath was just the permission he needed to give in to the temptation. Sweet warmth and lush softness were his as he took her mouth with his own. He felt his pulse in his head—or was it her heartbeat? He couldn't tell. He only knew how she made him feel, powerful and vulnerable at the same time.

He lifted his head just enough to speak. "Melissa," he whispered. It was all he could say, so completely did she fill his head and soul. She must have heard something in his voice, though, a call that spoke to her on the deepest level of her own soul. She made a tiny sound in her throat, almost a moan, and brought her lips to his again with a passion that melted his heart and hardened his arousal. Yearning to feel the curve of her breasts and hips against him, he tightened his arm around her. But with Jenny wedged between them, he couldn't pull her body against his own as he so badly wanted to.

Melissa backed away first, pushing a hand through her straggling hair. "Um, Jenny must be hungry, and I don't want to tire her out. I should feed her and put her to sleep."

Once again, the brief glance they exchanged was charged with unspoken purpose and need. He thought he might be wrong, that what he saw in her eyes was fatigue, or joy, or friendship.

But no. There was no mistaking it—each understood the other.

A better man might have walked away right then without taking the moment one step further, he supposed. But a better man would have lost out on the chance to mend his heart in the arms of this woman, and miss the privilege of honoring her with his own body. If Dylan was less noble, so be it, he thought.

He had slept next to her for weeks, fighting his desire for her, and he'd dreamed of her smooth, slender form more nights that he wanted to count. He'd promised her that he would never try to claim husbandly rights, but they weren't the same people they'd been that day outside the Yukon Girl Saloon.

Now, whether he liked it or not, Dylan had come to care for the woman whose freedom he'd bought for twelve hundred dollars.

He glanced at his bed, and then at the log-walled room. "Well, I guess I should go down and see about the store. I haven't looked in on it in a while."

Melissa touched his arm and let a timid, meaningful gaze slide up to his face before she looked away. "That's fine."

Feeling nearly as shy and self-conscious as he thought she did, Dylan turned and went to the door. His heart hammered in his chest. Then he looked back over his shoulder at her and Jenny. Melissa smiled at him, a sweet, beautiful smile.

He knew he was lost to her.

* * *

Do you know what you're doing? Melissa asked herself as she watched the door close. She believed she did, but even if she was wrong, she knew it would not be the worst choice she'd made in her life. Dylan Harper was a good man, a decent man, and the fires he stirred in her could no longer be ignored.

After she fed Jenny, the child fell into the exhausted slumber of a recovering convalescent. Cuddling her in one arm, Melissa lit the lamp on the table and lowered the flame to a soft glow. Then she carried the baby to the cradle that Dylan had bought for her.

"Good night, sweet little button," she whispered, then kissed the tiny hand that curled around her finger. Gazing down on the little girl with love, she tucked her blanket around her and said a silent, earnest prayer of thanks that her child had been restored to her.

Melissa went to the washstand and looked at her reflection. Her fatigue had left her as soon as Dylan had kissed her. Now anticipation and fear were at war within her, making her hands cold and her insides shaky. He hadn't swayed her with a lot of smooth talk or empty pledges. She knew there were no promises between them beyond what he'd told her the day she met him.

But Melissa was in love with him, an emotion that sent her to the heights of joy when she looked at him and the depths of despair when she thought of leaving him. Whatever might happen, she determined that she would know the touch of the man she loved. Taking off her clothes, she stood before the little mirror wearing only her untidy braid.

Her hair had come loose from its weaving, so she brushed it out and let it fall in soft waves over her shoulders. Expecting to hear Dylan's footsteps on the stairs at any moment, she soaped and rinsed as quickly as she could. What did a person wear in this situation? she wondered with a touch of giggling hysteria. On her wedding night the pretty white muslin nightgown she'd made for the occasion had gone unnoticed by Coy. He'd come to her room long after their quick courthouse wedding, stinking drunk. After a slobbering attempt to consummate their marriage, he'd passed out on the bed next to her.

She shuddered at the memory.

Tonight would not be like that.

She heard the door slam downstairs. Dylan would be up here any moment. Looking around, she spied a clean nightgown slung over the end of the bed. Normally, modesty would never have allowed her to leave her personal clothing in full view, but the last few days had made such details unimportant. Grabbing the gown, she threaded her arms into the sleeves and pulled it down over her head just as she heard Dylan's first footfall outside.

Melissa walked to the bed and climbed between the cool sheets. She'd followed this routine almost every night since she came to live with Dylan, but tonight she sat against the headboard in the semi-darkness, waiting expectantly for the man she had come to regard as her husband.

Then she eyed the barrier that took up the center of the mattress. Melissa remembered the night she'd dragged the sack up here. In a state of panic and certain doom, she'd hoped it would protect her from Dylan. But it had been his integrity that protected her, and the time for walls between them had long passed.

Considering the sack, she scrambled to her knees and pushed on it to roll it off the bed. It wouldn't budge. Slipping her hands beneath it, she put all her effort and will into lifting it, straining and grunting. Still she had no luck. Finally winded, she sat back on her heels, and flipped her long hair behind her shoulders. Mercy, her abject terror must have given her more strength that night than she normally possessed. Well, if she got it up here— She rose to her knees again with her determination and pushed.

The door opened, and Dylan stepped inside where he stood hesitantly, as if waiting for permission to come closer. Though only a low flame lit the room, Melissa could see that he'd shaved, and his long hair looked damp, as if just washed. His shirt was unbuttoned halfway down his torso, and his sleeves were rolled up, revealing muscle and sinew. The snug black pants he wore showed off his long legs and backside to shameless advantage, although she felt certain that he was unaware of his good looks. A flutter rippled through her—she swore he was the handsomest man she'd ever seen.

"Is she asleep?" he asked, nodding at Jenny's cradle.

"Yes, she's still weak and tired. I-I imagine she'll sleep for hours."

He approached the bed, and his gaze dropped to the rice. Melissa felt a searing tension between them, a powerful charge of desire and primitive need. The feelings were new to her, but they rose from ancient instincts and she recognized them.

"Melissa," he said, and his green eyes, as dark as a forest in the shadows, locked with hers, "shall I move this?" He gestured at the rice.

"Yes," she replied in a small voice. "I think it's time."

He lifted the heavy sack with easy grace and propped it in the corner, the muscles in his arms and shoulders flexing with the effort.

He turned and sat on the edge of the mattress. "God, I'm glad to be rid of that. I hated having it in bed with us." He gave her a crooked smile. "You know, that sack wouldn't have stopped me if I'd decided to give in to temptation."

She glanced down at the hem of the sheet. "I suppose not. Why did you let it stay there, then?"

"Because I knew it made you feel better." His smile broadened a bit, and his gaze trailed down the front of her nightgown. He reached for her hand. "And because some nights it worked."

An exciting flash of danger quivered through her. His touch was warm and vital as it trailed along her hand and wrist.

"Oh?" she said, feeling a little breathless.

He moved closer so that he sat cross-legged on the mattress, occupying the place of the newly discarded rice. His knee bumped her hip, and his hair brushed his shoulders with the movement. Taking her hand, he pressed a kiss to the backs of her fingers. His mouth, soft and hot against her hand, was tantalizing.

"Oh, yeah," he said, and his voice grew richer, huskier. He looked up at her with eyes that burned like green coals. "There were nights when I wanted so badly to jump over that damned fence you put up and hold you in my arms."

Melissa knew she'd had nights when she wished for the same thing. "I never knew."

"Well, it's true," he said, and suddenly rose to his knees on the mattress to take her face between her hands. "Melissa—" He shook his head. "I've tried everything I know to keep from thinking about you, about us together, but nothing works."

What he really meant she didn't know—was he talking about a future with her, or just this one night? She had no time to ponder it further, though, because he lowered his face to hers and kissed her passionately, devouring her lips with his own. His breath came fast as he held her. His hands moved away from her face and down her back, then he pulled her to her knees too, so they faced each other, body pressed to body. He rained soft, whispery kisses on her cheeks, her eyelids, her brow, her throat.

"Oh, Dylan," she whispered. Dare she reveal her heart to him? she wondered. It had seemed it would be an easy thing to do when she planned it, but now . . .

Dylan heard her voice, and the sweet sound of it was like kerosene on the fire she'd ignited in him. His pants grew painfully tight over his arousal, and he could think of nothing but how right it felt to hold this woman in his arms. He wanted to stroke every inch of her bare skin and follow with a trail of kisses. Realizing that, he pulled back and looked at her. Her hair fell around her like a rippling curtain of pale yellow satin, rich and shiny. Her simple white nightgown was, strangely enough, more alluring and exciting than the expensive silks and laces that Elizabeth had worn. He saw trust in her gray eyes, and maybe even something more.

"Tell me," he murmured against her ear, his breath short. "Are you sure you want to do this? If you don't, you'd better say it now."

She nodded solemnly, like a child. "Yes, I'm sure. It's what I want," she whispered again. Then she added, "And Dylan, I'm sorry for getting mad at you about the whiskey that day Rafe died. I was wrong to make such a fuss—"

"Hush now, Melissa. It doesn't matter at all. It's behind us." He enfolded her in his embrace and felt her breasts press against him. He wanted to do right by her, to conquer her with her own desire, as he'd once planned. To make up for some of what she'd probably suffered at the hands of Coy Logan.

Elizabeth . . . Logan . . . neither of their memories

or their names had any place in this bed. There were just the two of them now, Dylan and Melissa.

He dipped his head to her mouth to kiss her again, and this time she surprised him by meeting his tongue with hers. He groaned and pulled her down on the bed so they lay facing side by side, their arms wrapped around each other.

Dragging his mouth from hers, he pushed her over on her back and fumbled impatiently with the buttons on the front of her gown. He wanted to touch her, but not scare her. It took all of his dwindling self-control to keep from yanking the garment off over her head so that he could finally gaze upon her body.

Melissa reached up and gently pushed his hand away. At first he thought she would deny him access, and then he realized that she had unbuttoned the gown herself. Dylan had one glimpse of the creamy skin inside and placed a kiss on her breastbone, right over her heart. She arched against his mouth, and he felt her heart beating as swiftly as a bird's.

Covering her mouth with his again, he kissed her with all the desolate, urgent longing he'd kept inside for the past three years. Melissa lifted sheltering arms to embrace him and hold him close. He hadn't admitted to himself how lonely he'd been until now. This was where he belonged, he realized, with this sweet-voiced woman and the child he'd come to think of as theirs.

Dylan was no awkward kid—his experience reached far back to his early teens. But tonight he felt as if this were his first time. Maybe because he'd been months without a woman. Or maybe because this one meant more to him than any other ever had.

With a light, wondering touch he slipped his hand inside Melissa's gown and grazed the swell of one breast with his fingertips. Burying his face against her neck, he began a line of kisses that he strung down her throat and over her chest. Her skin smelled of soap and some other warm scent that was all her own. No perfume he knew of had a more enticing fragrance.

She threaded her hands in his hair to guide him toward her breast. His lips followed the path his fingertips had taken until he encountered her tight nipple. He closed his mouth over it and tugged, then was startled by a stream a warm milk that flowed into his mouth. Instantly, Dylan's raw need burned higher and hotter, and he rocked his hips against her thigh.

Melissa caught her breath and squirmed under the unexpected pleasure of Dylan's hot, moist mouth at her breast. Every nerve on her skin seemed alive and sensitive to the lightest touch. With each light pull of her nipple, she felt spears of fire shoot through her belly to the place that even now prepared the way for their joining. Everything female within her responded to him, and her desire sizzled like an electric current.

She breathed in the scent of his clean hair, and the smell of his skin that she had come to know so well in washing his clothes. Abandoning demureness, she wanted to touch him too, to feel his skin against hers. Reaching down, she struggled with his shirttail, but it was tucked in too tightly and she couldn't pull it out. She yanked harder. The sound of ripping fabric interrupted them.

"Oh, no," she cried, feeling the tear along the front of his shirt.

Grinning at her, Dylan bounced off the bed and looked down at the three-inch hole, then back up at her. "Hooee, woman, I'd better take charge of the undressing. You're one hell of a fiery she-lion, Melissa. Don't know your own strength, huh?" He cast off the shirt and his boots.

She stared at his shirt and up at him. Fiery—she'd certainly never thought of herself *that* way. She'd spent most of her life trying to remain inconspicuous. Mortified, she started to apologize. "Oh, dear, I'm so sorry—"

"I'm not." The teasing tone left his voice, and straightforward hunger glinted in his eyes, increasing Melissa's own craving for him. His belt buckle clanked as it hit the plank flooring, and he kicked his pants across the room. He stood naked before her then, the beauty of his muscled form emphasized by shadows and golden lamplight. She let her eyes trail over his broad chest, down his lean flanks and hips, to his powerful erection.

Feeling a little timid, Melissa sat up and made a move to pull off her gown.

"Not yet," he said softly, stopping her with a hand

on her shoulder. He put one knee on the mattress. "Not yet. I want to do it."

His hand brushed over her hair, down her back, along her leg, a caress of infinite gentleness. Grasping the hem of her nightgown, he slid it up her thigh and like a magician, swept it away from her. It landed in the corner, fluttering over the rice sack.

He eased her to the mattress and let his gaze touch her here and there. She felt awkward under his scrutiny and tried to cover herself with her arms. He nudged them to her sides.

"No, let me look, Melissa," he murmured. "I've wanted to look at you, touch you, for so long. Like I figured"—he kissed her forehead and her eyelid—"you're beautiful." He buried his mouth against her neck, thrilling her with soft, slow kisses that made her nipples stand erect.

Melissa forgot her shyness.

Running his hand up her ribs, he skimmed the side of her breast with his palm. His kisses made a leisurely path down her throat, and his hair brushed lightly over her skin, sending tantalizing shivers through her. Then he dipped to suckle her again and groaned as he took her milk greedily from each breast. His erection, heavy and full, pulsated against her thigh.

An insistent throbbing began between her legs, one that she had never known before. With it grew a demanding desire to have Dylan inside her, because she knew that only he could ease the ache. But too shy to tell him so, she shifted slightly and drew up one knee, hoping he would understand.

Instead, he let his hand drift downward across her flat belly, downward to delve her sensitive, swollen flesh with gentle, searching fingertips. Melissa gasped and arched against his hand. He began slowly, with a careful, deliberate touch. Soon though, she felt his breath coming fast and hot against her neck as he stroked her with increasing speed and intensity.

What was he doing to her? she wondered, half delirious. Nothing in her limited experience with Coy could compare with this feeling of excruciating pleasure and torment.

As if by instinct, she reached for the hard length of him resting against her thigh. He was hot and smooth and pulsing in her grip. When she closed her fingers around him, he made an inarticulate sound deep in his throat and sucked in a breath. He pulled his hips away, but she held fast, and he pushed back.

"Dylan," she moaned. Her voice sounded far away to her own ears. Helpless against his sweet onslaught, she could only press against his hand.

Seconds seemed like hours to her as the heat within her escalated until she was sure she could stand no more. Suddenly, Dylan batted her hand away from his own flesh and grasped her writhing hips. Melissa looked up at him, at his heavy-lidded eyes and the sheen of sweat on his face as he loomed over her.

"You've never made love in your life, Melissa," he ground out, his voice low and rough. "But tonight you will with me." Still holding her, he took her with a single thrust that filled her so completely, she nearly wept with the poignancy of their joining.

She felt as if there were a tightly wound spring inside her, and with each forceful thrust he gave that spring another twist. She looped her arms around him, consumed by the raging need that threatened to consume her.

She lifted her hips to him so that he could reach deeper into her. His thrusts came faster, harder, pushing the throbbing between her legs to a nearly painful extreme. If this didn't end—

"Dylan," she cried, "please—"

He lowered his head to kiss her again, and with the next desperate stroke he drove her over the edge, tumbling her into a dark gulf of sensation. Fierce spasms wracked her body as muscles contracted and pulled Dylan into her.

Melissa thought she called him again, but she was sure of nothing except him inside her and the feelings he'd ripped from her.

Rearing over her, his hair almost hiding his face, he plunged forward again and again, shorter, harder, more desperate. Finally, with one last fervent thrust, his own release gripped him. Wrapping her arms around his waist, she pulled him close. A low, tortured groan escaped him and his face contorted. The tendons stood out in his neck as he strained against her body, and she felt the hot, rapid convulsions that poured from him into her.

Dropping his weight to his elbows, he rested his head on her shoulder for a moment and panted against her neck. At last he breathed a sated, exhausted sigh.

Utter silence fell over them, and for a moment the ticking of the clock was the loudest sound in the room.

Dylan closed his arms around her and rolled them over together, so that he lay on his back and she was nestled against him. The sheets were in a tangled wad around their legs, and he reached down to cover them, enfolding them in a warm cocoon. Melissa thought she had never felt such security. In Dylan's arms, she was safe from the world.

He chuckled. It was a full, satisfied sound that reverberated under her ear. "This beats trying to cuddle up to that damned sack of rice anytime."

"Yes, it does," she admitted with a smile. Her heart brimmed with so much emotion, she wished she had the courage to say more, to tell him how much she loved him.

His chuckle bloomed into a laugh. "You're a different kind of woman, Melissa," he said, repeating the compliment he'd once paid her. He tightened his arms around her. "I wish I'd met you years ago, when I was younger."

She laughed now, too. "Ah, yes, I can see that you're an old man."

The amusement faded from his voice. "Not old, I

guess. But I'm not naive anymore, either. I don't assume that everything will work out just because I want it to."

Melissa had the distinct, uneasy feeling that he was talking about them, and she didn't want to pursue it. Never had she once suspected that a man's bed could be a place of such communion and sharing. It all felt so perfect she was afraid to ask any questions and break the spell surrounding them.

Their future was a mystery. They had tomorrow to face, and the days after that, and she didn't know what those days might bring. For now, she was content to lie here, with his arm holding her close to his warm body.

Dylan felt Melissa sigh. Her soft, smooth limbs tangled with his, and her head fit perfectly in the hollow between his neck and his shoulder. This . . . this sense of completion, of joining hearts and spirits instead of just bodies, this was what he'd missed. And the warm, unselfish woman who lay beside him had given that to him.

It lifted his heart. It scared the hell out of him.

He stared up at the dark, timbered ceiling overhead. He had to decide two things.

Would he spend another winter in Dawson? And if he did, would he keep Melissa and Jenny with him? Money was no longer the issue—he'd made enough to buy the land he wanted. He would have to make his decision soon. September was on them and winter came early to the Yukon.

But as Melissa burrowed drowsily against his

shoulder, he pressed a kiss to her forehead and pulled the wolf hide over them. Basking in the peace and contentment that had been strangers to him for most of his life, he let his eyes drift closed.

He didn't have to make any decisions tonight.

Chapter Fourteen

To Melissa's great relief, Jenny continued to make steady improvement over the next several days. Her rash had begun to peel like a bad sunburn, but Dr. Garvin told her that was part of the recovery process. Fortunately, both she and Dylan showed no signs of coming down with scarlet fever themselves.

After their night of lovemaking, Melissa felt a shift in her relationship with Dylan. Because she stayed upstairs to care for Jenny, she noticed that he found any number of reasons to come up from his store. He would claim to be searching for a ledger book, or a particular pocketknife, or a whetstone. One time he even came for the sack of rice, declaring he had a buyer for it. She suspected his true intention was to guarantee that it wouldn't be used again as a barrier between them in his bed.

With the Yukon's early autumn settling over Dawson, one afternoon Dylan brought Jenny a cashmere baby blanket. He'd traded a half case of whiskey to a Russian merchant captain for the costly, petal-soft white wool. It was the finest fabric Melissa had ever seen, and her love for Dylan grew accordingly.

As much as she wanted to believe that he actually came upstairs to see her, she refused to give in to the temptation. The lingering glances they exchanged, the half smiles, and brushes of hands and arms in passing meant nothing much, she maintained. They were only the natural results of their nights together.

Their nights . . .

In the evenings, with Jenny tucked into her cradle, they staved off the chill under the wolf hides on his bed. Dylan brought her body to heights of pleasure that she had never before imagined, and taught her wondrous ways to satisfy him. It gave her a heady sense of power to watch him lying next to her, groaning and struggling to maintain control as she caressed and stroked him to the point of near-climax.

"You're a heartless tease," Dylan said one night through gritted teeth. He lay with one arm thrown over his eyes and his hands clenched.

She took no offense at his accusation. "No, I'm not," she murmured with a sly smile next to his ear, "I only want to please you, and you showed me how to do it."

At that, he made an inarticulate sound that resembled a low growl, and rose from the mattress to flip her on her back. Then he parted her thighs and took her with slow, torturous thrusts to get even with her. He reduced her to whimpering his name over and over before he finally decided she'd suffered enough sweet torment and pushed them both to completion.

As much as Melissa delighted in making love with him, though, she liked it best when she brought the baby into bed with them. It was then that she let herself pretend they were a real family, and that Jenny, their daughter, was snuggled safely in the embrace of her two doting parents. It was a fairy tale, she knew, and probably the most dangerous kind because it involved her child's heart as well as her own.

And despite all the secret glances exchanged and the nights spent in fierce, breathless passion, Dylan spoke no words of love and said nothing about their future.

Melissa didn't need Dylan for support. Between the gold she had hoarded from her laundry business and the bequest Rafe had left her, she knew she and Jenny could go back to Portland and have a safe, comfortable life for the foreseeable future. She was far from wealthy, but with careful budgeting, the financial independence she had strived for would be hers. If the day came that she needed to earn a living again, she now had the confidence to do it.

No, she didn't need Dylan to keep the wolf away from her door.

She needed him for love.

He was doing it again.

His thoughts were drifting like slow-moving clouds across a summer sky, drifting to a blond woman and the child in her arms, drifting to cool nights under warm blankets, to a face whose prettiness he had not seen when he first set eyes upon it, a face he now couldn't get out of his head.

Dylan pulled himself out of his reverie and straightened away from the counter where he'd been leaning on his elbows, daydreaming like a kid with his first crush. He had all kinds of work to do—accounts to go over, stock to put on the shelves, a new shipment to check—and he'd done none of it. Every time he began a task, some distracting thought would cross his mind, like the way Melissa angled her head when she looked up at him, or her graceful hands, or the feel of her arms around him when she took him into her body.

This morning he'd heard her humming to Jenny again with a soft, mellow voice. He'd been so damned glad to hear it, his heart had felt as light as a feather. Disgusted, he kicked a ball of twine across the floor.

What was wrong with him, anyway? He was twice as distracted as he'd ever been over Elizabeth, and look what trouble *she'd* gotten him into.

He walked to the open door and, slouching against the jamb, looked out at the cold gray rain. It seemed almost profane to compare the two women—they were nothing alike. Even his own feelings for Melissa were not the same. She wasn't the mindless fever in his blood that Elizabeth had been. She touched him more deeply, reaching down to the corners of his soul he'd let no one into before.

Overhead, he heard her footsteps crossing the floor. Drawn to her, Dylan started down the duckboards and almost headed for the stairs again before he pulled up short in front of her abandoned washtubs.

She wasn't part of his plans, he argued with himself, gazing at the web of clotheslines. She had nothing to do with that plot of land he'd dreamed of and worked for all this time—not a damned thing.

Why, then, could he no longer think of it without picturing her in every room of the house he would build? He had to decide his future, and soon.

"Morning, Harper."

Dylan turned to see Big Alex McDonald lumber down the side street, carrying a bundle under one arm. He moved slowly and spoke even slower, as if talking were a difficult, unaccustomed thing he practiced. His heavy brown hair and enormous mustache concealed most of his face, making him look like a rendering of a Neanderthal. But while he seemed like a giant, awkward rube, Dylan knew that no shrewder man lived in the North. He'd amassed most of his fortune with the lay system Belinda had tried to interest Dylan in, the one Big Alex had introduced into the Klondike that reaped a portion of the gold that others mined.

"Hi, there, Alex. I haven't seen you in a while." Dylan propped one foot on a soap crate. "What brings you by?"

The towering Scotsman gestured up at Melissa's black and gold leaf sign. "I've been looking for your missus, the singing laundry woman, but I haven't seen her for a while. I brought her some shirts to wash."

Dylan shook his head. "The baby's been sick, and she's taking care of her. I don't think she'll be opening her business again."

The big man looked disappointed and paused before speaking, as if mentally stringing the words together. "That's too bad. Nobody in town does such a good job with shirts, or sings so nice." He rubbed his chin thoughtfully with a huge hand. "I got used to seeing her down here, working and singing to the babe."

He wasn't the only one, Dylan thought.

"Well, give her this for me, anyhow." Big Alex reached under his tidy bundle and withdrew a dog-eared newspaper. "She told me she grew up in Portland. I got it from a *cheechako* who just came into town."

Dylan glanced down at the masthead and read *Oregonian.* "Thanks, Alex. I'll tell her you stopped by."

Big Alex nodded and trudged back to Front Street. Dylan watched him go, then looked at the paper again. It was more than three months old, but it was good to see something from home. He was glad, too, for the diversion.

With a last glance at the stairway, Dylan walked back to the store and spread the yellowed newspaper on the counter in front of him. He'd never followed the goings-on in Portland, where the paper was published—the city was too busy and brash compared to The Dalles—but some of the topics were familiar to him. He turned the pages that looked as if they'd been soaked and dried in the sun, taking vague note of advertisements placed by general stores, carriage makers, and haberdasheries. He skimmed headlines concerning shanghaiing on Portland's docks, political disputes, and the war with Spain.

Then, just as he was about to fold up the thing, one particular item caught his eye. It was a small piece, located down in a corner and could have been easily missed, or dismissed, by a reader. But Dylan stared at it in stunned disbelief, reading and rereading the headline.

THE DALLES FATHER-SON BANKING MAGNATES
PERISH IN CARRIAGE ACCIDENT

He jerked the paper closer and read that Griffin Harper and son Scott, majority stockholders in Columbia Bank, were killed when the carriage in which they were riding apparently plunged into a deep ravine and overturned. The elder Harper suffered a broken neck, while his son appeared to have died of extensive injurious insults to the body.

Lowering the newspaper, Dylan swallowed and swallowed, but his throat was suddenly as dry as talc. God—his father, at least the only man he knew as his father, and his brother were dead? Forcing himself to finish the article, he read that Scott Harper was survived by his widow, Elizabeth Pettit Harper. The eldest Harper son, Dylan, had departed from The Dalles some years earlier, and his whereabouts were unknown.

He walked to the straight-backed chair next to the stove and sat down with his elbows on his knees, letting the newspaper sail to the floor. Dead—the man who had worked so hard to bend Dylan to his will, he'd nearly broken him. The man who had scrambled to grow wealthy on the misfortune of others. And Scott, the stolid *half* brother who'd followed in the old man's footsteps, who'd stolen his fiancée. Well, maybe "stolen" wasn't the right word; Elizabeth had probably piloted that event. But they were gone, their lives snuffed out like candles, and all their maneuvering and all the money in the world couldn't save them.

He looked at the date on the newspaper again—Thursday, May 12, 1898. That was more than three months ago. When he'd told Melissa he didn't expect to see his family again, he'd never once guessed that death would be the reason. Gathering the scattered pages from the floor, Dylan folded them up with hands that trembled slightly. Then he stood, walked outside, and rounded the corner to head upstairs.

He'd been trying to decide whether to spend another winter in Dawson or go back to Oregon.

With his fate turning on a brief visit from Big Alex McDonald, the decision had been made for him.

"I'm going home, Melissa. Back to The Dalles."

Melissa sat at the table, sewing a button on one of his shirts. Swept with astonishment, she dropped the work and her hands fell still. He looked as pale as milk, and all the expression in his eyes seemed to have disappeared. "When? Why?"

He pushed the newspaper across the table to her. Then with a heavy tread, he began pacing a short track in front of the stove, his head down, his hands jammed into his pockets.

"As soon as I can sell this place, I'm leaving. I have to go back. My father and brother were killed three months ago."

"Oh, dear God—"

He gestured at the paper. "It's all there on page seventeen."

Struggling to grasp this abrupt turn of events, Melissa glanced at the masthead, then opened the newspaper to the page he indicated. She read the opening lines of the story, then looked up at him. "Dylan, I'm so sorry. I know you weren't close, but—but this is horrible."

He walked to the window and looked out at the hillsides beyond Dawson, apparently lost in thought and time, with his arms crossed over his chest and his weight shifted to one hip. Finally, he shrugged, as if baffled by his own decision. "I guess old ties run deeper than I thought."

Melissa wondered if she would feel grief or sadness when her own father died, and didn't really know. Life with him had been so dreadful, all she might mourn is what could have been instead of what was. She looked up at his pensive, handsome profile. "I'd really be surprised if you felt nothing.

In fact, I suppose I'd be disappointed." But he hadn't said "we're going," she realized. *He* was going.

Reading further in the small newspaper article, though, she encountered one sentence above all others that stood out as if written in flaming letters six inches high, and perhaps explained Dylan's true purpose.

Scott Harper is survived by his wife, Elizabeth Pettit Harper.

"It doesn't make any sense to me, but I have to go and get back what's mine," he continued. "There sure was no love left between us. But death, somehow that puts things in a different light."

"Yes, I'm sure it does," she replied, feeling cold and hollow inside.

. . . survived by his wife, Elizabeth . . .

He turned for a moment and faced her. "Look, this doesn't change anything between you and me, not at all."

She gazed at him, but said nothing. Of course, everything had changed, at least from her point of view. She felt as if every wish and dream she'd had besides wanting a good life for Jenny were suddenly crashing down around her. She knew she'd been a fool to let her hopes run away with her common sense, but there wasn't much comfort in the knowledge. Maybe for Dylan nothing had changed because he had no feelings for her beyond their original agreement. Right now, she envied him that as much as she resented him for it. Better that she had stuck with her original goal, to achieve independence for herself and Jenny, and not depend on a man for anything. Not even love.

Pushing a hand through his hair, he began pacing again. Then he stopped and peered her. "You don't want to stay here alone, do you?"

"In Dawson? Certainly not."

He looked oddly relieved. "Good. I'll sell this place as soon as I can."

"That's fine. It's time for me to go back to Oregon and stand on my own two feet." She tried to keep her voice from quivering.

A slight frown creased his forehead. "Well . . . yeah, sure—if that's what you want."

"It is. It's what I've worked for." It wasn't what she wanted at all. But what choice did she have? She couldn't compete with his memory of a woman, even if that woman had been, by his own admission, treacherous and scheming.

"I'll book us passage on a steamer back to Portland. Once you're settled there, I'll go on to The Dalles."

. . . Elizabeth . . .

He walked to the door then, muttering to himself about finding a buyer for the store, or at least his inventory, about getting the details wrapped up before cold weather closed the rivers. "See you at dinner."

A chilly gust blew in when he opened the door. Then he was gone.

Melissa listened to his boots on the steps. She finished sewing on the button and carefully folded his shirt, smoothing the fabric with her hands. Then she hugged it to herself, burying her face in its folds, and wept.

"Sure, Dylan, I'll put the word out. I'll even take some of the goods off your hands if I can use them here in the hotel." Belinda Mulrooney waved off her bartender and poured coffee for Dylan herself.

Dylan leaned against the counter in Belinda's fancy hotel bar. With her ear always listening for business deals and deal makers, not much escaped her attention. He thought she'd be a good person to see about selling his inventory.

"Thanks, Belinda. I already talked to Seamus McGinty, too, so I'm hoping I can have this wrapped up within a week or two."

"Dawson will miss you," she said, smiling, "but if you have family affairs to settle, I guess you'd better go back. Myself, I've been on my own for so long, I can't imagine having family to worry about."

Just then, a fussy-looking clerk bustled over. "Miss Mulrooney, there you are. Count Carbonneau is here, asking for you."

Belinda blushed prettily, surprising Dylan. "Oh! Tell him I'll be with him immediately, Ambrose." She turned back to him. "Dylan, if you'll excuse me," and she hurried off with the clerk.

Although she was plain-featured, her wealth made her the best catch in the Yukon for an ambitious bachelor. But Dylan had never known one who could even get close, much less call on her. He thought back to the conversation he'd had with Ned Tanner the day that seemed so long ago now. "Belinda is too danged outspoken and too smart for her own good," Ned had complained.

"Count, my mule's rump," he heard an eavesdropper chuckle farther down the bar. "That Charlie Carbonneau is nothing more than a slick-tongued barber from Montreal who came up here to sell champagne. I heard it from a French-Canadian who recognized him."

"Maybe someone ought to tell Belinda," his companion suggested.

"Hell, someone did. She doesn't care." The man shrugged. "I guess she likes the compliments he pays her and the roses he sends over every day. I'll bet you she marries him."

"Belinda? Naw."

"I'll bet you a whole day of dust she does."

Even the smartest of women could be taken in by the right smooth-talking man, it seemed to Dylan. The conversation grew more boisterous then as the bar patrons debated Belinda's future marital status. But distracted by his own thoughts, he took a swallow of coffee and ignored it. With the load of regret resting on his heart, he would rather have had a whiskey, but decided that might be a bad idea. Sometimes liquor loosened a man's tongue and got him to admit things he wanted to keep to himself. With a couple of drinks in him, he might get the notion into his head to go back to their room and tell Melissa how he felt about her—that he didn't want to take Jenny and her to Portland and leave them there.

He'd hoped she wouldn't want it either. But regardless of the intimacy they'd shared and the crises they'd come through, she was determined to make it on her own. Well, let her go, then, he told himself impatiently. He wouldn't risk revealing his heart, only to have her reject him. He'd stick to his original plan, and so would she.

He wouldn't tell her that he'd grown accustomed to coming upstairs in the evening to the aroma of her cooking. Or that the sight of her nursing Jenny could, by turns, arouse him to a fever of desire, or put a lump in his throat that nearly brought tears to his eyes. He'd keep it to himself that her quiet singing was the sweetest sound he'd ever heard.

He could just imagine the startled look on Melissa's face if he were to tell her that sometime during their summer together he'd begun to think of her as his wife.

Three short days later, dressed in a navy wool traveling suit and an elaborate hat graced with an ostrich feather, Melissa stood in the doorway and took one last look at the room where she had lived for the past few months. She'd swept the floor and dusted the plain furniture to leave a tidy place for the next occupant. Dylan had found a buyer to take not only his stock, but the building and its furnishings, too. Now he was off to hire a wagon to take them and their belongings to the docks where they would board a steamer for home.

Home. She let her eyes follow the line of the rough log walls and the small area within them. Her gaze touched on the stove where she'd heated her irons and cooked their meals . . . the table where Dr. Garvin had examined Jenny that horrible night she got sick . . . the big, rough-hewn bed where Dylan had taken her with fierce, tender passion.

It all belonged to someone else now.

She closed the door with a quiet click and made her way downstairs where her belongings and Dylan's were stacked on the newly built sidewalk. They weren't taking much. Besides Jenny's cradle, Melissa hadn't owned more than what would fit in a big carpetbag, including her gold dust, and Dylan had his trunk. And of course, there was his gold. She didn't know its monetary value, but it was packed in two long rifle boxes reinforced with steel bands. And it was so heavy that Dylan had borrowed one of McGinty's bar boys to help him carry down each crate.

The early morning air had a decided nip in it, and she cuddled Jenny closer. The baby had fully recovered, thank heavens, with no discernable aftereffects. Dr. Garvin had examined her one last time and found her to be sound. For one lingering moment she stood in the side street and looked up at the sign that hung there.

MRS. M. HARPER'S LAUNDRY

It surprised her now how much that sign had

meant to her, and what it represented. She'd cursed Coy over and again for bringing her to this place, for mistreating her, for selfishly abandoning her. He'd given no thought to what kind of man he'd sold her and Jenny to. If possible, they might have been put in even more dire circumstances than they'd left, and to this day she didn't believe he'd have cared. Unintentionally, though, he'd done her a favor.

Dylan had given her the freedom to do what she wanted and to be herself. He'd encouraged her to express her opinion, and she knew he loved Jenny. Though she begrudged her child nothing, she wished he'd had enough left over for her, enough to make him want to stay with them instead of going back to Elizabeth.

Just then, she saw a wagon with low sides pull up in front of the store. Dylan sat on the high seat next to the driver, and she knew it was time to leave.

"Come on, Jenny," she murmured, lifting her chin, "we're going home."

When they got to the river, Melissa was stunned by the number of people, mostly men, swarming the dock, all of them apparently crowding the gangways to board the *Arrow,* the same steamer they had passage on.

"Are you sure we'll be able to get on?" she asked as the wagon pulled up.

"I got the last two cabins, and I paid twice the posted fare for them." His brow lowered ominously. "We'll get on, or the captain will have a hell of a lot of explaining to do." He left her and Jenny in the wagon to see to the loading of the gold.

Hoisting his trunk to his shoulder, Dylan took her arm and shepherded her through the crowd and up the gangway. Although she'd dealt with lots of men when she operated her laundry business, she felt overwhelmed by the jostling crush of so many. They eyed her with curiosity, or frank appraisal, or obvious respect.

At last Dylan hailed a harried-looking young purser who led them down the deck to the cabins. "Is the steamship company having a half-price sale?" Dylan asked, gesturing at the crowd.

"No, sir. But we've got orders to sell tickets to standing-room-only passengers. And believe me, some people are so anxious to leave Dawson they're willing to put up with almost any inconvenience." He stopped in front of a door and unlocked it, handing her the key. "Ma'am, I'm sure you'll be comfortable here."

Melissa opened the door and looked at a cabin so tiny, there was just a two-foot-wide space to turn around in between the wall and the single bunk. Comfortable, the purser had said? Compared to what? A place on the open deck?

"Well, yes, I guess—"

"Sir, if you'll follow me, your cabin is on the starboard side." The purser headed down the deck, obviously assuming Dylan would follow.

Dylan gazed at her for a moment and then at Jenny. It must have been a trick of the sunlight that fell in narrow beams across the deck—for just an instant Melissa thought she saw a trace of wistful longing in his eyes. Then it was gone, and she supposed she'd imagined it. Maybe she was the only one who felt it—after all, this was the first time they would sleep apart in months.

But sleeping without him was what she had to face for the rest of her life.

Dylan leaned on the steamer's railing and watched endless miles of shore slip by. Snow had already dusted the lower foothills, and he knew they were getting out just in time. Another three or four weeks, and they'd have been stuck in Dawson for the winter.

They'd been traveling for three days, and for the most part, he'd seen Melissa at meals—thanks to the captain's hospitality they were invited to dine with him. Otherwise, she and Jenny kept to their cabin. He supposed he couldn't blame her. As one of the few women aboard, she was outnumbered by men on the oversold ship, and every passageway and foot of decking was occupied by people.

It was all over, and as much as he'd disliked what Dawson eventually became, he didn't regret a minute of it. But while he'd gained more than he'd lost, the losses had been hard to bear. Sometimes when he was caught between wakefulness and sleep, he'd wonder if Rafe was with Priscilla, somewhere in a place where souls were finally reunited. And then his thoughts would drift to Melissa, slender, softly curved, and loving. He'd seen her emerge from a prison of fear and intimidation to reveal the woman she was meant to be.

But apparently, that woman wasn't meant to be with him, and the constant empty ache he felt was only a sample of what he had to look forward to for a long time to come.

Chapter Fifteen

Twelve long days later, under clear blue autumn skies and a mild temperature, the *Arrow* puffed up the Willamette River into Portland.

Melissa could hardly believe her eyes when she saw the familiar waterfront come into view through her cabin porthole. "Jenny, button, we're here!" she said and laughed. Plucking the baby from her bunk, she held her up to the window. "See? That's Portland, that's where Mama is from. At last, we're here."

The return trip had been faster and certainly less punishing than her journey to the Yukon. And with each port they stopped at, the ship's population thinned. But she and Jenny had spent most of their time in this cubbyhole, and she was glad to be leaving it. The bathing facilities had been less than adequate, and she felt as if every garment she owned was crushed and wrinkled.

She'd tried to avoid Dylan—even though every fiber of her being cried out to be with him. The time spent without him gave her a taste of the longing she would face. It would be hard, she knew. Her mind kept returning to the small oval photograph she'd found in his trunk that afternoon. If he still burned for the woman in that picture, after she'd betrayed him and jilted him, no matter how much Melissa loved him, there was nothing she could do about it.

Gathering their belongings, she moved with the remaining passengers down the gangway, intending to see about Jenny's cradle stowed in the hold. The dockside smells of river water and creosote struck her, and gulls squawked and hovered overhead, gliding on drafts.

"Melissa!"

She turned and saw Dylan striding toward her, wearing his slim black pants, a buckskin coat, and his knife tied to his thigh. The wind caught in his long hair, and his full mouth and firm jaw were highlighted in the afternoon sun. Oh, why did he still look so handsome? she wondered miserably. She'd hoped to somehow become immune to his good looks after being away from them. But if anything, he only looked more handsome, and she had to restrain herself from walking into his embrace.

"I'll hire a cab and take you to a hotel. You can stay there until you find a place to live."

It felt so good to have him standing next to her again, she wondered how in the world she'd get used to being without him. "Thank you, but you really shouldn't trouble yourself. At least I know my way around this town."

He took her elbow, turning her from the disembarking passengers, and she was forced to look up into his green eyes. "Come on, Melissa," he murmured in that rich, low voice she knew so well. "You've avoided me for most of this trip. I'll be leaving soon enough—let me keep my end of our bargain."

That bargain, she thought morosely. It had been her salvation and her curse. Maybe if the wedding Rafe performed in the Yukon Girl had been legitimate, Dylan would need to think twice about going back to Elizabeth. But, no—she didn't want him to stay with her because he was legally bound to do so, or felt obligated. She'd have him only if he wanted her and Jenny.

"Then you should let me keep my promise, too. I wanted to pay you for Coy's debt."

He sighed and rubbed the back of his neck. "I never agreed to that. Melissa, I don't *need* the money. You might. Just let me take you to a hotel. Then I'll say good-bye and be on my way."

It would be for the last time—the last time she'd see him. An ache knotted her heart. "But I have to see to Jenny's cradle."

"I'm having it sent to the hotel."

She looked around him. "But where are your things?"

"The captain has agreed to keep my gear in his quarters until I get back. What do you say, Melissa?"

In her life she'd had no dealings with a man who didn't laze around and wait for someone else to do work that rightly belonged to him. Dylan simply took charge of a situation and waited for no one. She would miss that, too.

"All right. Let's go."

He smiled at her, a sweet, tender smile, and she saw that trace of wistfulness again that baffled her. Then he led her to one of the cabs waiting along the docks. The driver jumped down to help her in while Dylan held Jenny. Handing the baby to her, he climbed in. "Take us to the Portland Hotel."

"Dylan! The Portland Hotel? It's too expensive." It was an elegant, luxurious, and extravagant establishment, or so she'd heard. She'd never been inside it herself.

"It's a good hotel, and I want you and Jenny to be safe."

Melissa could think of no argument for this. The horses lurched to a start, and as she gazed at the skyline of the city rolling past, she noted the changes that had taken place in the short year she'd been gone. She, too, was forever changed from the browbeaten woman who'd gone North with her loafing bully of a husband. That woman had never offered an opinion or spoken up to defend anyone but her child. She was no lionheart now—a lifetime of trying to remain in the shadows couldn't be unlearned in only a few months. But at least she'd begun to realize that what she thought and felt had value. And she had the man sitting next to her to thank for that.

They arrived at the Portland Hotel, a dark, imposing edifice, and Dylan told the cab to wait while he escorted her and Jenny inside. Men in fine suits and women wearing the latest fashions strolled the opulent, carpeted lobby, and Dylan, with his long hair, buckskin, and wicked-looking knife turned more than a few heads. It occurred to Melissa that she'd never gotten the chance to see him dressed up—their dinner at the Fairview Hotel had been canceled the day Rafe died.

Walking to the front desk, Dylan rang the bell to get the attention of the stuffy-looking clerk who let his disapproving gaze take in Dylan's appearance. His nostrils were cut so high, he had the look of someone sniffing a disagreeable odor. "May I help you—sir?"

"I need a room for my wife and daughter."

Melissa's head came up at this, but of course, how else could Dylan refer to them without raising eyebrows and suspicions?

Apparently, though, the clerk wasn't impressed. He stared down his long nose at Melissa and Jenny with that same condescending expression. Oh, she knew they were out of place, but she resisted the nervous urge to adjust her jacket and brush at the lap of her skirt.

"I'm sorry, but we've none available," the clerk replied.

An ominous frown drew Dylan's brows together, and he leaned over the counter. "What are all those keys on that board behind you?"

"I can tell you what they are not—keys to vacant rooms. Perhaps you should try one of the other hotels. They might be more suitable to your needs."

Icy and undaunted, the clerk looked Dylan up and down again.

Dylan leaned closer still, and she recognized his flinty tone. She'd first heard it when he talked to Coy, and even now it brought back that awful day. "I'm Dylan Harper, and I've just come back from three years in the Yukon. I made enough money up there to buy a thousand pinched-ass prigs like you. I want rooms and an adjoining bath for my wife and daughter, and not some damned broom closet, either." He nodded at the rows of keys on the walls. "Now I suggest you look again."

He never raised his voice above a deadly quiet murmur, so not even the most curious eavesdropper heard him. But it was enough. The clerk's pasty complexion bloomed with a ripe shade of crimson, and he looked as if he'd inhaled ammonia vapors through his high-cut nose.

"Mr. *Harper*, my most humble apologies. I didn't recognize you." He turned and hurriedly fumbled with the keys, his pale hands trembling slightly. "I am so sorry for the error. We were all very distressed to hear of the recent tragedy in your family. Of course, madam," he added, speaking to Melissa, "I'll have a boy take your things to a corner suite with a lovely view of the west hills." He rang the counter bell sharply, and a uniformed youth appeared to take her carpetbag.

Melissa watched the proceedings with raised brows. She wasn't sure what had happened, but obviously it went beyond Dylan's threatening demeanor. Once in the elevator car, she whispered, "How did that come about?"

He shrugged. "The old man stayed in this hotel a lot. He'd come to Portland on business, and he dragged me along a couple of times." He smiled wickedly. "There had to have been some benefit from carrying the Harper name."

When they reached the fifth-floor suite, Melissa put Jenny down in the soft cushions of the midnight blue velvet sofa. Dylan tipped the bellboy, who departed discreetly, and they were left standing just inside the door with an awkward gulf of silence between them.

Melissa spoke first, unable to prolong this painful farewell any longer. "Dylan, I appreciate everything you did for us. I don't know what would have happened to us if it hadn't been for you. And Rafe."

"You and Jenny made living in Dawson less . . . lonely." He almost whispered the word. Reaching for her hand, he held it and looked into her face with those green eyes. "Will you be all right?"

She lifted her shoulder slightly. "Having money is a big help. We'll be fine," she lied. She'd once told him that she wanted comfort and safety from life—she hadn't realized then that he was the embodiment of those things.

"Do you think you'll visit your family?"

Melissa was torn. "I'm not sure. I guess I owe my father the right to see his granddaughter."

He nodded. "Does he live nearby?"

"Oh, no, I grew up in Slabtown, closer to the river.

I'd never even seen this part of the city until Coy and I got married at the courthouse."

Dylan shifted his gaze to Jenny, who'd fallen asleep in the velvet cushions. "I'm going to miss you." Then he looked at Melissa again and pulled on her hand to bring her closer, closer, until she could smell his leather coat and the fresh-air scent in his hair. His arm slid around her waist and he tipped her chin up, trailing his fingertips along her cheek.

Oh, Dylan, she thought, please don't make this harder than it is. Please . . . But she could no more pull away from him than a starving child could refuse a crust of bread. When his lips touched hers, warm and soft and full, her heart filled with such torment and pleasure she thought it would break.

She wanted to beg him not to leave them, to stay where he was loved for who he was, not who he could be made into—loved without hesitation or reluctance.

Dylan broke away first, though. "I guess I'd better get back to that steamer. It's docking for only two hours, and it won't wait for me. Listen to me, now," he began, taking both of her hands in his, "if something should happen to you or Jenny, or if, well, there's another baby, promise you'll get in touch with me."

Startled by his last comment, she felt her face grow hot.

"Promise me," he insisted, and gave her hands a light squeeze for emphasis.

Her throat was so tight she could hardly speak. "I promise."

"Okay, good. That's good." He released her and opened the door. His eyes rested on her as if he were trying to memorize everything about her. She couldn't imagine why—Elizabeth was much more attractive.

Suddenly, he shot out a hand and grabbed her by the back of the neck to pull her to his mouth for one last, anguished kiss. "Good-bye, Melissa. Kiss Jenny for me."

Then he was gone.

Dylan pounded down the sidewalk, barely seeing the traffic and other pedestrians around him. He dodged a team pulling a Weinhard's beer wagon, making the animals shy. The driver shouted and waved a fist at Dylan, but he just kept walking, heading back to the *Arrow*. The tall buildings on Sixth Avenue, cut with diagonal shadows and bright streaks of late afternoon sun, faded away into the sharply blue sky. All he could see was Melissa standing in front of him, dressed in her dark wool suit and big hat, more beautiful than he wanted her to be.

After he left her, he paid off the cab driver and sent him on. He hoped that walking back to the boat would burn off some of the anger and emptiness he felt. As it was, he felt like punching a wall. He wasn't mad at Melissa. He was mad at himself.

He could almost understand why she wanted to be on her own. After years of being dominated by drunken bullies, first her father, then Logan, she wanted some peace and freedom.

He could give her that, but he just didn't know how to tell her. Willing himself to keep walking toward the river, he resisted the driving urge to glance back over his shoulder. If he gave in to it, he knew he'd run back to the hotel and be on his knees in front of Melissa, begging her to come with him to The Dalles. He could give her and Jenny a good life, and they'd make the family he yearned for. Of course she didn't know that. She had no idea how he felt because he couldn't tell her.

And somewhere, from whatever place his spirit had flown to, he suspected that Raford Dubois was laughing at him.

Where the Willamette River joined the Columbia, the *Arrow* turned east and chugged on through the night. It passed the high falls the Multnomah Indians told stories about, and the small towns that dotted both the Oregon and Washington sides of the big waterway—Troutdale, Stevenson, Hood River. Their lights gleamed like golden stars along the hillsides.

Dylan tossed and turned in his cramped bunk for most of the night, drifting in and out of a troubled sleep. Sometimes he dreamed that he was twelve years old again and in front of his father's desk, enduring a reprimand for getting his suit dirty in the stable. But in most of the images drifting through his mind he saw Melissa as she'd looked the first night he made love to her at Dawson. Her creamy skin tinted golden by low lamplight, her pale hair tumbling in waves around her, her gray eyes watching him with shy desire.

At last he gave up trying to sleep. Throwing off the rough wool blanket, he pulled on his pants and shirt and went out on deck. The air was sharp and brisk, driven by a riverborn wind.

He leaned on the railing just before dawn, watching the glow of a full moon in the rippling wake of the steamer, and asked himself what the hell he planned to accomplish on this fool's errand. He wished to God that Big Alex hadn't found that newspaper. Then he would have lived along in ignorance a while longer with Melissa and Jenny, instead of rushing off to The Dalles and a purpose that remained in the hazy distance.

There was nothing for him in The Dalles—there hadn't been since the night he left. Yet, from the moment he'd learned about Scott and the old man, he'd felt compelled to return, as if something drew him back to the place of his beginnings. So strong was the pull that he'd left behind the one woman who mattered more to him than any other, and the child he'd come to think of as his own.

As the sunrise glowed in the east, though, and revealed the landscape of sage and grasslands, he felt a quiet joy of homecoming. He wished he could have brought Melissa and Jenny here, to show them Celilo Falls, where the Indians, armed with dip-nets and spears, fished for salmon on rickety scaffolding over the churning river. He would take them back to the land where he grew up—not the house and its high-flown trappings—but the outdoors that he'd loved and which Griffin Harper had given so little thought to. Dylan supposed that land belonged to Elizabeth now.

Elizabeth . . . beautiful, sensual, widowed. Suddenly, he stood upright as the *Arrow* came into sight of The Dalles docks, and he realized why he'd come home.

He wanted to live on that land again, and he could think of only one way to make that happen.

Melissa had never lived in such luxury. The furnishings in her hotel room were upholstered in brocade and velvet. Her windows overlooked the high, wooded hills to the west and south. The bathroom had marble walls and a long tub of gleaming white porcelain, and the tall mahogany bed was intricately carved at head and foot. She and Jenny were warm, clean, and comfortable.

But she'd trade the velvet and marble to be back in the cramped, inconvenient little room in Dawson if she could be with Dylan.

He'd been gone for two days, and already it seemed that an eternity had passed. Although she'd always worked, now time hung heavy on her hands, and she didn't care about doing anything. She knew she ought to find a place to live and move out of this expensive hotel, but it was easy to let someone else wait on her for once in her life. And since the hotel staff believed that she was Mrs. Dylan Harper, they seemed especially solicitous.

Dylan—his face and form would not leave her mind or heart. Sometimes when Jenny woke at night, Melissa burrowed into the bedding in her half-sleep state, thinking that Dylan would get up and see to her. He'd done it so often. Or she'd wake up in the morning and expect to see him shaving at the wash-stand, barefoot and shirtless.

On the third day of her moping, she knew she had to break the cycle or she'd sit in the Portland Hotel indefinitely, and Jenny would learn to walk in the hallways.

It was time to get on with her life.

"Will you wait, please? I won't be too long."

"Yes, ma'am, don't you worry, I'll be right here." The cab driver glanced doubtfully at Melissa, then at the shabby street and dilapidated address he'd delivered her to. "Are you sure you want to stop here, ma'am?"

"Yes, I'll be fine." She must have lost her mind to ask a cab to wait—what a careless expense. If she kept living at the hotel and spending money at this rate, she'd be broke. But she didn't know what kind of reception waited for her inside the house they'd pulled up to, and she wanted the option of an easy escape.

With Jenny in her arms, she stared at the door, then took a deep breath and started up the walk. The yard was a ratty tangle of weeds, and the shrubbery nearly covered the front windows. The glass pane in the front door had been broken, and a piece of cardboard was nailed over the hole. The house's green paint had flaked off in big patches and showed the bare wood of the siding. Trash littered the overgrown flower beds, and an air of apathetic squalor hung over the property. It looked worse than she could remember, and certainly was the worst on the block. Even the mild September sun couldn't dispel the wretchedness.

For a moment she considered turning on her heel and getting right back into the carriage, taking Jenny away from here and never looking back again. But Melissa hadn't escaped this neighborhood and this life by being a coward. Tugging on the hem of her suit jacket, she lifted a hand and knocked on the door.

From within she heard thumping, unsteady footsteps as they made their way to the front. Finally, the door opened about six inches, allowing a gust of fetid odors—rancid cooking fat, unwashed bodies, and raw sewage—to reach her nose. Dear God, it was even worse than she'd expected.

A young man wearing only stained underwear stared back at her, and two suspicious bloodshot eyes raked her up and down. "Yeah? What do you want, lady?"

She recognized the hostile voice more than the face. "James, it's me. Don't you know your own sister?"

He squinted at her, looking her up and down

again, and then peered at her face. His mouth fell open with astonishment, revealing half-rotted teeth. At that sight, Jenny, staring solemnly at her uncle, jumped slightly in Melissa's arms.

"Lissy? Is it you?"

Melissa nodded, but couldn't make herself smile at him. She was already beginning to regret coming here.

"And this is your little tyke?" James turned and yelled to the back of the house, "Pa, Billy, get on out here. It's Lissy. She's come home."

There was something about that last—*she's come home*—that made Melissa very uneasy.

"Damn, I guess Coy has done all right by you. You're fixed up like a rich man's wife." He looked past her shoulder. "And hiring cabs, too. Well, well, Lissy."

Perhaps she was being petty, but Coy had not contributed to her welfare in any way, and she wouldn't allow the family to think he had. "I *earned* the money to buy these clothes, James. Coy didn't have anything to do with it."

He shrugged, then opened the door wider and stood aside to let her in. Inside the house clutter and downright filth made her hesitate to take another step. She certainly wouldn't sit down.

Waving in the general direction of their surroundings, James said, "Sorry the place is a mess. Since Ma died and you been gone, there's no one to tidy up." Then he called over his shoulder again. "Come on, Pa, come see your fancy-dressed daughter. Billy, shake a leg."

"Quit your yelling. Billy left early this morning." The elder of the Reed clan emerged from the back of the house, pulling his suspenders up to his shoulders as he shuffled to the parlor in stockings that both bore holes. Looking every bit as disheveled as his son, Jack Reed had more gray hair than brown now, and the stubble of his two- or three-day beard was almost white.

Melissa waited to feel her emotions stir; after all, this was her father, the man she'd grown up with, and she hadn't seen him for a long time. But she felt nothing more than dull anger rumbling to life for everything he'd done to her and the rest of the family.

He squinted at her, too, just as James had. Did she really look so different to them? she wondered. Perhaps as different as they looked to her.

"Well, Lissy, you're looking mighty prosperous. Mighty prosperous." His rheumy, assessing gaze took careful note of her dress and her hat.

"She came in a cab, Pa. It's still out there." James added.

Jack stumped to the window and pushed aside the grimy curtain. "So it is."

"Who's this you brought with you?"

She shifted Jenny in her arms. "This is your granddaughter, Pa. Her name is Jenny Abigail. I thought you'd want to meet her." But with every passing moment she became more convinced that she'd made a mistake in coming here.

He smiled at Jenny, showing new toothless gaps in his gums. "She favors you, girl." Melissa bit back a protest when he took Jenny's hand in his own very dirty one. Jenny pulled away from him and started crying.

"Oh, dear," Melissa said, and jogged her in her arms, "she's not used to strangers."

Pushing a litter of paper and an empty bottle aside, Jack lowered himself stiffly to a threadbare sofa that leaked its horsehair stuffing. "We're not strangers, we're family, and she damn well better get used to us," he grumped. His lack of compassion or understanding was so familiar to her. Then he fixed her with a stern look. "Where's your man, Lissy?"

She took a breath. "He died in Dawson. They said it was pneumonia." She supposed she should at least pretend grief for decency's sake, but she couldn't make herself do it.

"Died!" her brother and father both echoed.

"It happened earlier this summer."

After a moment of stunned silence, James spoke. "Well, by God, that's a tragedy." He sounded genuinely sorry. "He was a good man, the best friend I ever had." He slumped down next to his father and looked ready to cry.

Oh, she was tempted, so tempted, to tell them about the "good man" and how he'd settled his debt with Dylan. But she decided not to. She had the sick, uneasy feeling that they wouldn't find anything wrong with what he'd done.

"So you're a widow woman now." Jack glanced at the filthy house and nodded decisively. "A good thing you've come home. You belong here with your family."

"Say, that's right," James added, the benefits of her return obviously dawning on him.

Melissa gaped at them both in horror. "Oh, I'm not coming back here!" she blurted.

Struggling to his feet again, Jack advanced on her and pointed a shaking finger at her, apparently taken aback by her refusal. Melissa had never refused her father or spoken out in her life. "Why, the hell you aren't, Lissy. You aren't so big that I can't still whup you for your sass. You'll do as you're told and that's that. A woman gets into all kinds of trouble without menfolks to protect her."

Protect her? While threatening to beat her? She wished she could laugh at his ridiculous pronouncement. But fear made her clutch Jenny more tightly, the same gnawing, soul-withering terror that she'd grown up with.

"James, tell that driver outside to go along now. Girl, where are your belongings? When Billy gets home, he'll go with you to collect them."

"Well, I gotta put my pants on," James muttered, and climbed to his feet.

Melissa's heart pounded in her chest with a suffocating sensation. The image came to her of Coy standing at her washtubs in Dawson. *I'm giving you five minutes to get your gear . . . or I'll teach you a good lesson for talking back to me.* What she needed or wanted was of no consequence. The slow-burning anger that had ignited when she arrived continued to grow within her. Coy, her father, her brothers—none of them had cared about her. They saw her only in terms of the convenience and personal comfort she could provide. It was a startling realization that even her father didn't love her, but looking at him, she at last recognized it was true. With that knowledge came a new kind of freedom, and her paralyzing fear fell away.

"Don't you do anything of the kind, James," she said in her most commanding tone.

"Huh?"

She kept her eyes on her father. "I came back here because I thought you had the right to meet your granddaughter, and that she should know her grandfather. But I was wrong. I don't want her to know a man like you."

Jack Reed sputtered like a landed trout, but plain astonishment apparently kept him from stringing any words together, and Melissa plunged on, finding courage and growing fury with each passing minute. She'd grown up around men like her father and Coy—she hadn't known she should expect to be treated with more respect. But Dylan, while he offered no quarter to his enemies, had opened her eyes. His kindness to her and Jenny had proved to her that not all men were like the ones she'd known.

"You bullied me and Mama, and beat both of us—"

"I never raised a hand to one of you unless you had it coming," he protested indignantly. Jenny, responding to the tension of angry voices, began crying again.

"Who were you to decide that?" she demanded, her voice climbing in volume. "I know now that you didn't care about any of us. Your first love was the bottle, and you sent Mama off to work because you wouldn't. We would have starved if not for her!" Her breath came in short jerks, and Jenny screamed in earnest, adding to the chaos. "I'm never coming back here. Never." She spun around and strode to the door.

"By God, we'll see about that!" Jack lurched forward and grabbed Melissa's arm to stop her.

She looked down at the grimy hand gripping her sleeve, then met her father's eyes dead on. "Take your hand off me. Now."

Gaping at her with anger and genuine hatred, he released her. So icy and direct was her tone that even James backed up a step.

Melissa yanked open the door and hurried down the walk with Jenny howling over her shoulder. The cab driver, seeing her approach, jumped down from his seat.

"If you hadn't been holding that baby, I would have taken my shaving strop to you, you ungrateful bitch!" her father yelled after her.

"M-ma'am, are you all right?" the driver asked, helping her into the carriage.

"Yes, please . . . please just take us back to the hotel. Right away." Melissa felt her courage crumbling around her, and hot tears burned her eyes.

"Yes, ma'am!"

The break with her family was complete. Now she knew how Dylan had felt when he told her that he didn't want to see his own family again. If the earth opened up tomorrow and swallowed Jack Reed, she knew she wouldn't care a bit.

Chapter Sixteen

Allred Kaady straightened from the sack of oats he'd been cutting open. "Why, I can hardly believe my eyes—Dylan Harper! When did you get back into town?"

Grinning, Dylan stepped into the cool gloom of Kaady's Livery and let the tall, bony man pump his hand. "Early yesterday morning, Red. I'm staying over at the hotel. How are things here at the stable?"

Red shrugged, grinning back. "I ain't complaining. A couple of folks around here have bought one of those new horseless carriages, but hell, they make so much racket and smoke, their day will pass. Then those people will be on my doorstep to buy a real carriage." He sat down on a vacant hay bale and motioned Dylan to another one. "Tell me, where've you been these past two-three years? We were ready to give you up for dead."

Dylan sat and glanced at the cool, dark confines of the stable, inhaling the rich, familiar scents of horse and hay. "I knocked around for a while, but I was in Dawson for most of the time."

"Went up for the gold rush, did you?"

"I was already there when it got started. I owned a trading store. I bought and sold miners' outfits. I never saw so many men digging in the dirt in my life. You'd be surprised what people will do for the chance to get rich."

Red looked wistful. "I was tempted to give it a try myself, but then I figured, what would happen to my boys and girls if I went? I couldn't leave 'em with just anybody, and you weren't here to take 'em." A stranger wouldn't realize that he was referring to his horses and not his children.

Good old Red, Dylan thought. Still here in his baggy overalls and battered straw hat. "That's okay. It's good to see that some things don't change. Anyway, I was trying to decide if I wanted to spend another winter up there when I happened to come across an old copy of the *Oregonian.* I read about my brother and the old man."

Red fidgeted a bit. "Say, I'm sure sorry about that. It was a surprise to the town." Dylan thought he was being especially tactful, given that Columbia Bank had nearly foreclosed on him for being one day late with a loan payment, after he'd established a long history of paying on time. Dylan never knew for sure what had happened, but he suspected that Griffin Harper had extorted some kind of bribe from the liveryman that didn't go on the books. A bachelor in his mid-fifties, Red's whole life was tied up in this stable, and he would have done anything to keep from losing it to the bank. The old man had probably known that.

"You know we were always at odds, the three of us. Especially just before I left." Dylan stood and walked over to the stall containing Red's sweet-tempered sorrel mare. Sticking her head out, she bumped her nose against his chest and sniffed at his shirt pockets. He laughed, then to the mare he added, "I swear, Penelope, you'd follow anyone home if you thought you'd get an apple. I don't have anything for you."

Red laughed. "But she knows a soft touch when she sees one."

Dylan's smile faded. "Like some women I know."

The older man pulled a straw out of the bale he was sitting on and stuck it in the corner of his mouth. "She's still living up there, if you're wondering." The whole town had known that Elizabeth and Dylan were engaged, but only Red really knew how much he'd cared about her.

"I thought she might be."

"But maybe not for long. It turns out there were a few years' worth of taxes that haven't been paid on that property. The county assessor aims to collect."

Dylan stared at him. That was startling news. "And if they aren't paid?"

"Well, I guess the sheriff will put it up for sale. I think they've held off as a courtesy to your brother's widow."

This put everything in a new light. The plan that Dylan had formulated during the trip over from Portland became more firmly fixed in his mind.

"Red, can I rent Penelope here for a little ride? I'd like to take a look at the home place."

Red studied him for a moment, then stood up to get a saddle. "Sure, go ahead and take her. If you don't bring her back tonight, I won't worry."

The mare was a sturdy, dependable mount that didn't need much control, so Dylan had time to think as he rode out to the house. Regardless of the circumstances, or how many times his thoughts turned to Melissa, it was good to see these grasslands again. The Yukon had been majestic before the stampeders arrived, but not beautiful like this. The last of the day's sun was warm on his back, and off in the distance he heard the twitter of meadowlarks as they winged toward their nests for the night.

Remnants of summer's wildflowers edged the road, and to his left the Columbia River stretched out below. Dylan could think of no place else on earth that looked so good in all seasons, even in the gray, rainy spring. He wished Melissa were here to see it.

"Damn it," he swore aloud, "let's get going, Penelope." He had to stop thinking about her, wondering about her, envisioning her. She and Jenny were part of his past, and he had to try and keep them there.

But thinking about his impending meeting with Elizabeth was no more comforting. How would he feel about seeing her after all this time? After . . . everything? Would the pain of her betrayal, once exquisitely sharp, spring to life again when he saw her?

At last, he reached the long, graveled drive that led to the house where he'd grown up. He couldn't think of it as a home—he'd always felt alone and out of place there. Passing the stables, he saw the stall doors hanging open, swinging lazily on the light breeze. The stalls themselves were empty and run-down, and the entire structure needed to be cleaned and painted. Remembering the fine, blooded stock that had occupied the stables before, and how tidy and well kept they were, he felt a flash of white-hot anger. It was as if Griffin Harper had done everything he could to obliterate Dylan's hard work, and his very existence.

But he got the biggest surprise of all when he rounded the last turn in the drive and saw the house. The stately colonial seemed just as desolate and forsaken, and in little better condition, as the stables. What had happened here? he wondered. Red hadn't said anything about the property going to ruin, but it looked as if no one had lived here in months. The lawn had grown into a wild tangle that fell over the flagstone walk, and weeds grew through the gravel. For as long as Dylan could remember, the old man had kept two gardeners busy six months out of the year tending the grounds. No one had touched these in a long time.

Dylan climbed down from his saddle and led Penelope to the hitching rail by the back door. Tying her up, he walked slowly around the place, looking up at the windows, searching for signs of life. Maybe

Elizabeth was away or had moved back to her father's house. But where was the staff?

Finally, he walked around to the double front doors, turned the knob, and stepped inside. There he found the entry hall and parlor as he remembered them, although he thought a piece or two of furniture were missing.

"Ada, did you forget something?" a familiar female voice called from the dining room.

His heart began thudding in his chest, and his hands suddenly grew damp. "It's not Ada. It's me, Dylan."

A moment of silence that seemed to stretch into an hour was followed by soft, hurried footsteps. Elizabeth rushed out to the hallway and stared at him. She stood with her hand at her throat, utter surprise and perhaps a little fear stealing the color from her creamy cheeks. Her black wavy hair was swept into a coronet at the back of her head, and wispy tendrils curled in front of her ears. He saw no sign of mourning dress, though. She wore a beautiful white gown made of gauzy organdie, decorated with panels of inset lace. Looking as if she were preparing for a dinner party, she was as breathtaking as ever.

"Dylan!" She took a step forward, and then another. "Wh-what are you doing here?" Her voice was still sweet and deceptively childlike.

"I used to live here," he reminded her softly.

"When did you get back?"

"This morning. I heard about the accident, and I caught the boat down from Dawson."

She came closer still. The familiar scent of roses followed her. "You've been in the Klondike? At the gold rush?"

"For over two years. Look, Elizabeth"—he gestured at her hair and dress—"if I'm interrupting some plans of yours, I'll just get on my horse and ride back to town." Were those *tears* in her dark eyes? he wondered.

"Oh, no, please stay! I have no plans at all. None. In fact, I—" She hurled herself into his arms. "Oh, Dylan, I'm so glad you're back! Everything will be fine now."

Melissa looked at the scrap of paper in her hand, then at the address on the house. Yes, this was the right place. It was a nice-looking home, with a neat lawn and window boxes, on a quiet tree-lined street.

She was so nervous about this interview. Was she dressed correctly? What if she made a bad impression? She'd spent an hour or so each day sitting in the hotel lobby with Jenny, watching women pass by, studying their clothes and their manners, hoping to learn the ways of a lady. Certainly, her mother had taught her manners, but etiquette had been in short supply in her old neighborhood, and she hadn't learned much in Dawson.

Taking a deep breath, she proceeded up the walk and climbed the stairs to the front porch.

When she rang the bell, from within she heard a clamor of children's voices and a thunder of running feet that reverberated through the floorboards on the porch.

"I'll get it!"

"No, you always answer the door, and the telephone, too! Let me."

"Ma, someone's at the door—"

"You girls hush now and go back to your schoolwork, or you'll be doing all the cooking every night for a month!"

"Aw, Ma—"

"Lordy, don't call me 'Ma' in front of company! It sounds rude. Go on with you—"

After the sound of more giggling and scampering feet, the front door opened, and Melissa saw a little bird of a woman with high color in her cheeks and smiling brown eyes. She wore her rich chestnut hair in a luxuriant knot on top of her head that added perhaps another three or four inches to her diminutive height. Without knowing anything more about her, Melissa instinctively took a liking to her. Perhaps it was the kindness she saw in the woman's eyes.

"Mrs. Keller?"

"Yes, yes," she replied eagerly. "And you're Mrs. Logan?"

Melissa tried not to cringe, but she knew she couldn't use Dylan's name any longer. After all, Logan was Jenny's name, although nowhere was it recorded as such. Birth certificates had been in short supply on the frozen banks of Lake Bennett when Jenny was born.

"Yes, I'm Melissa Logan."

"My nephew, Tommy, telephoned about you." Mrs. Keller reached for her hand and shook it, practically pulling her in over the threshold. "Please do come in."

Inside, the house was as neat as a pin. The furnishings weren't extravagant, but there was such a homey atmosphere, Melissa began to relax a little.

The bustling little woman ushered her to what appeared to be the nicest chair in the parlor. Then she sat down opposite Melissa and poured coffee from a pot that stood waiting on the side table.

"Tommy said you want to rent a house." Tommy Keller was a polite young man who worked in the dining room at the Portland Hotel. Melissa had struck up a conversation with him a few times, and he'd told her about his aunt. Only to him had she confided her legal last name.

Melissa accepted a cup of coffee and nodded. "Well, yes, I've just come back to town from Dawson. My husband died while we were up there, and I didn't want my baby to spend another winter in the Yukon. Now I'm looking for a place to live."

"Oh, dear, to be widowed so young—" She reached over and patted Melissa's hand. "I know how you must feel. I was young when I lost Mr. Keller. Fortunately, he left me with a little income and some property, or I'd really be in a fix."

Melissa couldn't very well reveal that Coy's death hadn't devastated her. Her separation from Dylan was a thousand times more painful. But she wanted to make a good impression, so she admitted reluctantly, "It's been hard, but I think Jenny and I will be fine if we can just settle someplace."

Mrs. Keller nodded sagely. "A woman's instinct is always to make a nest, and I can well imagine how difficult that would be in a hotel, especially with a child. Um, where is your baby today?"

"The hotel staff has been very kind to me. When I told the manager about this appointment, he offered to have one of the chambermaids watch her for me. She's such a good-tempered child, I don't think she'll have much trouble with her." Of course, except for Tommy Keller, the staff all believed she was Mrs. Dylan Harper.

"I have four girls myself, and they're quite a handful, I can tell you!" From the hallway came the sound of muffled giggling. "Of course, they know if they don't behave," she went on in a louder voice, "their chores will double for six weeks."

A scuffling in the hall was followed by the sound of feet pounding up the stairs.

"I'm sorry," Mrs. Keller said. "They're really good girls most of the time, but they tend to be a bit too exuberant. But enough about us—let me show you the house. It's just next door."

She followed Sarah Keller outside to a house of identical design just to the right of her own. Leading Melissa on a tour of the unfurnished three-bedroom dwelling, she pointed out its recent improvements, such as wallpaper and new paint.

By the time they were back in Mrs. Keller's parlor, sipping coffee, Melissa had fallen in love with it. It would be hers—well, perhaps not hers in the sense of ownership, but she would shop for some modest furniture and put her own identity into it. She and Jenny would have peace and quiet. A baby carriage—she could buy a baby carriage and take Jenny for strolls to the park. They would be warm and snug on winter nights by the stove or the fireplace, and she would teach Jenny her ABCs. The only thing missing from the picture in her mind was Dylan. If he were with them, it would be perfect. For a moment she felt such a wave of grief and loneliness for him, it was almost as if he were the one who had died. Oh, God, she knew she'd never see him again.

"Mrs. Logan? Are you all right, dear?"

"What? Oh, oh yes, I'm sorry. I guess I was just remembering . . ."

Mrs. Keller sat back in her chair. "I understand. There are some losses that nothing can make up for. But having good friends will help."

Melissa looked at her and gave her a watery smile. "I guess you're right."

At least she hoped so.

"Dylan, I can't tell you how good it is to see you again. I'm so glad you agreed to have dinner with me." Elizabeth directed him to the dining room table and went out to the kitchen. It felt odd to be treated like a guest in the house he grew up in.

He plucked the linen napkin from his plate, and memories of a thousand tense mealtimes at this very table came crowding back. "I agreed to it because I want you to tell me what's been going on around here, Elizabeth. Why is the place so run down?" He gestured to her as she carried a roast chicken to the table. "And what happened to Ada and the rest of the help? Are you living here alone?"

"Oh, we can talk about that in a minute. I want to hear all about the Yukon. Was there a lot of gold up there? We heard reports, of course, but they must have been exaggerated. They talked about millions of dollars. Isn't that silly?"

"There *are* millions of dollars in gold up there. I wouldn't have stayed if I weren't making money." He was fully aware of what she wanted to know, and he didn't mind baiting her a bit. Especially when they were discussing a subject so dear to her heart. "Now tell me about this place."

"Dear, dear, where to begin," she sighed prettily, toying with one of her earrings. "Well, after you left, Scott and I married. Of course, you know that." She had the decency to look embarrassed, and poured each of them a glass of wine. "Oh, Dylan, it really was a dreadful mistake." She dropped her breathy pretense and sounded earnest. "I know he was your brother, and my husband, and now he's gone, but . . . I never should have listened to my father. He was the one who insisted that Scott and I marry."

His stomach knotting, Dylan put down his fork. He didn't want to hear any of that, not now, not if he was going to sit at the same table with her. "Elizabeth, never mind about that. What happened is in the past, and nothing is going to change it. I want to know about this property. In town I heard the taxes haven't been paid."

She dropped her gaze. "No, they haven't. There's no money to pay them."

"Why not?" he demanded. With every minute that passed, he felt he knew less and less.

She didn't answer.

"Goddamn it, Elizabeth!" Losing his patience with her coy game, he pounded his fist on the table, making her jump and the glassware rattle. "You own only half of this place. I own the other half, and I want to know why I'm about to lose it!"

"You don't need to shout at me," she said coldly.

"It seems I do—"

"I only wanted to spare you the pain."

He shook his head and gave her a sardonic smile. "Why? You didn't before."

"Dylan, I tried to tell you about that. I loved you. My father—"

"Not now, Elizabeth."

She lifted her wineglass and took a big, unladylike swallow. "Scott and your father made some bad investments. When they ran through their own money, they solicited other investors to put up more, and lost that too. My own father lost everything. This house and the land are all that's left."

Dylan slumped back in his chair and laughed. He laughed until his side ached and tears came to his eyes.

She stared at him as if he'd lost his mind. "My

God, how can you laugh? What can you possibly find in this that's funny? It's a tragedy!"

Throwing his napkin on the table, he snorted. "Tragedy—if I believed in divine retribution, that's what *I'd* call it. Griffin Harper made his money by taking advantage of other people, calling their notes, throwing them out of their homes. And Scott followed right behind him. I'm not glad they were killed, but I'm not surprised by the way this is ending."

"Well, I can tell you that unless some miracle occurs, this place will be sold by the county for the taxes. I've just been scraping by here. I can't ask my family for help—they're worse off than I am. Ada comes by sometimes out of the goodness of her heart, but I can't pay her. The rest of the help left right after the funeral. I've had to do the housework and even my own laundry. It's so degrading."

Laundry. Dylan thought of Melissa washing clothes for dozens of miners while she sang to Jenny, handling those heavy flatirons, working harder than Elizabeth had ever dreamed of even in a nightmare. On top of that, she'd taken care of a baby and done the housework too. And through it all, she hadn't lost courage, she'd gained it. She had never complained when she had every reason in the world to do so. Some inner grace, he thought, must have sustained her through a hard childhood and her life with Logan. A grace that Elizabeth would never have because money couldn't buy it. It wasn't her fault—she'd led a soft, spoiled life and now couldn't adjust to the loss of luxury. He almost felt sorry for her. Almost.

"It's getting late, and there's no moon tonight to see by," she added, taking another drink of wine. "Will you stay?"

Drinking his own wine, he replied, "Yeah, why not? I'd hate to end up like Scott and the old man."

Dylan lay in the darkness on a feather tick, thinking that the last thing he'd ever expected to do was sleep under this roof again. The bedding was scented with lavender, and the furniture was expensive. It all was a far cry from a handmade bedstead and wolf hide blankets.

It was at times like this, late at night, when he missed Melissa the most. It had started on the trip down from Dawson. He could imagine her singing, sweet and clear, as she worked or rocked Jenny, and an aching emptiness swelled in his chest that made him feel like crying. Damn it, anyway, he thought impatiently, he had to get over this. Grabbing the other pillow, he wrapped his arms around it and rolled to his side, trying to shut out her image. But it was hopeless. She was burned into his heart, and she would remain there always, even if he lived to be a very old man. And someday, he might find himself giving advice to another man, just as Rafe had tried to advise him. If that man was smarter or luckier than Dylan had been, he'd listen.

He thought he wouldn't be able to sleep, but soon he found himself in the misty world between consciousness and slumber, where half-formed dreams came to life. Melissa was with him then, lying soft and warm against his bare body. He felt her hand sliding up the inside of his thigh as she whispered his name and rained soft, moist kisses down his back. When her hand closed over his erection and quickened him with long, slow strokes, he groaned and rolled slowly to his back.

"Melissa, Melissa . . . oh God, honey, I love you." He reached for her soft, fragrant flesh, and she smelled like roses—

Dylan was awake in an instant. "Elizabeth, damn it, what the hell do you think you're doing?"

Pushing her hand away, he fumbled with a match and lit a bedside candle. She lay beside him propped on one elbow, naked, her long wavy hair flowing over her like black satin. "Don't send me away," she pleaded. "It was always good between us, Dylan. Scott couldn't make me—I mean, he—you were the only one who knew what I needed."

He sat on the edge of the mattress and stared at her, incredulous, wondering if he'd ever really known her. "Don't you realize that there's *nothing* left between us? I don't care what your reason was—you broke off our engagement to marry my brother, Elizabeth, for money. There are some pretty ugly words for women like you."

"Oh? And who is Melissa?" she demanded, flipping her hair behind one shoulder. "Your wife?"

Startled, he realized he must have called her name

in his sleep. "None of your business. Look, you just get back to your own bedroom."

Making no attempt to cover herself, she rose to her knees and looked at him with her big, dark eyes. "Dylan, think how it was between us. Don't you remember those nights I came to you in your rooms over the stables? Sometimes you were so satisfied when we finished that you couldn't move. We could have all that again. I never stopped loving you. And you loved me once—we can start over, from the beginning."

He shook his head, hardly believing his own ears. "What makes you suppose I want you?"

"Think," she continued as if he hadn't spoken. "If we married, we could restore this house and the grounds to their past glory. You'd have horses back in the stables again."

"Are you crazy? This is the last house I'd want to live in. And you're the last woman I'd want to live with!" He jumped off the mattress and reached for his pants and shirt, so furious he was almost afraid to say anything more.

"Are you leaving?" Her lower lip was actually trembling. Finally, she drew the sheet up to cover herself.

"Yes, damn it, of course I'm leaving." He jammed his arms through his shirtsleeves. "And I've got one proposition for you, Elizabeth, so you'd better listen. I'll make a settlement on you so that you can move out of here and get a new start somewhere else. Or you can wait here and let me buy you out when the county puts this house up for sale. If you do that, you won't get a dime from me. But make no mistake—I'll get this place one way or the other."

She clutched the sheet to herself. "But you said you don't want to live here."

"I don't."

She reached for his arm. "Are you doing this just to spite me? Dylan, don't be a fool. I could make you happy."

He disentangled his arm and pulled on his boots. "Elizabeth, spite hasn't got a thing to do with it. You're nothing more than a beautiful viper. You did me a favor by marrying Scott. Christ, I actually feel sorry for him."

"Where will you go? What are you going to do?"

He walked toward the door to the hall, then turned to look at her. "I almost made the biggest mistake of my life a few days ago, and tomorrow night I'm going to catch a boat back to Portland to see if I can fix it. In the meantime, I'm staying at the hotel in town. I'll give you till noon to let me know your decision. If you decide to take me up on my offer, there'll be ten thousand dollars in the bank in your name by tomorrow afternoon."

"T-ten th-thousand . . . ten thousand dollars?"

"It'll be the best money I ever spent."

Chapter Seventeen

"Mrs. Logan, is this all you have in the world?" Sarah Keller gestured at the few bundles piled on Melissa's empty parlor floor. She'd brought a basket of warm bread and fresh butter as a welcoming gift. Rectangles of burnished October sun gleamed on the polished hardwood and reflected off the light striped wallpaper, making the room bright and cheerful. But there was no way to disguise its lack of furnishings.

Melissa smiled and rocked Jenny in her arms. "I know it doesn't look like much, but I think it's safe to say that most people left the Yukon with a lot less than they arrived with. I have clothes for Jenny and a few things for myself. And of course, she has her cradle to sleep in. As soon as my new furniture is delivered, the house will look more lived in."

The older woman gaped at her. "But what about you? Where will you sleep in the meantime?"

"I have the bedding—at least that much was delivered. I'll sleep on the floor until the rest of the things get here." Melissa honestly didn't mind. Solitude wasn't what she'd wanted, but since it had been thrust upon her, she was determined to make the best of it now.

"Oh, dear, no. You must come to my house and stay. I'll make the girls double up for a night or two, and you can have one of their beds."

The memory of warm wolf hides skittered across Melissa's mind before she had a chance to push it away. If Dylan didn't stop haunting her thoughts, she worried that her heart would never heal. She put a hand on Sarah's arm. "I appreciate it, but really it isn't necessary. On the trip to Dawson, I was expecting Jenny and I slept in a tent. Everyone camped in tents. In fact, she was born in one during a blizzard, weren't you, button?"

Jenny was far more fascinated by the tiny earrings Melissa wore than anything her mother said, but Mrs. Keller made a horrified noise.

"Lordy, how terrible! I had no idea— But at least you had Mr. Logan with you then. It's so tragic that you lost him."

Remembering that awful night with vivid clarity, she said nothing. Coy had left her in the care of an Indian woman, and had gone off to gamble and get drunk. The blank-faced woman, who spoke almost no English, had been more frightening than a comfort. Melissa had been sure she would die—she'd never been so scared or lonely in her life. And she never wanted to be in that spot again.

She shifted Jenny to her hip. "Maybe it won't be easy to make it by myself—I think the world can be very cruel to women alone. But believe me, there are far worse situations a woman can find herself in. We'll be all right. Making sure Jenny grows up in a safe, loving home is the only thing that matters now."

Mrs. Keller gave her a searching look, then nodded. "I've survived with just my girls, so I know it can be done. I hope you won't be too lonely, though." She sighed. "Some nights are a year long."

Melissa drew a deep breath. "But loneliness doesn't leave bruises or scars. At least not the kind you can see."

Dylan made his way back to town in the darkness, blessing Penelope for her calm plodding every step of the way. After turning her loose in Red's corral, he went back to the hotel and tried to sleep, but he only tossed and turned.

At least he was alone in the bed, he thought sourly. If he'd held any ragged remnants of esteem for Elizabeth, she'd erased them with the little stunt she'd pulled at the house. Why he'd never seen through her before remained a mystery to him. But if everything finally went the way he'd like, he'd have just one last dealing with her.

The single good thing that had come of seeing her again was he'd realized what a fool he'd been to let Melissa go. He loved her—and now he believed that she loved him too. She had good reason to be afraid of being dependent on a man, but he could prove to her that he was worthy of her trust. They belonged together.

Somewhere toward morning, Dylan rose and sat by the window to watch the sun come up, edgy with anticipation. He had plans, great plans, wonderful plans, for the land here. He would bring Melissa and Jenny home to it yet.

As the morning grew older, Dylan paced his room like a restless dog, waiting for word. Sometimes he'd go to the window and look down at the street, hoping to see Elizabeth approach. Then he'd go back to pacing. He must have pulled out his watch a hundred times to check the hour. At twelve-ten he flopped into a chair. Well, damn it, they could have done this the easy way—easy for both of them, and certainly less humiliating for her. But if the sheriff had to get involved, then so be it.

Suddenly, there was a knock on the door. Dylan strode across the room in three steps and found a boy standing in the hall.

"Mr. Harper? Are you Mr. Harper?"

He nodded.

The boy whipped an envelope out from behind his back and thrust it into Dylan's hands. "A lady downstairs paid me a quarter to deliver this to you. So I went to the front desk and asked what room—"

Dylan dug into his jeans pocket and pulled out a silver dollar. "Here, son, I'll give you a dollar for doing a good job."

The youngster's eyes lit up as he stared at the coin. "Gee, thanks a lot!"

"Go buy yourself some candy," Dylan called after him as he ran down the hall.

He looked at the creamy envelope and his name written in Elizabeth's flowing script, and his hands actually shook a little. He ripped open the flap and pulled out a single sheet of vellum that smelled faintly of roses.

Dear Dylan—
I accept your generous offer to move from this house. I think I can be out within the month. Please believe me when I tell you I didn't want to hurt you by marrying Scott. But I have a lifetime to review my regrets.

Love,
Elizabeth

"Yeah, a lifetime and ten thousand dollars. That makes it a little easier, doesn't it?" he said to her handwriting.

By four o'clock that afternoon, Dylan had made the bank deposit and was standing on the dock, waiting to board a steamship bound for Portland. The biggest challenge of his life lay at the other end of this journey.

He hoped he was ready for it.

Melissa stood in her parlor, critically studying the location of her new settee, and shook her head. She looked up at the two burly draymen who'd delivered it to her. "I'm really sorry, but do you think you could put it back the way we had it before? I promise this will be the last time. Really." Jenny watched everything from her cradle with an expression of solemn curiosity.

She heard a muffled sigh, but they picked up the settee and carried it back to the bay window, turning it so that it faced the street.

"Oh, much better. Thank you for your help! Would you like some lemonade before you go?"

The older of the two said, "No, ma'am, but thanks. We've got two more stops to make before lunch. We'll have to come back this afternoon with that lamp we left at the store."

"That's fine. Just so I have it by evening."

They left then, and Melissa went to the doorway to admire the room and its new furnishings. They weren't fancy, but they looked very good in this house. Everything was clean and bright and newly painted.

"What do you think, button. Isn't this nice?"

Jenny smiled at her and waved both arms.

This was a new beginning for her and Jenny, too. Not one that she'd wanted, but given time, Melissa hoped she might stop thinking about Dylan twice an hour. Maybe she'd eventually be able to think about him twice a day, and then once a day. She might even be able to sleep nights without seeing him in her dreams, or feeling as if he still lay next to her. As it was now, sometimes she woke up in the darkness certain that if she put out her hand, she'd find him on his side of the bed. He was the only loose end left in her life. She'd taken care of everything else.

Thank God Pa didn't know where she'd moved to.

That was the one fear she had, that he'd somehow find her and try to drag her back to Slabtown, or demand money from her.

For now, though, her life was as good as it could be without Dylan. She and Jenny were well and happy, they had good neighbors in Mrs. Keller and her daughters, each of whom competed with the others to hold Jenny, and they had money.

It wasn't until she moved into this house that Melissa had found a poke in Jenny's clothes. She knew Dylan had hidden it there, probably supposing that she wouldn't accept it from him otherwise. And he'd been right. But since he'd left it with Jenny's things, she intended to use part of it to open a bank account for the baby. Added to what she'd already accumulated in Dawson, the gold would keep them comfortable and safe for a good long time.

Carrying a bouquet he'd bought from a cart on the street, Dylan walked into the lobby of the Portland Hotel and approached the front desk. Once again, he turned some heads, but he took little note of their rude curiosity. He felt all the nervous anticipation of a boy plotting his first kiss. On the trip downriver, he'd envisioned the scene— The surprise on Melissa's face when she opened her door, and the joy. She'd be so glad to see him that she'd fall into his arms and save him the agony of having to bare his soul to her with words. Or maybe being with her again would make it easy to tell her how much he loved her. He'd tell her whatever she wanted him to if she would only be his true, legal wife. He'd happily spend the rest of his life making up for everything she'd missed.

He didn't recognize the desk clerk behind the counter—what kind of reception would he get *this* time?

"May I help you, sir?" The tone was a bit brittle, but not downright hostile.

"My wife, Mrs. Dylan Harper, is a guest in the hotel. Could you ring her room and tell her I'm on my way up?"

The clerk glanced down at Dylan's knife and blanched. "Well, sir, you see, Mr. Harper . . ."

Foreboding washed over him like a powerful wave. Feeling as if his stomach were trying to grab his ankles, Dylan put both elbows on the countertop. "What's the matter?"

"I'm afraid your wife checked out yesterday."

"Checked out! Are you sure?" It never occurred to him that Melissa would leave the hotel so soon. He'd supposed that she'd want to stay there for a month or so and let the staff pamper her a bit.

The clerk nodded. "She paid her bill and left with your daughter. I handled the matter myself."

"What forwarding address did she give you?"

The clerk swallowed hard and looked as if he wished he could crawl into one of the pigeonholes behind him. "None, I'm afraid, Mr. Harper." Obviously, he thought that Dylan was an abandoned husband.

Disappointed and frustrated, the pain of loss sliced

through Dylan with a sharp, ruthless blade. He swung around and gazed unseeing at the guests wandering the lobby. *Damn it!* Why had fate conspired against him like this? Now that he'd finally realized what a dunderhead he'd been to let Melissa go in the first place, he'd come racing back to Portland, only to lose her completely.

Rage and the stirring of grief made his heart thump in his chest. He turned to the clerk and demanded, "Doesn't anyone in this hotel know where she's gone? Is she still in Portland?"

The clerk glanced around the curious onlookers and shook his head. He lowered his own voice to a whisper, as if hoping to suggest to Dylan that he lower his. "No, Mr. Harper, we have no idea. I'm sorry."

"Goddamn it!" he erupted, then turned sharply. He wished there were someone to place the blame on, he'd *love* to point a finger at an individual or a group and accuse them of having lost the one true love of his life. But there was no one to blame except himself. "Have you got a wife?"

"Y-yes, sir, and three children."

"Here, give these to her," he said, and shoved the flowers at the clerk. "Where's your bar?"

Like a drowning man spotting a life preserver, the clerk spied a hotel employee, a young man passing by in a crisp, white jacket, and snapped his fingers at him. "Keller, please escort Mr. Harper to the hotel bar immediately."

"But Mr. Stickle, the dining room—"

"Now, Keller. I don't care what you were doing."

"Yes, sir." The young man faced Dylan. "This way—" He studied Dylan for a few seconds as he turned to lead him across the vast carpeted lobby. "Your name is Harper?"

"Yeah, that's right," Dylan grumped, but at that moment, he thought it should be mud.

Glancing at the new mantel clock, Melissa saw that it was almost lunchtime, and she started toward the kitchen. Jenny would be hungry, too. It was wonderful to have a regular schedule and a sun that rose and set at decent hours.

Just as she brought out a loaf of bread to slice, she heard a knock at the front door. Maybe the draymen had found her lamp in their wagon after all. But when she opened the door, she saw neither the draymen nor her lamp.

She saw a man in a black suit that fit him perfectly, following the line of his broad shoulders and his long legs. His heavy sun-streaked hair still brushed his shoulders, though, and his clear green eyes considered her as if they could see through her heart to her soul.

"Dylan!" she whispered.

"Hi, Melissa."

She stared at him in amazement, as if he were a dead man come back from the grave.

"How did you find me?"

"It wasn't easy. I looked for you at the hotel, and most of the staff knew Melissa Harper, but only one knew about Melissa Logan. I got lucky when I happened upon Tom Keller. Um, can I come in and talk to you?" He seemed nervous and hesitant. Maybe he thought she would order him from her porch.

"Yes, of course." She opened the door wider.

He stood in the entryway and looked around. "This is nice, really nice. Homey."

"Thank you . . . um, please . . . do sit down," she said, motioning him to the new settee.

Jenny let out a loud noise of recognition then and grinned at Dylan, showing off two little bottom teeth just coming through her gums.

"Hey, Jenny," he said, and stooped to give her a kiss. Then he settled lightly on the slick fabric of the settee.

Melissa perched on a side chair, feeling as nervous as he acted. God, please don't let it be bad news, she prayed. She eyed his clothes again. "You look very nice, like you're going to a wedding or a funeral."

He smiled at her, that sweet, tender smile that she'd seen once or twice before. It went straight to her heart and made it ache. "I'm hoping to go to a wedding."

The ache turned to sharp pain. She glanced away from him, hoping she could get control of the tears that sprang into her eyes. "Oh, you and Elizabeth patched your differences?"

"Elizabeth! God, no! Melissa, I want to marry *you*." He startled her by sliding off the settee to his knees in front of her. He took her icy hands in his.

"But—but isn't that why you went back to The Dalles? To marry Elizabeth?"

"No, honey, that was never the reason. I wanted to see the property and figure out if there was a way I could get control of it again. It wasn't the house I wanted, it was the land. It's beautiful there." He explained to her what had transpired with the taxes and the condition of the house, and what he'd learned from both Elizabeth and checking around on his own.

"You want to live in that house?" she asked. "I thought you hated it."

"I do hate it. I'm going to have it torn down so I can build a new house on the land. *Our* house." He looked down at their linked hands. "I understand why you don't want to have anything to do with marriage again, and that you want to make it on your own." He leaned forward. "But, damn it, Melissa, we were good together. I love you and I love Jenny. I really do. Tell me there's at least a chance you'll change your mind about living alone."

Flabbergasted, Melissa stared at him. She could hardly believe what she heard. "You have some idea of how hard life was for me with Coy. I never wanted to be married again," she began, and he sat back on his heels. She went on to tell him about the incident with her father and her brother, and saw anger smolder in his features. "As horrible as that day was, I realized that if not for you, I probably would have let them bully me into going back there. I'd grown up with being ordered around and treated like an indentured servant—I didn't know any different. Until I met you. You proved to me that I was worth more." She smiled at him, but she couldn't stop the tears that ran down her face. "I told my father that I didn't want Jenny to know a man like him, even if he was her grandfather. But I want her to know you and have you in her life, Dylan. And I want *my* new life to be with you."

He smiled up at her—it was a grin that lit his whole face. He rose to his knees again. "Does that mean yes? Yes, you'll marry me?"

She nodded. "It means yes. I love you so much. I loved you long before we left Dawson. And now that neither of us has any family left—"

"We'll be our own family." He leaned closer to her and kissed her then. His lips, warm and soft on hers, hinted at passion yet to come, and the tenderness that had always been there.

Dylan broke away and rummaged around in his pocket, relief and bone-deep gratitude washing through him. "I admit I took a chance and hoped things would go my way." He pulled out a small box and opened it. "I never gave you a wedding ring that day in the Yukon Girl. So I figured I should back up and start from scratch with an engagement ring."

He would have given a day's worth of gold to see that expression on her face—delight and wonder. She reminded him of a kid opening a Christmas present.

"Oh, Dylan, it's beautiful!" He put it on her finger; lucky for him it fit perfectly.

"What kind of wedding do you want?" he asked.

"Neither of your previous ones were much to write home about."

She shook her head and stared down at the diamond ring, still smiling. Then she looked up at him with those gray eyes, eyes that had haunted his sleep from the first day he met her. "It doesn't matter what kind of wedding, it's who you marry. The courthouse will be fine. Just as long as we're together." Her smile faded then.

"What's the matter?"

"Oh, I signed a lease on this house for a whole year! And this furniture, it was just delivered. In fact, I'm still waiting for a lamp."

He waved off her concerns. "Oh, hell, that doesn't matter. We can afford to buy out the lease if we decide to. But we can stay here for a while. Have our wedding night . . ."

They'd have all the nights of the rest of their lives. At last they had found what they'd always been searching for.

A family of their own.